The Pet Boutique

By Suzie Carr

ISBN-13: 978-1-7336857-0-2

Also by Suzie Carr:
The Fiche Room
Two Feet off The Ground
Tangerine Twist
Inner Secrets
A New Leash on Life
The Muse
Staying True
Snowflakes
The Journey Somewhere
Sandcastles
The Dance
Beneath Everything
The Curvy Side of Life

Keep up on Suzie's latest news, projects and podcasts:
www.curveswelcome.com

Follow Suzie on Instagram and Twitter:
@girl_novelist

For Bumblebee, my spunky and spirited sidekick.
You're in my heart forever...

Acknowledgements

Writing a book is a team effort, and I'm so grateful I have an incredible team by my side. They see me through moments of doubt and anxiety, and also through moments of elation when the words start to click into place and I feel I have a story to tell.

To my beta team, Jennifer Morris, Felicia Haggerty, Dana Holmes, Alakshendra Tripathi, and Ted Beveridge, I am incredibly grateful for your honesty and support through this writing process. Thank you for taking my work seriously and for helping me to turn it into something I'm proud to share with others.

To my editor, JoAnn Collins, thanks for combing through every single word and helping to right the wrongs. Also, thanks for teaching me something new each time.

To Joanna Darrell, for your continued support. You keep me going, always reminding me why I do what I do. Thank you for being my friend and my greatest ally in this literary world!

To one of my best friends, Michelle Grondin, thank you for sharing your adoption story to help me better understand how Stephanie might've felt. I'm grateful that you helped me understand the intricacies of the adoption process and the emotions that go along with it.

To my sister and dear friend, Debra Ferranti, for always believing in me and helping me to heal after the loss of my sweet Bumblebee.

To Dorina Jasparro, for always being my cheerleader and for being the best auntie to Bumblebee, a.k.a. your sweet Cashmere.

To Hector, for being you and encouraging me to be me.

To my readers, for opening your hearts to me with your support and encouragement.

And finally to my lovable and loyal Bumblebee, for bringing so much joy to my life and to this story. May this tale honor you in the very best light and allow your sweetness to remain in the hearts of all those you touched with your silly and exuberant spirit. Thank you for being my best friend and sidekick through it all…

Chapter One

TAYLOR, *age 18*

Taylor excelled at pretending. She'd been doing it for the better part of her so-called gap year after high school. Not only did she leave sweet Ms. Peabody's halfway home as a changed person, but she did so as one with a story to tell. A story accounting every last tear she had shed and the emotions that fed them.

Taylor trusted in Ms. Peabody's encouraging words. She especially trusted in them the day Taylor placed her newborn baby in the arms of the strangers who would adopt her.

A week after that tearful afternoon, Taylor and Ms. Peabody stood alongside a bus that would take Taylor back to the life she'd left behind many months earlier. Right before Taylor boarded, Ms. Peabody hugged her goodbye and whispered, "You did right by her."

Taylor couldn't speak. All the words she had planned to say lodged themselves in the back of her tight throat. She sobbed into Ms. Peabody's comfy cotton shirt. She smelled like rain on a spring day. So fresh and alive. "Thank you for everything," she managed.

Taylor pulled out of her embrace and climbed the steps of the bus, carrying a heaviness she'd undoubtedly lug around for the rest of her life.

Taylor selected a seat next to a friendly-faced man. He wore a stylish fedora hat and a sharp business suit, the kind fancy financers from New York City wore in the movies.

He offered her a *National Geographic* magazine from his briefcase.

"No thank you. I'll close my eyes and nap instead."

As she traveled down a dusty road, sitting in the eleventh row of that Bonanza bus, Taylor's thoughts jumbled. One second, a sense of relief washed over her. Relief that she could still go to college and build a successful life. Another second, dread squeezed her chest, dread that her baby would one day wrestle with the idea that the first person who ever loved her had abandoned her.

Taylor peeked at the man sitting beside her. Then she asked him, "I'll take that magazine after all, if it's okay?"

He handed her an assortment. "Have your pick."

A sudoku book slipped out from the pile, so she grabbed that.

"Do you have a pen?" he asked.

Taylor bent for her backpack under the seat. "I'm a writer. So I always have several."

"What do you write?"

"I'm working on a novel."

"Young adult?"

Not with her experiences. "No. Only adults will want to read this one."

Joy sprang from his eyes. "Will you write under a pen name?"

Taylor tapped the pen to her lips. "I'm not sure." She enjoyed pretending to be someone with purpose. To be someone other than herself. That's what she loved about writing. She could be anyone and slip into any kind of life she wanted.

"I'd prefer to use my real name," he said.

Taylor chuckled. "I can't imagine my name on a book."

"Oh, but you have to. That's how you build a writing career."

"Do you write?" she asked.

"I write magazine articles. Not as fun as novels, but it pays the bills."

"You should imagine your name on a book, too."

"I always wanted to write a science-fiction novel."

"Why don't you, then?" Taylor enjoyed escaping her anguish. Talking about writing watered her soul and sprouted creative ideas.

"Maybe one day I will."

"What kind of magazine articles do you write?"

He handed her a *National Geographic*. "I wrote the article on invasive fish in Florida."

Taylor opened her mouth wide. She sat next to a real life published writer. "How does it feel to be published?"

His dimple deepened. "Amazing."

She glanced at his byline and picture. Roger Lyles. "I'll look for your name on a science-fiction book one day."

"And I'll look for yours, Ms.?"

"Taylor Henshaw."

He extended his hand. "It's been a pleasure."

She firmly shook his hand before settling into the sudoku puzzle.

A few hours into her bus trip, they stopped at a rest area.

Taylor picked up a package of hard-boiled eggs wrapped in flimsy, soggy plastic. Then she scanned the snack aisle. A mother pushing a baby carriage passed her by. The baby gurgled and kicked her chubby legs up and down. Her downy, brown hair spiraled in all directions. She was adorable, loved, and happy.

Taylor fell from her writer's high.

She tossed the eggs back onto the shelf. It no longer mattered if she filled up on a good source of protein.

A wad of sadness stole the moment. It crept in like a sneaky cat and pounced on her soul, kneading all the acceptance she'd worked into it over the past few days into sorrow. She missed her baby, and it had only been a week since she last kissed the top of her velvety head and smelled her innocent love.

She needed more than hard-boiled eggs to fill her emptiness. She snatched a jumbo bag of Cool Ranch Doritos, then picked up a Coke on the way to the register.

She took it another step, figuring she should pick up her smoking habit again from before she got pregnant. "I'll take a pack of Marlboro Lights and a book of matches, please."

3

The woman, with a face covered in wholesome wrinkles, peered down at her. "You don't need those, sweetheart. They'll kill you."

She didn't care. "A pack of Marlboro Lights, please."

The woman scanned her face with a loving, concerned sweep. "If you're going to gamble, why not gamble on something hopeful?" She pointed to the lottery tickets. "They're cheaper, too. And they don't stink." Her gray eyes shimmered.

Her kindness comforted Taylor, relieving the pressure from her chest. "Why not?"

A few minutes later, comfort food in hand, she walked back to her seat on the bus next to Roger. He scanned *The Wall Street Journal*. When she plopped in the seat next to him, he looked up from the newspaper and at the lottery ticket she gripped between her teeth.

She opened her bag of Doritos. "Want some?" she mumbled.

He shook his head. "Do you need a coin?"

"Excuse me?" she mumbled again. "Oh, right." She removed the ticket from her teeth. "Sure."

He plunged his hand into his suit's front pocket and handed her a coin. "I've got this one quarter. If it's a loser, you can keep it."

"And if it's a winner?"

He arched his eyebrow on a twinkle. "I'll let you determine that."

Taylor took out her journal from her backpack, then proceeded to scratch off the lottery ticket. As the odds favored her, her fingers tingled. "I won something." Taylor stared at the matching numbers.

Roger leaned over. "Well, I'll be damned." He pointed to one last area to be scratched. "That's how you find out how much."

Taylor hovered the quarter over the spot, enjoying the hope that suspense brought to the moment.

Hope was like the sun. It eased out the darkness, casting warmth and possibility onto those lucky enough to be in its path. The tease of it played a tender melody in her, lightening the load of burden.

Taylor resisted scratching her prize for a few moments longer, allowing the joy enough time to wrap itself around her heart.

"Come on," Roger said. "The suspense is killing me."

The suspense filled Taylor with a life force. It erased the sadness.

Nonetheless, she scratched it and revealed the number.

Five thousand dollars!

"Wow," Roger said. "You can do so many things with that. You can buy a computer and write from anywhere."

That. Or she could start at the community college right away. She had planned to wait tables at Daniel's Pub for the year. Now, she had options.

She stared at the quarter, admiring how it shone. Then she handed it to him. "Here you go."

He regarded it between Taylor's fingers. "It's always good to have loose coins when traveling." He nudged her hand away. "Sometimes it's better to pay it forward."

Taylor waited a second longer in case he changed his mind. He didn't. He went back to reading his paper. So she placed it in the zipper pocket of her backpack. "Well, thank you."

He nodded, then he continued to read the newspaper.

She stared at the lottery ticket. Five thousand dollars. She had never seen a thousand dollars, let alone five. Instead of taking a full class schedule, she could take one. Then she could learn to drive and buy a used car. Or buy some new clothes.

Her legs bounced. She had to press her fist against them to stop the jumpiness. She never had so many choices, fun choices, ahead of her.

The longer she sat and contemplated that, the less shiny it became, though. She'd done nothing to earn that other than *not* buy a pack of cigarettes.

She rolled her neck to work out its kinks. As long as she kept the past in the past, she might do okay in life.

Somewhere down the road, Taylor hoped she'd come to see that Ms. Peabody was right when she told her that she'd acted with courage and selflessness.

She stared at the lottery ticket again. What could be more selfless than donating

5

that lottery ticket to someone who deserved it more than she ever would?

She would mail the lottery ticket to Ms. Peabody.

She deserved it.

When the bus stopped at her station, she stood, gathered her belongings, and waved at Roger.

"Write that book and pay it forward," he said, arching his eyebrow.

"I'm going to go do that right now."

He tipped his fedora hat. "I'll keep an eye out for your book."

"I'll do the same." With that, she walked down the aisle, carrying a new emotion, one filled with determination. She disembarked the bus and laid her eyes on her excited mother who had already begun her skip toward her from the crowded platform.

Just as she placed her backpack down, her mother tossed her arms around her and squeezed. "The gap year did you some good." She pulled away. "You finally padded that skinny body of yours."

Taylor picked up her backpack and pressed it against her bloated belly.

Her mother, in her bulky six foot frame and animated expression, scanned her from head to toe. "So how was your gap year, really? It's hard to tell over phone calls."

She hated to lie to her. But how could she be sure her mother would not hate her for what she had done? After all, when she told her mother she was bisexual, she stopped allowing her to have her best friend from childhood over to the house. Imagine what she'd do with her newest news?

Some imperfections were best left hidden from loved ones. So she settled on the partial truth. "It was defining."

"Defining." She taste-tested the word, like she would a new dessert. "I like that."

If she only knew.

She grabbed Taylor's backpack.

Taylor stole it back. "I've got it, Mom. I'm used to carrying it around."

"Of course." Her mother smiled. "So what would you like to do first? Get some lunch? Go home and freshen up?"

"I'm kind of tired."

Disappointment leaked onto her mother's face. "Okay, let's get you home, then."

Guilt stabbed Taylor. She couldn't stand to disappoint her mother. "You know what? Lunch sounds good. First, can we go to the post office? I have something I need to mail to a friend."

"A new friend from your travels?"

"Yes. An excellent friend."

Her mother placed her hand on the small of Taylor's back and led her off the platform toward the parking lot. "To the post office we go, then."

Chapter Two

Present day, TAYLOR, *age 36*

When Taylor first met her editor, and now best friend, Maya, she wanted to run. In an email, Maya had warned her about her tough side. *I'm going to massage your words, toying with them until they writhe on the page and demand release into the world.*

Yeah. Maya might've been a wizard with a red pen, but hot damn, she scared the living crap out of Taylor with that first email welcome.

They met at a coffee shop in historic Annapolis, Maryland. Taylor's late husband, Nate, had to prod Taylor around the corner of Main Street to get her in the front door. Taylor wanted to bolt, but Nate wouldn't let her. Instead, he pulled her toward the door. Before he opened it, he kissed her forehead and whispered, "Go get your dream."

Within a blink of first shaking Maya's hand, Taylor felt at home. Her kind, sparkling eyes and nurturing manner allowed Taylor to relax into the booth seat and take on a new confidence. Maya had a way of bringing that out in her. In fact, within an hour, Taylor cracked lighthearted jokes and even found herself amusing.

In one way, Maya parted a pathway for them to be collaborative, but in another way, she laid out the terms of their partnership to be that of sincere tough love. Maya could critique Taylor and open her up to greater success. Thankfully, she had that touch and ability to get the most out of Taylor without killing her spirit or mojo at the same time.

When Maya had something to say, Taylor always believed every single word to be true. Maya didn't sugar coat and didn't let any word slide by without proper assessment and evaluation.

Taylor's writing would be crap without her friend marking up every sentence with her red pen, challenging her to get the fuck out of her own way and let the characters set the course and speak their minds. Taylor eventually got to the point where she'd ask herself while writing a dialogue scene—*what insults will she slap onto my snappy phrases?*

So when Maya called a meeting that morning, Taylor knew she had screwed up something and better steady for the bumpy ride.

Taylor knocked on Maya's front door. Her dog, Toby, a cairn terrier with an attitude the likes of a crazed teen pumped up on too much soda, raised holy hell in the front window.

When Maya opened the door to her, Toby jumped up into Taylor's arms and barked a mouthful of hysterics into her face.

Taylor came prepared. She pulled his favorite treat from her pocket.

He played that game every time she visited. He screeched and whined probably because he feared he wouldn't get his treat if he showed up all calm and collected. Kind of like Maya.

"Here you go, Mr. Grouch." Taylor handed him the crunchy marrow treat and he gobbled it up. When he finished, he screeched at her again. Taylor adored the little guy's attitude. So she played along like any good auntie, revealing another one from her pocket.

"Where are the other dogs?"

"Out back, digging holes."

When the mighty greeting ended, Taylor let him down and he circled around them. He ushered them into the foyer.

It had been several months since she had been to Maya's house.

Maya kissed her cheek and squeezed her. "I have a surprise for you."

"Please tell me it's Tahini and Almond cookies."

She stopped her elegant stroll across the shiny, colorful granite floor and cupped her hand around Taylor's thick upper arm. "Oh, darling, I'm sorry. You should've told me you were craving them. I would've baked some."

Maya was a great friend. She would walk barefoot across hot coals if Taylor asked her. Her shimmery white hair, cropped in an elegant feathering at the nape, and wild and free to do as it pleased toward the crown and front, reflected her attitude on life—who gives a fuck!

"I gained my thirty pounds back, so it's best if you didn't. I'm better off with a rice cake."

"Oh, nonsense." She scanned Taylor's stocky build. "You're healthy. That's all that matters. Let's leave the stick figures to the cover models while we enjoy a treat now and then."

She strolled through the foyer and toward her office on the left side of her home. Toby trailed behind her, matching her happy gait.

"Where's your new houseguest?"

"Lexie's out at the park with her dog. Don't worry, you'll meet her very soon." She pointed to a picture on the wall of an attractive blond woman with pretty blue eyes walking a cute white boxer. "That's her and her adorable sidekick, Cashmere."

Taylor nodded and continued to follow Maya toward the office.

"She's out under this blazing sun with no sunscreen, so she'll come home with blistered skin as red as a lobster and need me to rub aloe all over her damaged face. It's what happens with a stubborn niece who refuses to agree that there's an issue with the ozone layer. I can tell her over and over again, and yet, she acts surprised when her skin starts to peel."

"You love taking care of others. Who are you kidding?"

She did a little skip and squeal like an eight-year-old playing hopscotch in the schoolyard. "You're right. She's a messy tornado and a charming delight all wrapped up in a shiny present that I get to toy with."

They entered her office and Maya waved to a small, delicate Bonsai tree. "Meet Cashy Poo, your surprise." She handed her the small tree.

"I don't get it."

"It's a money tree."

"Why are you giving me a money tree?"

"Why do you always question me?" Feigned hurt crawled across her smooth, dewy skin and settled into the fine lines around her playful eyes.

"Do you foresee a money issue with this next book?"

"You're in a slump, sure, but that's not why I'm giving it to you." Maya took the plant from her and placed it back down on a small tray with pebbles. "I got it for you to teach you how to nurture yourself better."

"I'm fine. I just need more time."

Maya fingered one of the tiny leaves. "There's nothing wrong with seeking counsel from someone you trust. I'm a pretty awesome role model. I'll get you back on track. I've done it before."

"By giving me a tree?" That tree would be dead the next day under her care. She couldn't remember to flush the toilet, let alone water a plant.

"You'll need to talk to it. Plants have feelings and respond to sound. You're going to be amazed at how healthy and happy this plant will be once you learn to pay attention to it."

"You're nuts."

"You need to learn this, Taylor. You need to learn it fast before you break down or worse, hand me a sappy, depressing hollow manuscript, killed by lack of love. Your latest chapter depressed me. You're supposed to be funny. I cried and blew my nose the whole time I read it. My eyes turned all puffy and I got a few more wrinkles from the ordeal."

That didn't shock Taylor. Her writing sucked big time since her dog, Oscar, died. "You've got a lot of faith in the plant."

Maya combed her over with concerned eyes. "You've got some work cut out for you. A lot of work if you want to get this straightened out."

"Your critiques wear me down."

They both plopped down on a set of cushy chairs across from each other.

"I'm not talking about your manuscript anymore."

Taylor covered her mouth with a tense fist. "I'll keep trying to move forward."

Maya stretched her long arms between her legs. "I hope so. As far as your writing, restart your story from wherever you desire. Start a new chapter and correct the wrongs. Tie up the loose ends. It's your story. You can do whatever you want with it so long as you get to writing it. But nothing's going to happen if you sit around and wallow over this latest block in your writing."

"I'm not wallowing."

"Well, I am." Maya arched her manicured eyebrows. "You need to create something new to nudge things in a different direction. Fill it up with something worth investing time in. You wouldn't expect a reader to commit to something boring, would you?"

Taylor groaned.

Maya continued her diatribe. "You wouldn't expect me to sit idle and let you turn it into something dreadful, right?" She tapped the top of Taylor's nose. "Write a new story. One worthy of time, and one so exciting that you'll not want to stop writing it. Don't you deserve that?"

Taylor shrugged. The regret of a failed manuscript crept onto her shoulders and weighed her down. "I'm not sure about that."

Maya took her hands and squeezed them. Then she stared straight into Taylor's eyes with earnest fortitude, maybe even desperation. "Don't the memories of Nate and your adorable little furbaby, Oscar, deserve it?"

Their memories meant everything to her. They kept her going, and reminded her that when they were alive, they loved living life. If it weren't for that constant reminder in watching videos of them or browsing through pictures, Taylor would've wanted to die, too, so she could be with them. "Well, when you put it like that."

"I have a suggestion."

Maya tightened her grip on her hands, gazing at her with dramatic pose.

"Go on."

"I've got a project for you."

"What kind of project."

13

Maya squeezed Taylor's hands more, and then she let go of them. "One that will open you up and allow the magic to flow again." She ran her fingers through her glistening white hair.

"Let's hear it."

Maya folded her leg up to her chest. She had the flexibility of a five-year-old. "You love building things, right?"

Taylor sighed. "Come on. Get to the point."

"See, that's your problem, right there." Maya pointed to Taylor's face. "You're always in such a rush to get to the end. Like with that disaster of a story that you expected me to fix with a little backspacing. You need to pour your heart into it."

"I try to."

"Sorry, my friend, but your life is sinking in the middle. It's sinking because you need to add some substance to it. You need to entertain, remember? You must keep it light and fun so it can catch wind and float on the merits of good placement between setting and prose."

"I'm confused. Are you talking about a new story?"

"I'm talking about the story of your life." Maya raised her chin. "Words alone aren't going to keep your life fresh and dynamic. Despite your love of words, they aren't enough."

Maya got up and grabbed two dainty coffee cups from the ebony-toned credenza. "You need to have a fun adventure. Get out of your routine. Your current one reeks of dullness because you lock yourself behind your office door all day. You need new ideas, new experiences. You need to get outside and do something youthful and something that'll get your adrenaline pumping. You need to find a new story."

"What kind of new story?"

"Oh, darling," Maya said with pity. "I'm your editor. You have to write the story. I'll be here like I am now to tell you when your writing stinks like Brussels sprouts or shines like the pearls on my necklace." She ran a manicured nail over her set of pearls. "You need to wake up and take action. Take back your ability to create something magical."

"You said you had an idea."

"Yes. You need a purposeful activity that sparks you back to life, like after Nate passed. Because if you don't, your words will fall to shit. Then you'll turn into a blob of shit too. I don't want that. Please," she stretched her voice out in a plea. "Please don't let yourself become a blob of shit. I love your work and am craving something entertaining from you again."

"So what activity are you proposing?"

She poured them each some coffee, and then she handed one to Taylor.

She sat tall, and her eyes took on a new, brighter sparkle. "Help me and my niece, Lexie, rehab a storefront. We're going to open a pet boutique together."

Taylor laughed and sipped bitter coffee with her honest friend, brooding over her suggestion. "Is my writing that dreadful?"

"Rehab this building. Help us create The Pet Boutique. You'll come back to life."

Taylor sipped the bold coffee. She lingered over the idea of working on The Pet Boutique. She did enjoy working with her hands. The last time she picked up a hammer, the words began to flow again. "Are you going to pay me?"

"Would you settle for a token gift?"

"Cashy Poo?" Taylor laughed.

Maya didn't.

"Do you remember when you and Nate lost those thirty pounds and rebuilt yourselves?" Maya asked. "You emerged changed, more vibrant, more in tune with life. You need to rebuild again. But not your body. This time you need to rebuild your spirit."

By the time she walked out of Maya's front door, the idea clicked and offered much more promise to jumpstart her creativity than going back to her dark office and staring at her blank screen.

Chapter Three

"I hate to break it to you, Auntie, but I doubt that even a rat would want to hang out in here."

Lexie winced at the dreary walls and ugly gray-beamed ceiling of the empty storefront. Historic district? More like prehistoric district. How long had it been since those walls had been treated to the soft bristles of a paintbrush?

The store reeked of mildew and cat pee, and it stung her nostrils. Lexie pulled her shirt up over her nose.

Her aunt, lost in the possibility of the place, didn't seem to notice the stench.

Her white boxer, Cashmere, yanked her toward the oversized grimy front window. When Lexie let the leash go and Cashmere cut loose, a cloud of dust dispersed in a chalky haze. She flopped her legs on the front sill, scanned the street, and then bolted toward the back of the store to where Auntie Maya had placed a bag of muffins.

Cashmere sniffed the bag and dug her head into it, almost winning a mouthful. But Lexie, gaining the reflexes of an Olympic athlete since adopting her, stopped her. Cashmere twirled, chasing her wiggly butt, instead.

Boxers were clowns dressed in fur.

Lexie's aunt had tricked her into the deathtrap with great ease, tempting her into downtown Annapolis to get a fun psychic reading. Leave it to her auntie to cast a white lie for the sake of chasing an idea. A big, fat, outrageous idea, at that. Lexie had banked that the psychic would confirm that her job interview that afternoon would pan out. That she'd finally be able to lift her head a little higher than she had over the past few months. Oh no. Nothing of the sort. Instead, she stood a silent

17

sentinel to her aunt's big vision of taking that smelly storefront debacle and turning it into a pet boutique.

The boutique idea could've been a whole lot worse. Like that time her aunt dragged her halfway across the state of Maryland to dig in the mud for shark's teeth to give to her future grandbabies one day. They came back with rocks Lexie could've plucked up with her toe in the backyard after a good soaking rain.

Lexie wrinkled her nose and glanced at her watch. She'd need to go home and shower before the interview if she didn't want to smell like she'd rolled around in a litter box. If she landed that job, she'd be able to keep her car. If not, she'd have to sell it. If only she had planned her departure from her job more effectively.

She needed that interview.

"What do you want me to say, Auntie? That I love it? I see potential?" Her face creased into painful folds from the stench. "I can't. There, I told you the truth. Now can we go?"

Cashmere raised her head higher than normal.

"Even she can't take it."

"Wait until we get done with it," her aunt said. "You'll see. Where there is love, there is life."

Her aunt breezed around the room on a dancer's high, swinging her arms wide as she spun. Her silky floral poncho celebrated each of her swings. She glanced around the dingy space with love in her eyes, seeing the potential take shape in that sharp mind of hers. She glowed and mirrored a woman half her age.

Auntie Maya had great taste, typically. Her home always smelled like fresh flowers. She always appeared so balanced and free, like a leaf floating on a mountain breeze. She swept into a room on a graceful sashay, charming young and old with her zest for life. Except when she dropped the occasional F-bomb. Once in a while she'd let one rip, and shock anyone within earshot.

"There's a lot of potential here. Look at that crown molding." She pointed to it, dragging her finger through the air as she traversed the length of the room. "Things don't last anymore. They construct everything with a cookie-cutter approach and dull, fake wood nowadays. This molding has personality. It energizes the room. And once it's painted, it'll pop. People will enter to buy their home-baked dog biscuits and admire it. It drapes the place in sophistication. You know, back in the day, I bet fancy people lived here. They likely sipped fine teas from England and nibbled on delicious crumbly blueberry tarts in this room. We can do the same with the boutique, serve delicious human and canine treats at artsy tables decorated with mosaic tiles."

Lexie used to be a staff photographer for a home décor magazine, so she could spot good space. As of late, though, she took selfies in front of her meals and attempted to create the illusion that she had it all together. So any opinions she braved to share shouldn't be trusted.

Her job went belly-up after she asked for a leave of absence when her aunt had a heart attack. Okay, not a heart attack exactly. More like a long, drawn-out, but realistic, panic attack. Someone stole her laptop right from her desk at home. Who wouldn't panic? Of course, by the time the paramedics sped her off to the emergency room, she remembered she had forgotten it at the café at Barnes and Noble. But still. That laptop served as her lifeline.

Lexie didn't discover those details until she arrived in Maryland, and unfortunately after she requested and was denied the leave of absence.

The job stressed out Lexie anyway. All the deadlines drove her batty. And she didn't enjoy living in snowy Lincoln, New Hampshire, either. The time she landed in a ditch off the Kancamagus highway and a moose ate its breakfast a few hundred yards away had done her in. Of course, had she not forgotten her camera at home that day, maybe she would've gained an incredible collection of photos from the incident.

Cashmere didn't much care for walking in the deep, unrelenting snow, either. She'd skip around it, yapping at its torture to her sensitive paws.

All ended well. Sort of. On one hand, she liked being closer to family. And on the other hand, her girlfriend's job could eventually transfer to Maryland. They banked on that happening. Now, at least Lexie could get them settled in just in case that dream did pan out. At the moment, her girlfriend, Christine, was temporarily working out of the Miami office, trying to get one of her company's teams up and running. So Lexie didn't mind leaving lonely New Hampshire.

Though, Lexie did miss her friends. And happy hours. Oh, she loved those watermelon martinis at Louie's Grill. And those crunchy, fried asparagus spears.

She also missed her cool apartment with the big windows that opened to an exquisite view of the quaint shops lining the center of town.

If Lexie squinted out the big, dirty window before her, the view did have a similar appeal. Well, maybe the word appeal stretched the truth a bit. She'd be willing to settle her word choice on *look* instead. Yes, a similar *look*.

"I've arranged the boutique in my mind already," her aunt said. "The reception counter can sit by this wall. I'll place large buckets, like the bushels we get from the apple orchards in New England when I visit, right next to it. Oh, I have another idea." She cupped her hands under her chin and spun to face Lexie. Her blue eyes twinkled. "We can hire an artist to paint a mural of dogs. Lots of dogs running free on a grassy hill. I see it, all clear as day and am ready to arrange it."

Her aunt liked to arrange life on the fly—no thought of consequence. She just went after things like she could erase the negatives later on down the road. But life wasn't an electronic document. She couldn't arrange life like she could a manuscript.

She approached new ideas with delight, treating them as the sparkly, action-packed words in a document that she could copy, cut, and paste. If they sucked, she could hit delete, add an action verb or italicize on a whim. Like the time she wanted fresh eggs and arranged to turn her backyard into a haven for guinea hens. She paid someone to build an open coop and pen for them. A week later, her homeowner's association plastered a notice on her door. She had to find a new home for the hens and tear down the coop.

Did she learn her lesson?

Duh! Did the room smell like a spring garden in full bloom?

Lexie glanced around the space, trying to see what her aunt did. She spotted something toward the back wall that turned her skin into a goose bump party. "What are those sticky pads for? Are they for rats?"

"No. Don't be silly, darling." Her aunt moved to her side and twisted Lexie's

20

cheek between her fingers. She laughed. "They're for cockroaches, I would think. How's a rat to fit on such a small thing?"

Her aunt walked alongside one of the long walls, sliding her finger on it. Curiosity sprang in her eyes, like she'd just discovered cave drawings. What mesmerized her so? The asbestos inches from her fingertips?

Cashmere sat tall, statue-like, following Auntie Maya with her big dark eyes. She perked her ears with each of her aunt's inflections, seemingly as confused as Lexie about what Auntie Maya saw in the place.

"You're an editor, not a pet boutique connoisseur. Caring for your four dogs requires patience, sure, but it doesn't come with the skills to run a brick-and-mortar business. What are you going to do? Edit manuscripts in between selling bags of dog treats?"

Her aunt's wrinkled, pink-glossed lips puckered as she headed back over to Lexie's side. "I didn't know how to inject Toby with insulin when I took him home from the shelter, but I figured it out. Jab and press my thumb against the doohickey. It isn't rocket science. Honestly, darling. Your auntie is smart." She took a Superwoman stance. "If you stand with hands on hips, feet wide apart, shoulders back, gazing ahead with laser focus, you'll gain confidence."

"You can't keep that pose forever." Though Lexie figured she ought to try it for herself. After repeatedly failing at securing a new job, confidence kept its distance.

Why would her aunt want to start over at her age? She should buy a sports car and take up smoking pot if she wanted to recapture her spunky side. Turning that place into a boutique would require that she disastrously lunge into scary things like power tools, paint thinners, and tall ladders. The place should've been condemned. Pour some gasoline and strike a match, save historic Annapolis from the eyesore. Perhaps people did at one point drink from fancy teacups as they sat in wing-backed chairs and smoked cigars. But in the present moment, it resembled the underneath of her hiking boots after trudging through muddy, gritty, wet leaves.

Her aunt dropped her pose and placed her hands on Lexie's shoulders. "I got this place for a steal. I already met with the zoning department, lawyer, accountant, and hardware store. Everyone agreed that I stepped into the right place at the right time. Sure, it needs some cosmetic love and creative business planning. Once I pour some ingenuity into it, I'm golden. I might even end up the front page of the *Gazette* if I'm smart about it."

Her auntie's eyes bore into hers. *Watch out world, Auntie Maya's on a mission. If anyone could set a plan on fire, Auntie Maya could.* She didn't plan well at all, unless she was editing. But zoning department? Lawyers? Accountants? Not only had she already set the plan into motion, she did so with a seriousness Lexie had never seen.

Like it or not, Lexie would be hearing all about The Pet Boutique on every morning walk. She hadn't seen her auntie's face pink up since Tony Robbins tapped her hand as he ran past her down one of the aisles at his convention in Washington, D.C.

How would Lexie ever break it to her that she had dived right smack into the deep end of the pool without a life jacket?

"This place needs too much work, Auntie. You're in over your head on this one."

She lifted her chin and turned on her heel. "Not if you help me."

Lexie shook her head. "I'm interviewing. Today. That's right. I'm interviewing today for a job in Bel Air. The commute will be an hour on a good traffic day. Which means, I'll be moving from your house soon. Very soon." Her bra strap scratched against her back. "Trust me, don't put anything down on this place. It isn't worth it, even if I don't get the job in Bel Air."

"Too late."

Lexie's face burned. "You already purchased it?"

"No," her aunt said on a tiny whistle.

Lexie eased her shoulders down. "Well, thank God."

"I leased it. From Goldie. My psychic. She owns it. She runs her studio next door and lives upstairs. She sees its success too. She foresaw that the fudge shop that used to be here would crash and burn from day one." She placed her hands on her wide hips. "She's intuitive. She said the sun was shining all over The Pet Boutique. Then her best friend, Emma, freaked a little because Goldie told her the same thing about getting together with Haley and becoming an artist." She placed her finger over her lips. "Oh, Emma can paint the mural. They'll be here from Denver for a month to do an art show in Baltimore. See, it's all perfect."

"Why are you doing this? You don't even like to pick up your dog's poo in the backyard." Living with the guinea hens in her home would've been better than this.

Auntie Maya bowed her head. Her face drooped and depressed Lexie right away.

"I won't live like an aardvark for the rest of my life."

Her aunt banked on her asking how an aardvark lived. It's how she conversed. Bait and reel in for the sheer fascination of spitting out useless facts.

"Go on. Tell me how an aardvark lives."

"Alone. It spends its life digging its snout into the earth to eat and burrows itself in the cold dirt. Their kids leave after six months and it's so long family. No one on the planet cares where it sleeps, how it eats, or if it lives or dies. The poor aardvark doesn't exist to anyone but itself." She kicked the air with her toe.

"You're surrounded by family and by some of the literary world's top writers. You'll never be alone."

Cashmere nudged Lexie's calf with her wet nose, done with the boring talk. Ready to move on. Ready to pounce around the new streets and meet new friends. Friends who didn't hang out in places with sticky floors.

Lexie stooped to pet the back of her neck.

"I eat, sleep, and fantasize along with their characters," her aunt said. "I spend my days alone in my home with the computer as my friend. Having you here lately has been eye-opening. You infuse life into my world. It's incredible to sit and sip a glass of wine with someone besides the dogs. I love having conversations in our pajamas. Nothing lasts forever. So I need something to ensure I don't ever end up an old woman holed up in the burrows of my down-comforter."

"So a pet boutique? How about a bookstore instead, and in a better location?"

"A woman of my age needs more than the company of books. I want visitors. Lots of them. The kind who wag their tails and don't give a fuck if my hair sticks up, if my roots are gray, or if I forget to brush my teeth. I don't want to stare at a bunch of people with their noses buried in books. Books. Books. Books. I need to spread my eggs to more than one basket."

"The kind of work this place needs will take months."

"My friend and writing client, Taylor, is going to help. You can help us both! It'll be fun. We'll crank up the music. Drink margaritas. Order pizzas."

Her temples pulsed out a category five beat. Her mother warned her about sleeping in Auntie Maya's attic loft. She'd reel her into her crazy ideas. Her persuasive weight strengthened in the limelight of anyone who accepted her ideas. She could drown them both in a sea filled with nothing more than idealism.

Lexie needed to get her life in order. She needed a new job and an apartment so when Christine finally arrived they'd be settled.

Lexie stared at her aunt's makeshift composter on the grimy counter.

"Why do you have a full composter here?"

"I eat a lot of fruits and veggies. So does Goldie. We spent the last two days rifling through paperwork and ideas. We needed fuel. So I brought lots of snacks. I don't waste scraps."

True. Nothing went to waste with Auntie Maya.

Lexie contemplated the composter. Inside represented the unwanted—the tips of celery stalks, the bruised parts of an apple, the used up grinds from a coffee pot, the cracked shells from hard-boiled eggs, and the pokey tops of pineapples. If those scraps could talk, would they ask her why they'd been tossed away, out of sight, leaving them to find home in a place where they hadn't started off.

Lexie discarded things with ease, like her side dresser or her pleated curtains with the brown and orange stripes she carried out to the curbside last month. For years they hung out with her in life, and in a blink she decided that they no longer served her life plans for a bright and cheery home. What would happen to them? Would they spend years decomposing in a rotting pile of trash at the landfill or might they be plucked up with saving grace from the love of a stranger yearning for such décor in her life?

Lexie didn't always waste things. She loved saving things when she could. Like

24

that time when she was a teenager and she rescued a baby squirrel from the storm sewer on her street and found someone willing to nurse it back to health. She could've walked right past it. But when she saw Auntie Maya's face distort in a pain she never wanted to see, she jumped in.

Hell, she adored her aunt. She would fling neon paint on the walls if she asked her to.

Her aunt deserved to be happy.

Lexie would dig in and get her hands dirty.

"I can do some until I get a job."

"Screw the job. You don't want it anyway. Do you want to take pictures of babies in front of backdrops all day?" She bent forward and petted Cashmere's white chest. "Cashmere," she said on a high inflection. "You and your momma can be my business partners instead. She'll be able to keep her car that way. Would you like that?"

Cashmere rose off her haunches and turned in a few circles, wiggling her bum.

"See? Cashmere likes the idea."

Business partner? Lexie couldn't blink in the seconds that followed, even if someone handed her a million dollars for doing so. "I'm not in a position to be a business partner or screw the job thing."

Auntie Maya twisted her mouth. "I disagree. But sure. Okay. You don't need to screw the whole job thing. You can still interview. In the meantime, though, we can enjoy the process together." She took Lexie's hands and swung them. "If a job comes along, fine. You can remain a silent partner, and we'll have fun with marketing meetings on the back deck as we grill steaks and boil potatoes."

She swung her arms high. So high Lexie's neck cracked.

"I don't know anything about running a pet boutique."

"You order from Amazon. So there you have it. Inventory. Check. You love dogs and they love you. Check. You're good at handling unruly people. Check." She squeezed Lexie's hands.

A plea sat in the blue of her aunt's eyes, the same kind her aunt used on her years ago when she begged her to go with her to Disney World during the middle of summer.

Auntie Maya offered her home to her. She didn't take money for rent. She wouldn't let her buy groceries or clean the bathroom. She took Lexie in like a wounded squirrel, and Lexie didn't even try to run free. She snuggled up to that comfort without regard for the consequences. Say "no" and be a horrible human being. Say "yes" and forfeit her life for a while.

"Let me sleep on it."

Her aunt's eyes lost their twinkle. "Sure. Of course."

Auntie Maya dropped her shoulders and aged ten years. Lexie couldn't even guess her age. She fibbed about it. Ten years ago she turned fifty-eight and last year she turned fifty-two. She could be seventy for all Lexie knew.

"It's got a fenced-in backyard."

"How big?" Lexie asked.

"Big enough for dogs to enjoy puppy ice-cream and parents to fling balls to them. Cashmere will be able to spend her days frolicking in the grass and playing host to new friends. Go have a look." She skittered away. "I'm going to tinkle."

Her aunt headed to the bathroom at the far end of the store.

Lexie walked down the dank hallway to the back door, pulling out her cell to check her notifications. Then she tripped over a piece of dislodged wood and her phone flew out of her hand. "Shit." She bent to pick it up. The sticky floor caught on her shoes, causing her to topple onto the grime. "Oh, for heaven's sake." She climbed to her feet and stepped right into a ginormous spider web. She felt a spider drop onto her head.

She screamed and smacked her head, flinging herself in circles before bending over to shake her ponytail.

Cashmere skidded to her side, flinging her head every which way and barking for reinforcements as she did anytime a deliveryman dared drive their truck down the street.

The front door opened and closed.

"Are you okay?" A woman's voice echoed across the empty room.

26

Through her legs, Lexie caught the sight of a sporty-looking woman wearing an orange baseball cap and carrying a bucket from The Home Depot.

Cashmere stopped barking and rushed toward the woman, wagging her whole body.

The skin across her hairline pulled. She screamed again, flinging her hair around and raking her fingers through the remnants of the spider web.

"Get out," she wailed, snarling her fingers in her hair.

Her scalp itched.

The spider could be weaving itself a new home in her wavy mess of hair.

She wanted to run. But then, the skin on her chest itched. Maybe it went into her shirt. Still bent over, she lifted her shirt over her head and tossed it to the sticky ground.

She rose. "Spider. There's a spider," she managed.

"It's on your shirt."

Lexie panicked, wiggling and tamping her shoulders, chest, stomach, and back.

"On the floor," the woman said.

Cashmere, her trusty sidekick, launched into rescue mode, snorting and pawing at it.

Lexie caught her breath while attempting to straighten her tangled hair.

The woman moved in, brushing past Lexie's exposed skin, and bent to grab her shirt from under Cashmere. She shook the spider from it, then handed it to Lexie with a slight smirk on her face. "Are you okay?"

Lexie tore the shirt from her hands and pulled it over her head. "I'm fine. It surprised me that's all." She scanned the sporty woman wearing an Orioles baseball cap with a thick ponytail sticking outside the back hole of it. "Who are you? You're not the psychic are you?"

"I'm surely not psychic. I didn't see this coming," she murmured, wrestling with her growing smirk.

"Well, me either. Surprises have popped up all over the place today."

"Maya asked me to come by."

"Are you the writing friend?"

The woman nodded.

"She's in the bathroom," Lexie said.

"You've got a bit of the web still in your hair."

Lexie whacked her head again, and the web twisted around her fingers.

The woman's smirk continued to get bigger with each of Lexie's attempts to shake the web off.

"You can wait for her in the main room." Lexie waved her away with a snarl. "Auntie Maya," she yelled out. "You've got a visitor."

Auntie Maya opened the bathroom door and danced toward the woman. "Now before you say anything," she clasped her hand around the woman's bicep. "Remember what I told you about keeping an open mind. Oh, and you've met my niece, Lexie, I see."

The woman scanned the tall ceilings. "You can say that," she said without looking at her.

"I told you that Taylor's going to help us, too. She needs, well...how can I say this?"

Taylor swiped her hands together. "Some inspiration."

Maya clapped her hands. "Yes, inspiration. Perfect word choice. Talk about a clean palette to get the juices flowing. Taylor researched rehabbing old places for a novel she released last year. She went all in. She's going to help bring this place to its full potential while she works out her writing kinks."

Taylor cocked her head. "She's got it all planned out," she said to Lexie.

"She always does."

Taylor and Maya walked around the center of the room.

"We have our work cut out for us," Auntie Maya said. "I have no clue what our first step should be."

Taylor laughed. "Maybe calling an exterminator."

Chapter Four

The next day, Auntie Maya had invited Lexie to the monthly breakfast celebration of life for her late husband, Skip. Lexie adored her Uncle Skip and was honored to attend.

All three of her aunt's kids and their spouses also joined in the picnic celebration at the gravesite, each bringing a breakfast dish and a story to tell. Even Cashmere tagged along for the celebration at her aunt's insistence. They all hung out on a couple of blankets, ate, and caught up with each other.

Her aunt shared her news about The Pet Boutique, and no one applauded the idea.

Meanwhile, Cashmere chewed on a marrowbone as she lay on her favorite heart covered blankie. Gnaw. Grunt. Yack. Back to gnaw. She enjoyed the sunshine, unaffected by the tension brewing as Auntie Maya tossed in a lie to smooth everyone's concerns over her finances.

She had told them all that Lexie tossed in half the investment as her silent partner.

Lexie braced for impact, and with good reason. Her extended family was quite the mixture of sweet and salty.

The saltiest of the bunch, her cousin Jack, looked about ready to punch her for allowing his precious mommy to get involved in such a ludicrous idea. Lexie would've agreed had her aunt not sent her an SOS from the other side of the blanket.

Jack nearly passed out at the news. His husband, Nico, the sensitive pleaser, cradled his hand and calmed him down.

Nico brought out the best in Jack. Lexie adored them as a couple. They worked together like a well-oiled machine. Nico always softened Jack's pretentious ways with his empathetic personality, and Jack protected Nico from being taken advantage of. Over the past decade, they learned how to navigate each other's quirks with great skill.

Her cousin, Ally, and her husband, Tom, typically shared sugary, loving gazes. Not after Auntie Maya got through shoveling her news onto them though. After that, those sugary gazes turned into way too many eye rolls. Even still, they belonged on an anniversary greeting card. Tom with his wavy, golden head of hair and Ally with her shiny, coifed ponytail and brilliant scientific brain always highlighted the space.

Then, came Rex. The rebel. The adopted one. Lexie's favorite. He responded with a good old fashioned *Fuck yeah!* And then added, "I've got some big news myself. My girlfriend's preggo!"

Responding to his elated voice, Cashmere leaped, dropping her bone and picking up her favorite stuffed orange duck instead. Then she broke out into her *bounce off the walls because a cool person is here* dance, launching into spins that defied gravity. She bobbed her head from side to side, swinging her rear end as she bolted from him like a strung-out coke addict to her Uncle Skip's headstone and back to him again. She did this all while gripping the belly of her duck in between her teeth. Then, after she got that out of her system, she pounced on Rex's chest and licked his face. He let her, even lifting his chin for easier access.

Jack scoffed.

Ally marked the scoff with a chuckle.

Auntie Maya clapped.

Then, Nico elbowed his hubby, and a fake smile spread across Jack's face.

Lexie could smell the jealousy. Jack would never be Rex in Auntie Maya's eyes. Fun, adventurous, cool Rex with his dreads and knack for charming even the most miserable of old people. He had that ability to be the tough guy one second, and the softy the next.

Rex was a foster kid, adopted by Lexie's aunt and uncle when he was five years old. He claimed the title of wild child, experimenting with skateboarding, marijuana, and forgoing the college life to open a business with one of his friends, growing medical marijuana at a renovated mill in downtown Baltimore.

He lived a full, fun life.

And now, parenthood had blessed him before the rest of them.

Go Rex!

~ ~

"The fudge shop that used to be here stopped caring about cleanliness," Auntie Maya's psychic friend, Goldie said. A fit Latina woman, she stood in the center of the dingy room with her hands positioned on her tiny waist. Everything was tiny about her. Even her ears. She craned her neck and squinted at a blinking light fixture above her head of kinky, dark brown curls. She stretched on her toes and lengthened her four foot frame by at least two inches.

Rex had come along to check out the place. He rubbed his scruffy chin. "How does your psychic gift work? Do you know what's running through my mind right now?"

"I wish it worked like that. Then I'd be able to know if Charlie remembered to deposit my checks yesterday." Goldie lowered her eyes from the light fixture and pointed them at Rex. "He's my husband."

"Ah ha. Your husband." Rex rubbed his scruff harder. "You answered my unstated question. She is a mind reader," he said to Lexie.

"I'm pretty sure we all questioned that." Lexie punched his arm.

"I'm not some weird, freaky lady reading your thoughts." Goldie's kinky ponytail bobbed up and down on her tiny head. "I only do that if you pay." She exposed a set of dimples that lifted her entire face and brought out a beauty that hid in the deep laugh lines along her cheeks. "I'll offer you this, though. In a few months, you're going to be one of the happiest men alive." She walked toward the front window.

Rex turned to Lexie. His jaw hung, and he mouthed a silent OMG.

Auntie Maya giggled. She twirled toward the folding table where her notebook lay and picked it up. "You're so easy, Rex. My innocent little wonder boy." She shook her head and jotted in the notebook. "We're going to need some supplies. Also, a few kennels so we can offer doggy staycations."

"Let's get some shelving and a register set up before we jump into the dog retreat business, too," Lexie said. "We haven't even swept the floor and you're expanding."

"I love seeing my mom so happy," Rex said.

"Me too." Though, Lexie still didn't agree with how her aunt tossed her in the middle of the business with her white lie, as she called it. Lexie got it. Her aunt had to feed her children white lies if she ever wanted to jump into another adventure. With Lexie as a co-partner, they couldn't block their mom's journey.

With less shock than when she first visited the place, Lexie glanced around the room. The idea of a pet boutique grew on her. Annapolis did attract lots of tourists and locals. She couldn't walk past a café or restaurant and not stop to pet a dog. They walked around, lapping up the sun and earning their right to a home-baked delicious and nutritious doggy biscuit. Their target market flooded the quaint streets, and if they set it up right, the door would swing open with hungry pups leading their humans to treat paradise.

Lexie had to admit that spending her day hanging with tail wagging furry friends could be a lot more fun than taking pictures of pretentious houses and the people who owned them.

So the question remained. Could they pull it off?

Lexie had the benefit of time on her side. Her last interview in Bel Air hadn't gone well at all. She blanked when they asked about her greatest value. Taking great photos? Really? A photographer. No shit. She hated interviews anyway. She hated being placed on the hot coals and flipped to char. Self-employment appealed to her. No more fluffing up the résumé or asking her friends back in New Hampshire to pretend they were her former employers.

Her life headed in a dangerous new direction. She could only hang on and hope she didn't fall into a ditch. She didn't want to spend the next few years of her life rotting away along with the passing seasons.

"World to Lexie Tanner. Hello?" Rex knocked on her head.

"What the hell, Rex?" Lexie flicked his hand away.

32

"You went blank. I saw no other way to get in. So I knocked."

Since the day he got comfy with the family, Rex flung his way through conversations without regard like a wrecking ball, smacking into whatever sat in his path. He spoke unfiltered and rough, and approached life in much the same way, stepping one haphazard foot in front of the other to cross to the other side of the room. He climbed on whatever and whomever landed in his way.

He tossed an arm around her and stuck his phone in their face. "Let's get a selfie. The future mother of my kid wants to see the progress." He snapped it before she could straighten her snarl.

"Show her this wall." Auntie Maya pointed to the peeling dark green plaster. "We have an artist who's going to paint a mural on it."

Rex pointed and shot the ridiculous picture.

"Emma and Haley should be here from Denver next month," Goldie said, rejoining them in the center of the room. "Haley's got a few sales calls in the area, so the trip works out. Emma's happy to help."

"How much will this mural cost you, Auntie?" Lexie asked.

"Cost *her*?" Rex raised his eyebrow. "You're paying half, right?"

Lexie scoffed. "I can't do this, Auntie."

"Can't do what?" Auntie Maya asked.

Lexie wouldn't lead her to her own death march. "Lie. Especially to him." She flung her thumb in Rex's direction.

"How much, Mom?" He bypassed the trivial stuff, and stormed right into the meat and potatoes of the standing issue.

"It's my gift to her," Goldie said, then turned on her heel and headed toward the back. "I need to use the little girl's room." Her two inch heels clacked against the sticky floorboards.

Auntie Maya waved Lexie and Rex's blank expressions away with a flip of her jeweled fingers. "Stop gawking at Goldie. We have work to do. First things first."

"No," Rex said. "First things first is I need to know what you lied to me about, Mom."

33

Her aunt exhaled a dramatic sigh. "Alright fine. Lexie didn't help me finance this place."

Rex glanced at Lexie.

"Like I have that kind of money hanging around," Lexie snapped. "I didn't know she was going to launch that lie, either. So I'm not at fault here." Lexie opened her arms, exacerbated. "You two work this out."

"You know how your brother and sister are, Rex, honey." Her aunt's face whitened and sagged. "They worry too much about me and they take all the fun out of being spontaneous and entrepreneurial. If I lived by their strict codes, I'd shrivel up into a wrinkled old ball of muckiness."

Rex's face softened. "So you expect me to keep this a secret from them?"

Auntie Maya stretched her eyes. "Just until it's up and running and they see I'm profitable."

"This is kind of reckless." He stared up at the exposed ceiling rafters.

Her aunt perked back up. "Yes, and that's the whole point. Go in big or don't go in at all."

"You're certain this will turn a profit?"

"Well, not if we stand around here all day contemplating how I live my life." She picked up her notebook again. "Lexie I need your help with selecting paint colors. I'll need you to take a trip to the hardware store to get some color swatches. No peach. I hate peach. My grandmother had painted her pantry peach and it smelled like Lysol. Rex, come out back with me. We need to consider a higher fence."

Before they could take a step, the front door opened on a whoosh. In walked Taylor Henshaw, the so-called famous author turned fixer-upper specialist. "That door's going to need some reinforcements." She examined the metal frame. "It's seen better days."

A small gasp, call it residual shame from her spider web freak out the other day, escaped from Lexie. She swallowed it when Rex snapped a funny gaze her way.

"Ah, she shows." Auntie Maya crossed her arms over her chest. She glanced at her watch. "Only forty-two minutes and twenty-three seconds late."

Taylor landed her playful eyes on Lexie. "Imagine if she had a red pen between those fingers?"

Lexie pulled in her bloated stomach from the blueberry muffins that she wolfed down that morning, and a slight buzz filled the space between her temples. Then the heat of a demanding blush burned across her cheeks, right on cue.

Cashmere spotted Taylor and catapulted toward her, ears back, nub wagging, body wiggling. Taylor stooped to her knees and scratched behind her ears. Cashmere bowed her head and enjoyed the attention treat.

When Taylor stood back up, Rex leaped forward and extended his hand. "I'm the runt of the family, Rex. And you are?"

"The only child in my family, Taylor." She shook his hand like a woman who meant business. No frills. Cut to the chase. Alpha woman in the room who doesn't take shit from anyone. The vibe spread clear across her golden kissed face, into the lazy tilt of her half-smile, and into the deep pocket of her well-endowed cleavage.

She had presence. Kudos for that. Who wouldn't with a path extending behind her that included a contract with one of the top American publishers to keep her company?

She suffered writer's block, her aunt had said.

Not as bad as unemployment, but still distressing. That much Lexie could agree with.

Well, put on your gloves, grab a paintbrush, and smear that roadblock until the walls shine, Lexie thought.

Goldie emerged from the back. She cupped her hands over her mouth. "Oh my goodness. It's you. I've read everything. I still can't believe you killed off the husband in *The Widow Maker's Journey.*" Goldie landed before her. "What are you writing now?"

"My creative mind quit on me," Taylor said. "It took a long coffee break and refuses to get back to work. That's why she ordered me here." She pointed to Auntie Maya who still stood hugging herself.

"By the way, you're not going to be able to wear those heels around here," she said to Goldie. Then she glanced at Lexie's feet. "Nor those sandals. Unless you want a splinter in between those pretty toes."

Rex extended his leather-booted foot. "If I had said something to them, Pfft."

Taylor walked around the storefront, drifting toward the area where Lexie scrambled around the floor like a wiggly piece of dessert gelatin that first day they met. Auntie Maya followed.

Lexie bit her lip, dropping her eyes to her naked feet. The same foolish spasmodic rush from the spider assault zapped through her. "I plan on wearing sensible shoes once we get started," she said with force.

Taylor continued to walk and glance at the walls, carrying paperwork under her arms and ignoring her. Cashmere trotted beside her new friend, inspecting the walls as well. "We can either work some serious elbow grease into scrubbing, scraping, and spackling these walls or cover them in sheet rock and start from scratch."

"You're the one who spent time on a rehab project to research this kind of stuff." Auntie Maya dropped her typical know-it-all attitude and followed Taylor like a kid trailing behind her parents at the mall.

Lexie didn't want to spend the next two months of her life fishing paint chips out of her highlighted waves. "I vote for sheetrock," Lexie called out.

"There's no way she's going to go for sheetrock." Rex stole a glance their way. "She likes a good challenge."

"What do you know about that?" Lexie nudged him with her elbow.

"She's not going to want this project to end fast."

"We all want this project to end fast."

He chided her with one of his famous lip curls. "You're so clueless. Either that or I'm a psychic, too."

"What are you talking about?"

He motioned toward Taylor. "She's into you. She checked you out when you turned away."

Lexie's face reddened all over again.

"Is she your type?"

"I've got a girlfriend."

"Christine forgot your birthday last year. You need to upgrade. Hell, I bet the dog doesn't like Christine as much as she adores Taylor. Dogs know people. She clearly approves."

Cashmere adored Christine. Whenever they Skyped, Cashmere would perk her ears at the sound of Christine's high-pitched greetings to her. Of course, their online time together didn't happen as often as Lexie would've liked. Lately, Christine's texts and calls lessened because of her job demand. But Rex didn't need to know that detail. "Once again. I've got a girlfriend."

"Where is she?"

"In Miami."

"More business travel?"

"It's her job. Once she gets that office up and running, she's going to come here and work out of the Baltimore location. She's great at what she does, so she's in high-demand. What can I say?"

"Why are you back here and not traveling with her?"

"Because I'm getting us settled in here first. Besides, I don't like the humid Miami weather, and Cashmere would die in that heat."

Rex scrunched up his cheeks and then loosened the tension, creating a weird vacuum draining noise. "Just be mindful, that's all."

"You're the expert relationship advisor in the family? What are you on right now? Your twentieth love? I lost count after ten."

"This time it's real."

"Because you knocked her up?"

"Because she hasn't asked me to change. I can grow pot. I can ride a motorcycle. I can get more tattoos. No fights. She loves me for me. No one's ever done that before."

Lexie couldn't argue the logic. Thankfully, Christine never asked her to change. The few girlfriends she sifted through over the years always asked her to gain weight, dye her hair a darker shade, or wear brighter lipstick. "Look alive," they'd say.

Apparently, they didn't like her skinny body, blonde hair, and natural lips.

Lexie changed the subject as they headed out. "So you're going to be a father, huh?"

Rex opened the door for her, and before Lexie could walk through it, he pulled her into a hug. A tight, appreciative hug. "Thank you for always accepting me for me, too." He kissed the top of her head. "I love you, cuz."

Lexie swallowed the ball of emotions that lodged itself in the back of her throat. "I love you too, goofball," she mumbled into his leather jacket.

~ ~

When Taylor's dog, Oscar, died a few months earlier, her creativity vanished along with his ashes when she spread them over his favorite stream in Patapsco Valley State Park.

Grief was a funny thing. It stole the breath right out of Taylor's lungs and left her gasping, tongue flagging to the side, eyes bulging, chest heaving. It snuck up, curling around her and squeezing until she surrendered to it. Taylor excelled at using the tools of grief, wails, and pleads. With enough force, she overcame the first wave and braced for the next.

It had been several weeks since her last wave broke her down. She and Maya giggled about a garden gnome with a hat that resembled a shriveled up penis. Then the guilt over laughing smothered her because poor Oscar could no longer join in with his momma's good times.

Well, that little meltdown, along with handing over a set of poorly written chapters afterwards, landed her in a dilapidated historical building, warding off the sharp eyes of a psychic and a few untrained helpers. Granted, Maya's niece, Lexie, was sexy as hell with her tight jeans and sandals. But who showed up to a rehab project wearing sandals? At least the guy with dreads had the sense to wear boots. Though, that leather jacket would be speckled in primer before he could twist the ball of his lip ring.

God only knew what kind of paint colors they'd come back with from the

38

hardware store.

Ah well, all in the spirit of getting her brain refocused and back to writing. It worked when it struck the first time after her husband, Nate, died. It would work again. Something about spreading the creamy side of a paintbrush over a blank wall released the blockage.

She couldn't wait to get back to words. But for that to happen, she needed to work some magic with the building.

She scratched the back of her neck as she glanced around.

Maya counted on her. What if she failed her? Sure the walls could be redone and the floor re-sanded. She could do those things with her eyes closed. Once you rehab a building with horsehair plaster and termite-infested wooden beams, you could pretty up any place with the right tools and a bit of patience.

Taylor agreed to Maya's demand for two reasons. One, she cared for Maya. The woman treated her like family. Maya went out of her way over the years to ensure Taylor's growth as a writer. She set up interviews for her. She introduced her to hands-on professionals living and breathing the life of her characters. Once she even figured out a way to worm Taylor into the hidden underground of Denver airport to research her suspense novel *Under God's Ground*.

Second reason, Taylor needed to work out her writing block kinks. She'd never experienced writer's block to the extent of her latest episode. So she couldn't grasp this latest round's intensity until it struck her down with its piercing tip. It gutted her of words, thoughts, feelings—hell, even the ability to sit in one place long enough to turn on her laptop.

Taylor decided she'd start off the rehab project by issuing a strict warning to Maya. Stay away from the saws and drills. Maya needed her fingers to edit again soon. With any hope, Goldie, the psychic, would already see danger lurking and stand far away from the energy vibes of Taylor's ever-going internal dialogue about life and her past screw-ups.

At the very least, that white freckled boxer would be fun to hang with. Rex might also be cool to have around. He, at least, didn't have a filter. Taylor enjoyed keeping the company of people who spoke with truth and conviction. Rip off the bandage and get it over with. But the sexy spider lady. God help her. She could end up leaping onto a freshly-painted wall if an ant crawled past.

She was adorable though, with her messy blonde spirals and freckled nose.

As Taylor sorted through the supplies she'd brought in that day, her mind tangled up with images of Lexie's long, milky-colored legs and sharply focused blue eyes. Her red-hot toenails complimented those string-laced sandals, even if that sexy combo didn't belong on a rehab site. She was willing to lend a hand for Maya's sake, which meant she had an empathetic side to her.

Taylor liked a woman who could empathize.

A beautiful woman with a caring heart always weakened Taylor's knees.

"Let's make a list of everything you envision," Taylor said. "Then, we'll figure out our game plan."

"Like a well outlined book," Maya said. "It'll keep us in check."

Taylor swiped her hands together. "Let's outline."

"Charlie and I can help with that," Goldie said, marching in from the backroom carrying a bucket with paint rollers and brushes. "My hubby dug these up from the basement. She placed the bucket down next to a paint-speckled folding table. "It pays not to toss everything out. He loves to purge. I won't let him." She lifted one corner of her mouth. "I drive him nuts."

"I still love you." A tall man with a tiny ponytail at his neck walked in. He wore cargo pants splattered with paint and a twinkle in his eyes. The step ladder he shouldered matched the speckles on his pants. He leaned it against the wall and turned to them all. "I'm Charlie."

Taylor stepped forward. "Nice to meet you. I'm Taylor."

He extended his hand, but then spotted dirt on them. He rubbed his palms on his pants. "The writer?"

Taylor liked him right away.

Goldie rushed past them and over to the closet door. "I've got some folding chairs in here." She placed them in a circle, then motioned for Taylor to join her. "Grab a cup of coffee on the table there and have a seat."

"Do you know what I'm thinking right now?" Taylor asked, cautiously.

"Sit. I don't bite. I just nibble a little." She laughed, then added. "I'm a professional. I dig when I'm paid to dig."

Taylor bit the inside of her cheek and poured a cup of coffee, then paced the small area next to the chairs. She considered asking her about Nate and Oscar.

Charlie dug into the bucket. "I'll be measuring." He walked into the backroom.

"I'll help you," Maya said and followed him.

"He's going to help install the DIY wash basins," Goldie said.

Taylor sipped her coffee. "He's a plumber?"

"Eh, he's a lot of things. Sit. Please. My heart skips when you pace like that."

Taylor sat on command. "Are you able to connect with those who have passed?"

"Of course. If they're willing to come through."

Taylor drew a deep breath. "My husband and dog both died."

Goldie stretched her eyes wide. "I'm so sorry. That has to be difficult."

Taylor nodded.

Goldie studied her for a moment. "They don't always come through."

A heaviness settled in around Taylor. "It's okay. I didn't expect anything. But I had to ask."

"I believe when they don't it's because they're happy on their journey," Goldie spoke softly, reassuring her.

"I like that." Taylor smiled, even though a part of her felt sad that they continued on a journey without her. What a selfish way to look at it, Taylor thought. But she couldn't help it. The emptiness always stole her breath.

"If you stay aware, they may give you a sign from time to time. Like a song that reminds you of them might start playing when you need it most. Something like that."

Taylor eased back in her chair, still not comforted. She hadn't received a single sign.

"You must've loved them a great deal."

Taylor nodded. "Yeah."

"You know, when I first met Charlie, I didn't like him." Goldie relaxed back in her chair. "He was scraggy. And he was with someone else at the time, so I didn't think anything of him. But a year later, he was single and asked me out. I hesitated. But he was sweet and patient. So eventually I said yes. I thought for sure my daughter, Tatiana, wouldn't care for him either. Then he brought her a stuffed teddy bear and introduced the bear as Apollo. She took Apollo and hugged it. Then she asked if we would take her to McDonalds. I opened my mouth to say no. How could we go when I had agreed to go on a date to a steakhouse with the scruffy man that night? But then he said he'd be honored."

Love spilled upon Goldie's face, softening her features even more. "I fell in love with him and it's been history ever since. He's a walking, talking, eating teddy bear. Tatiana, is no longer that little girl. She's in college and she still has Apollo. She refers to Charlie as her other teddy bear, Zeus."

An odd peace connected her to the eccentric woman. "That's a great story."

"When Tatiana left for college, we were so lost. And depressed. We ate everything in sight." She patted her slightly round belly. "And it shows."

Goldie was petite and had nothing to worry about with her weight. Taylor, however, folded her arms across her belly, regretting the fried eggs and pancakes that she ate at the diner that morning.

Goldie stretched her legs out in front of her and opened her mouth to say more. Then Lexie and Rex came back in the front door.

"We made it halfway to the store, then I realized I forgot my pocketbook," Lexie said, flushed and radiant.

She came up from behind Taylor and grabbed her pocketbook from the folding table. One of her golden spirals tickled Taylor's upper arm.

Taylor sealed her eyes closed for a moment. When she opened them, Goldie sent her a crooked, knowing smile, as if she really could read her thoughts. Taylor couldn't deny that the touch of Lexie's hair on her arm sent a flutter of trills up and down her spine.

The last time a woman tickled her like that, she was a freshman in college and in a breakup with Nate. The woman lived next door for a summer, visiting her grandparents. They shared a bottle of wine on her backyard swing while staring at the full moon. They explored more than the lunar surface that night, and Taylor was never the same again.

The rehab project would change her too, no doubt. Between the work and expectations, Taylor would need to focus harder than usual.

Lexie would be a distraction that she'd have to overcome if she ever wanted to get any work done.

Chapter Five

That night, Taylor opened up a bottle of red wine and sat on her couch. She grabbed her old journal book, the keeper of beautiful memories from the life she used to have.

She opened up to an entry she wrote a year before Nate died.

Oscar is the ultimate encourager of family time. We can't refuse those perky ears or playful tilts of his head when he wants us to group hug or go for a walk. No matter if my characters are singing me a million-dollar song, I must hit the save button, lace up the hiking boots, and follow my family out the back door and toward the wooded path by the river. As our feet crunch pebbles and fallen tree debris, we connect through the shared love of that crazy, fun-loving Oscar who demands we nurture the time together. Oscar fills in the nooks and crannies where anxiety tries its darnedest to sneak in. He has a way of turning anxiety away and filling life with so much joy. I don't fear the quiet with Oscar around. Memories of my past mistake from years ago don't show up because he fills that scary space with his crazy barking, chasing, and mud rolls.

When Oscar passes, he's going to break my heart. He's going to take a piece of my soul with him. I dread that scary space, the space where my past catches up with me. A time I can never go back and fix.

When Taylor's husband, Nate, passed away several years ago in a motorcycle accident, she took it hard. She had Oscar to help her through the grief cycle. He would sit there with his beefy belly and offer his stoic posture for Taylor to sob into. Nights

45

and early mornings still echoed the silence of Nate's chuckles when he watched *That '70s Show* on Netflix while he rode the spin bike in the living room.

Thankfully, Oscar stood in, forgoing a comfortable spot on the couch or bed to nurture Taylor during a breakdown. They usually occurred on the unforgiving ceramic tile in the kitchen or breakfast nook where they used to share sections of the newspaper before he shuffled off to his job at the hospital.

No doubt, those years had been filled with great memories. Especially toward the beginning of those years, back in high school, when life took on a glow that could only be seen through the eyes of budding friends that eventually turned into lovers years later.

Then, somewhere along the way, life and all that came along with adulting blew in and covered them in a veil of protection on one hand and distraction on the other. They had settled in over the years, into their ideal home. They celebrated things like furniture, curtains, paint colors, smartphones, and smart televisions. Everything was so darned smart, yet Taylor sat like an ignorant fool. Thanks to technology's ease, she no longer needed to even calculate things on her own.

All those times spent mulling over unimportant things, things that killed rather than elevated their souls, acted as a piece of clothing that covered the hidden parts.

After Nate's death, Taylor needed a reason to get out of bed, brew the coffee, and brush her teeth. Exercise had slipped way down the priority list at that point, even though Maya insisted it would help her push through the cobwebs in her brain.

So to rid herself of those cobwebs, and much to Maya's dismay out of concern for her well-being, Taylor retraced her steps from many years earlier to a farmhouse out in North Carolina. The trip didn't amount to much other than finding out Ms. Peabody had passed away.

The halfway home for single women turned into a bed and breakfast, complete with horse-drawn carriage rides and basketball courts where Taylor used to sit with Ms. Peabody and talk about the life she would live after she gave birth.

Reminiscing about such things, combined with grief, congealed into a dangerous situation. It caused people to do foolish things like dig up a past they promised they'd leave alone.

Taylor's eighteenth year had branded her in shame. When she handed her baby over to a set of strangers with wide grins and designer clothes, she died at the hands of remorse.

Her daughter would've been fourteen years old at the time of Nate's death.

She crossed her mind every day. The girl might be lonely in need of family. She might have questions about why she gave her up. No one could answer those questions except for Taylor.

Some answers she might not want to hear, though.

The father was a boy she hardly knew. She couldn't even remember what he looked like. She did remember that his name was Tim Flurry and that he drove a red Camaro. She remembered that because that's where they conceived their daughter. If she did get the chance to meet with her, then that detail would remain buried.

Some things were better left unstated.

But she wanted to share so many other details.

How she craved to pull back the blinds and peek through the window at her life. Was she safe? Did she study hard? Was she a cheerleader? Did she have nice friends? Did she turn out to be a good girl or someone who bullied others? Were her parents still alive? How many siblings did she have? Or was she an only child like Taylor? Did she look like Taylor?

God help the child if so. Taylor hoped she didn't have her stubby feet or lack of a singing voice. She would've liked to see her with dark hair and the same brown eyes as her, though. Those had always served her well in pictures for her book covers. Except if they shot the picture from the left too much. Her nose tended to protrude out on that side more than the right.

The week after she had returned from hearing about Ms. Peabody's death, Taylor took an even braver step. She contacted the adoption agency to let them know she wanted to unseal the adoption records.

"It's not that easy, sweetheart. You'll have to send a letter stating you're willing to be contacted should the adopted child decide the same thing. As of today, the adoptive party hasn't signed any such agreement. So until she does, the records will have to remain sealed."

Receiving that kind of news, twisted Taylor's heart. Her daughter wanted nothing to do with her. Not even curious? Didn't she question her origins? That question poked her every day, every minute, every second. Then she'd remind herself that her daughter, being only fourteen years old at the time, wouldn't have been able to decide for herself. Her parents would've needed to make that choice to unseal the records for her.

That little tidbit, in fact, did help Taylor get out of bed again. As for her creativity, that had died. Thus began her first trudge through the dreaded land of writer's block where words piled up like roadkill along the side of a rocky and tumultuous path toward nothing. It dragged on forever, that trudge, toying with her, stealing her mojo until she surrendered to Maya's plea to get out of her own way and go into hands-on research mode rehabbing an old building.

It worked. Even Oscar seemed less depressed when she'd return home from hours spent nailing wood and painting walls. Life had taken a turn, and she had put the past behind her. The next few years got easier.

Then, just a couple of months ago, Oscar passed away.

Maya to the rescue again.

A pet boutique.

~ ~

It had been five days since Christine had last contacted Lexie with more than a one sentence message to let her know she was busy, but wanted to say hello. Lexie grew frustrated. Living so far apart took a lot of effort, and lately Lexie was the only one offering that effort.

Lexie sent Christine a third text that night. *I'm heading to bed, so I guess no Skype chance again tonight.*

Christine responded a second later. *I'm still out with clients. Maybe tomorrow? Oh, and by the way, I'm taking three days off the week after next to visit you.*

Oh my gosh, really? Tell me when, and I'll clear my schedule. Cashmere is going to go berserk! Wait until you see. She's going to do pirouettes for you. Be prepared!

Lexie waited another thirty minutes for an excited reply back. When one didn't come, she turned out the lights and settled into a gnawing feeling, one that hinted that disappointment would soon follow.

~ ~

As the days passed, Taylor began to envision great ideas for the boutique. She enjoyed the mental and physical work, and the relaxation it provided each night when she returned home.

Working opened up her mind more, even if the work at that point only entailed purchasing supplies from the hardware store and delivering them into the vacant room.

Rehabbing a building was a lot like writing a book. You had to first plan out the details. Then you had to organize them into a logical sequence. Next, you had to get your feet wet by trying things out. Too much emphasis on perfection at that early stage would paralyze any turn toward necessary change. Get too attached to an idea by spending too much time with it cornered a person.

Taylor couldn't wait to get her hands dirty. The idea of working on The Pet Boutique thrilled her, and she hadn't been thrilled in some time.

That night, as she washed and rinsed her thermos from her lunch at the job site, her cell rang. Probably a stupid sales call. Or maybe her mother. It had been a while since Taylor talked with her. The calls usually turned into canned answers to her mother's tired questions about how she was doing and how her writing was coming along. Her mother tried to connect despite the distance Taylor had wedged between them through the years since her supposed gap year. So many times she wanted to tell her mother the truth. But as the years passed, so too did the opportunities and courage.

She watched the suds slide down the slippery surface of her thermos.

Then her phone beeped a message alert.

She placed the thermos in the strainer and wiped her hands. If it wasn't her mother calling, it may have been Maya checking up on how she enjoyed the day.

Maya knew Taylor's secret and nurtured her even still, and Taylor loved it. Everyone needed someone they could count on. Maya was her coffee on a blistery, snowy morning. Always warm and comforting, able to ease the chill away with a delicious honey coating.

Sure enough, Maya helped mark the end of a pretty good day with a caring message, wishing her pleasant dreams and hoping she was just as excited as her about The Pet Boutique.

Chapter Six

For the next week, Lexie helped her aunt and Taylor decide on some initial floor plans for the boutique. They had ample space to place shelving, a small café-style area, dog-washing stations, and open areas for socializing and enjoying the ambiance. But Lexie feared they lacked manpower to get it all done in time for the holiday shopping season.

Lexie didn't know a drill bit from a screw, let alone how to help lay a new floor and refinish ceiling rafters.

Even though her aunt overwhelmed her with her outrageous deadline, Lexie planned to sneak out for a few hours. Christine would be flying in that morning, and Lexie couldn't wait to see her. First, Christine had to pick up clients from the Baltimore office. They'd be joining them for lunch at Pusser's Caribbean Grille.

Later on, they'd catch up more intimately over drinks and movies in Lexie's makeshift bedroom in her aunt's attic loft.

"I love Pusser's," Auntie Maya said. "They have the best view in town, overlooking the boats. Can we tag along?"

"I don't think we should impose," Taylor said.

"Will we be imposing?" her aunt asked, arching her eyebrow, innocently.

Lexie couldn't say no to her aunt. Besides, it would be good to show up to the restaurant with someone in case Christine and her colleagues ran late. "You're both welcome to join us. It's not an imposition at all."

"Oh, good! Time away from the dust will do us all good," her aunt said.

A little while later, they headed out the front door, leaving Cashmere with a very willing and excited Goldie as pet-sitter.

They arrived right on time, and Christine and her colleagues had not. A familiar sinking feeling lodged itself in Lexie's belly. An entire thirty minutes past their scheduled meeting time had passed. So Lexie excused her absence to likely getting stuck in traffic. She texted her for the second time since arriving at the restaurant, and then put her phone face down and ordered a chicken sandwich.

A few minutes later, Auntie Maya drizzled ketchup on her Caribbean jerk chicken. "Jack and Ally want to come by and see the boutique."

"You're going to need to tell them the truth."

"I'll tell them the truth, soon. Right now, I need some wiggle room. If I let them control my life, I'll be like one of those birds with clipped wings stuck in a cage in someone's living room. I want to fly. I want to see the view from a tree."

Lexie dug her fork into some rice pilaf. "I get it. Tell them what you need to for now. Understand, though, that if a job offer comes through, I need to take it."

Auntie Maya bobbed her head. "Of course."

Lexie turned to Taylor. "Can you pass the salt, please?"

Taylor passed her the salt shaker. "What kind of a job are you looking for?"

Lexie salted her roasted vegetables. "Photography, preferably."

"Do you have a specialty?"

"I'll take pictures of grass growing out of sidewalk cracks if it'll pay me more than unemployment."

Taylor swigged some water and opened her eyes wide.

"I'm kidding." Lexie forked more pilaf into her mouth. "Tell her I'm kidding, Auntie. I'm anxious to work again, but not that desperate. I can be patient. Christine won't be moving here for a few more months, so I've got some time to get the job situation in order."

Her aunt shrugged. "You don't need to be desperate at all, dear. My mind is overflowing with ideas." She leaned in. "Speaking of ideas, I had an incredible one on how we can bring some attention to our boutique."

Lexie braced herself. "What now?"

Auntie Maya wiped her mouth. "Cashmere inspired me the other day. I noticed

52

her in the front window and that song "How Much Is That Doggy in the Window" popped into my head. Of course, I don't believe in buying a dog, but I do a million percent support adoptions. Let's have dog adoption days! Each month can be a different shelter. They can bring a troop of their most desperate dogs, and we can help them find homes." Her eyes twinkled in the sunlight.

Lexie had to hand it to her aunt. Her idea did sparkle. "I like it." She turned to Taylor. "Do you like it?"

Taylor nodded. "It has a ring to it."

Excitement over the new venture finally filled Lexie. "We can call them Shelter Days and call in the local press for free publicity."

Auntie Maya leaned in and clutched Lexie's hand. "See. That's why you need to stick with me. Partners. If you want to work the camera, take pictures of the dogs." Her eyes flew open. "Oh, wait. A calendar! For charity! Oh my God, the ideas keep coming. We need to write them down. God only knows what'll happen to them if I don't." She pulled out an outrageously large, spiral notebook from her tote bag.

Lexie laughed. "Do you have a laptop in there, too?"

She plopped the spiral notebook on top of the bread crumbs on her side plate and foraged inside her tote again. "I do."

"Don't. I'm joking." Lexie smirked. "Let's stick to the paper and pen, otherwise we'll need a bigger table."

"Very well." Auntie Maya jotted down her ideas.

Meanwhile Taylor sat back, chewing on her bread, taking them in as if she'd never seen two women brainstorm before.

Lexie sipped her water. "Does she get this excited about editing?"

Taylor chuckled. "Not with my writing lately."

Lexie dropped her fork and wiped her mouth with her napkin. She turned her attention to her aunt and took in her zestful attitude. Her mother poked fun at her aunt's eccentricity, but she never complained when Auntie Maya took Lexie in each summer when she was a kid. That allowed her mother and father a chance to spend their summers traveling abroad without her.

She glanced around the deck dining area, attempting to enjoy the light breeze from the bay. Then her cellphone rang.

Christine. Thank God.

"I'll just be a minute. I'm going to take this call from Christine." Lexie climbed to her feet, answering. "Hey, where are you? We're almost done eating."

"We?"

Lexie headed away from the table. "My aunt and her friend."

"I'm glad someone is there with you." Christine's voice softened like someone about to deliver bad news.

"Why?" Lexie stopped walking, placing a hand over her other ear to hear her better.

"Please don't be mad."

"About what?" Lexie asked.

"I can't make it."

Lexie walked toward the railing overlooking the harbor, smiling back at her aunt and Taylor to hide the embarrassment rising.

Lexie's stomach balled up into a tight knot—its usual position when it came to Christine lately. "Why not?"

"I'm really sorry, Lexie."

"That's not an answer," Lexie snapped, tired of being tossed into the second-place position.

"Everything got jumbled at the last minute. The clients I was supposed to meet in Baltimore showed up here instead. And I've been in meetings with them for the past two hours. I had a text message in draft mode to you that I thought I sent. I never sent it, Lexie. I'm so sorry."

"So you're in Miami, still?"

"Yes. I'm not going to make it up this month. But I promise, I'll aim to visit at the beginning of next month."

"Next month?" Lexie's voice reached soprano levels.

"There's a lot going on, Lexie."

Anger spun in her. "Yeah, well, for me too."

"Please don't be upset, okay?" Christine used her most gentle tone with her as if she would crack open. "Things are more complicated here than I thought."

"With the job or between us?" Lexie asked, flatly.

The cruel silence hung between them.

"Let's make time this week to talk, Lexie."

"Okay," Lexie released her voice, like if she spoke too fast or too loud, she might set off an alarm. "Actually, why not tell me what you need to tell me right now?"

Christine cleared her throat. "I can't now. The clients are waiting for me to get back in the meeting."

"Go, then," Lexie snapped again. "Go tend to your clients."

"I'll call you tonight," Christine said, ending the call without confirming with Lexie if she'd even be available.

Lexie clung to the railing. Her ego shriveled and flopped like a wet squid on the floor. Never in her life did she ever plan to end up such a fool, waiting idle on someone who so obviously wanted to run the other way. Since Christine landed in Miami, she acted aloof. She treated Lexie like she was an inconvenience in her schedule on the path to career success—like Lexie was in her way.

Well, Lexie wasn't a cage. She'd never trap her. In fact, if Christine needed space, she'd make it easy on her. She'd open the damned gate for her and let her run free.

She texted her before she lost the courage that rejection gifted her in that moment. *We need a break. Stay in Miami. It's best that way.*

After a few deep breaths, Lexie walked back to the table.

Taylor busied herself by dabbing a french fry into a puddle of ketchup repeatedly. Auntie Maya stared up at her with a question on her face.

"Christine won't be joining us," Lexie said, then sat down and folded her napkin over her lap.

"We figured that from your tone of voice," Auntie Maya said.

Lexie's face flushed. "Well, she couldn't hear me. She's in a loud place."

Auntie Maya wouldn't let up the stare.

"Okay, fine." Lexie tossed her hands up in the air. "She's still in Miami, and I told her to stay there and enjoy her life. Now let's finish eating so we can get back to work."

Her aunt sipped her iced tea with a super sucking force and Taylor continued torturing that poor french fry.

~ ~

Christine texted Lexie five times that day, sending her long messages about not wanting to hurt her. That night, she called and left a desperate message, pleading with Lexie to return her call so they could talk.

Lexie lay on her bed, staring up at the ceiling. Cashmere snored gently next to her. She rested her head against Cashmere's side, lulled by her deep and relaxed breaths. The only reason Christine would want to remain in her life was because she didn't know how to fail at things. She'd rather find a solution than give up. She'd rather torture herself and succumb to a life of pleasantries than risk walking away from something that she committed herself to.

Christine would never be the one to cut the tie, regardless if she was miserable.

If Lexie didn't want to live her life as a sidekick, a mere incidental Christine had picked up along the journey, then she'd have to stay firm.

Lexie sat up tall and called Christine out of respect for herself as a decision-maker and a noble person for doing the polite thing.

They exchanged hellos.

"When I said we needed to talk, I didn't mean I wanted us to break up," Christine said.

Lexie pet Cashmere's back and steadied herself. "We both know this isn't going to work."

"It can work," Christine said with force.

On her terms, it might. But what about Lexie's? "Christine, I don't want it to. And you don't either."

The silence that followed branded Lexie's decision. Christine needed an out, and Lexie had given it to her.

"They asked me to stay on here, but I—"

"Then, you should."

"But what about you?"

"I've got a pet boutique to build." Lexie swallowed the cry in the back of her throat, as tears rolled down her cheeks. "And right now, Cashmere needs a walk, so, I'm going to say goodbye." Cashmere continued snoring, oblivious that Mommy Christine would not be coming home and joining them for a walk ever again.

"How about we don't say goodbye, but instead we say until next time?" Christine asked.

Christine hated to fail, even at goodbyes. And Lexie didn't have the heart to ruin that for her. "Fine, until next time…"

"Until next time," Christine whispered.

Lexie hung up, and dropped her head back against Cashmere's relaxed softness. As the hours passed, the anger from earlier that day disappeared, as did the sadness. Relief slipped in and replaced the bad feelings. It opened the window for her. She floated through it, suddenly free to decide for herself where to go from there.

~ ~

A little over a week after having lunch at Pusser's with Lexie and Maya, work began to show a little bit of progress. Taylor loved deconstructing things. That day, she began to pull up some of the creaky floorboards in the backroom. Lexie and Maya discussed plans out in the front room.

Mid-pound with the sledge hammer, Taylor's phone rang. She let the unknown number go to voicemail. A few moments later, she listened in.

A woman's voice she didn't recognize introduced herself as Tabatha, a clinical aid with the center for family services. Taylor's cheeks numbed. Her heart beat with wild intensity. "Ms. Henshaw, about four years ago you contacted us about unsealing adoption records. Well, I have great news. Please call me back."

Taylor gawked at the phone, expecting it to explode in her hands as part of a dream she still needed to wake up from. After about ten rapid breaths, the reality sank in. Her daughter wanted to connect.

She'd secretly dreamed about sharing such a moment with Nate. But Nate worried that opening up the past might hurt Taylor and her daughter. So Taylor kept her past far behind her where she had long before promised to keep it. Besides, she had waived her rights, and had no business barging into that young woman's life. What did Taylor expect? A loving hug from the beautiful person she handed over to strangers? Best to keep the past where it belonged, Taylor had told herself and wrote another book.

She could lose herself in a story when she had Nate and Oscar.

But with no one left to care? How could she not at least dip her toe in the possibility of her own story? Swirl it around and see what kind of ripple effect it might have?

Taylor paced the backroom.

She opened up her wallet and dug out the quarter the nice man on the bus with the fedora hat had given her eighteen years ago. The tiny black dot in between the words United and States still remained.

She rubbed it between her fingers, as she did anytime she needed to calm down. It soothed her. It always had. The man had helped Taylor to see herself as someone other than the monster she had believed herself to be after handing over her baby to strangers. For one brief moment of time, his kind eyes and thoughtful words reminded Taylor that life wasn't all bad and that hope still existed in the big, scary world that lay before her. Rubbing his quarter always brought Taylor back to that moment of solace when she snuck a small peek at hope.

Taylor paced and massaged the coin, considering the possibility before her.

The second she picked up her phone and called, both of their lives would change. She wouldn't be able to rewind the action. The power in that call could possibly endanger the lives of everyone in its path. Or it could sweep in like a breeze, nurturing them with the lullaby of forgiveness and compassion.

58

Taylor called the lady back and fell to her knees in panic when she answered.

After stumbling through her introduction, the lady filled her in. "The adoptive party has signed to accept the unsealing of the adoption details. So, congratulations. We're just waiting on her to send us her birth certificate for legal purposes. Until then, we have to sit tight."

Taylor's face numbed. "Okay. Sure."

"She lost her birth certificate in a house fire a few years back."

"A house fire?"

"That's what she said. So it may take a little longer than you expect. We'll reach back out to you when we have more details."

A house fire?

An inferno?

Did she lose her home, her clothes, everything?

What if it had left her an orphaned teenager?

Had she been shoved into foster care?

Did she live under a roof with people who didn't love her?

Too many questions and horrors to consider.

Chapter Seven

Lexie had circled around a few stages of grief in the weeks since her final call with Christine. She went from happy to sad, accepting to judging, and peaceful to angry. A breakup was a lot like death. Parts of life were scattered, never to be put back together again. Shared lives were cut down the middle and separated for good. The past became a harsh reminder of time that could've been spent building a better, more sustainable future. That kind of pondering left a person dry and bitter.

Lexie's strength from the initial moments of the breakup turned into a dull thud, warning her that life would speed by her. Lexie caved one day in the first week, sending Christine a text to check in on her and ask how she was doing. Sort of an olive branch extended to help Christine through the whole guilt of failing thing.

Well, that text went unanswered.

As each day passed with still no reply, the anger grew. Had Lexie just been an inconvenience to her all along? Was Christine happier now? Was she already dating someone new? Had she secured an apartment on her own and ordered furniture? What if she had already moved on? What did that say about Lexie?

Two weeks into her sour mood, Ally stopped by. She brought her a plate of cookies and told her Christine didn't know her ass from her elbow. For Ally to use the word ass instead of butt, meant sincerity. They may have grown apart over the years, due in part to her turning elitist when she earned a full ride to Brown University while Lexie enrolled at the community college, but when it came down to the nitty-gritty of things, Ally was still compassionate toward her family.

After Lexie ate ten of the cookies, the sugar rushed to her brain and warped it, causing her to invite Ally out for a drink. Well, Ally drank virgin daiquiris. She wanted a baby, and soon, now that her brother had one in the oven. Meanwhile, Lexie nursed five mojitos. A lot of surprises flew when alcohol ran the show. For instance, she had forgotten how much she hated how Christine smacked oatmeal around her mouth in the morning and how she slurped soup. Christine also had forgotten her last birthday. Sure, thirty-five didn't reign in as a milestone like thirty or forty. But still. A card and a kiss would've sufficed. But she flaked and even stood her up. She later apologized and blamed it on her mother chewing her out for neglecting to visit her the Sunday before. Apparently, Christine was a forgetful girl.

Working at the boutique did begin to help Lexie. Focusing on dismantling something, helped her work through the kinks in her heart. Within a few weeks, she began to feel more like herself again.

~ ~

"If we rag roll the paint on the walls, you won't need to start from scratch with sheetrock."

Taylor educated Lexie's aunt on the finer detail of decorative painting. Rag roll the damned wall, Lexie thought as she pulled up tiny staples from the creaky underlying floorboards. She had pulled up about fifty in the first hour, and had about ten thousand more to go. Her knuckles bled from scraping against the splintering floor. Why couldn't they just plop plywood over the existing boards? The plywood was a half inch thick. Wouldn't it cover up the stupid staples?

Taylor assured her no. So she dug them out, one painful staple at a time, propping her sore ass on one of the pillows from her aunt's couch. A woman had to do what she had to do to get by.

Lexie shoved the edge of her tool under the next staple and pulled it up. It flew in the air and narrowly escaped hitting Taylor's knee. She wore loose cargo pants, and the edge of a handkerchief hung out the side of one of the pockets. She wore a Mt. Saint Joe's baseball cap and looped the dark wavy wisps of her ponytail through the back hole of it.

Taylor and Auntie Maya continued to discuss the walls. Auntie Maya flapped the edge of her silk shawl from India, a present from another one of her bestselling authors. "Very well. I trust you. I'll head back to Lowe's and grab what you need."

"I can go," Taylor said, folding her arms over her baby blue V-neck.

"Nope." Auntie Maya flicked away her offer. "You can help Lexie with the staples while I go. I can't get down on the ground like that anymore."

Taylor glanced at Lexie, and that same little smirk from their first meeting returned to her face. Cashmere tilted her head. Bright and attentive, she followed Taylor as she moved across the room and grabbed a roll of painter's tape.

"I'm fully capable of pulling staples in a timely manner." Lexie adjusted her ass on the pillow. "I finished piling the scrap wood in the back, didn't I?"

Taylor simply nodded and tossed her another smirk.

Once her aunt left, Taylor busied herself with taping off the crown molding. Lexie pushed her speed past breakneck. The staples flew, her knuckles bled, but dammit she covered some serious ground. She wasn't some crazy, spider-swatting woman. She could pull her end of the work. When she committed, she went all in. If Lexie was nothing else, she was determined.

Taylor was also determined. That much Lexie surmised as she watched her. When she fixed the blue tape around a challenging bend in the wall, she stuck her tongue out the side of her mouth and did a weird squinty thing with her left eye.

Lexie guessed that Taylor didn't much care for casual conversation. When she asked Taylor if she went to St. Joe's as a high-schooler, she blushed and her words twisted like a train wreck. She excused herself and went to the bathroom. Then a few minutes later, Lexie asked her if she had a dog.

A curt head shake followed.

Sorry, Lexie mumbled to herself.

Of course, though, Lexie couldn't stop there. It drove her batty when someone treated her like a wallflower. So she asked her a rehab question. She couldn't care less about how to touch up plaster-swirled ceilings, but damned if she didn't toss that baby out as kindling. Low and behold, the woman grabbed onto it and talked her ear off for five full minutes about the boring intricacies involved.

Talk about asking the wrong type of question.

Time for Lexie to take one of those escapist bathroom breaks. Or even toss a spider at her. Anything to avoid more nervous chatter about plaster swirls.

Taylor may not have been a great conversationalist about anything other than plaster, but she did have a spark to her. Something in her eyes, maybe? Or could've been the way her t-shirt clung to her sweaty torso. Ever since the summer she turned thirteen and she experienced her first kiss with a girl named Lucy at day camp behind the firewood cabin, the female body, with all its curves, captivated Lexie.

Taylor had curvy features. Her cheeks plumped up like shiny nectarines when she eased. But something else about her intrigued Lexie.

After spending a few weeks cleaning and prepping the space together, she still couldn't put her finger on what exactly intrigued her.

Lexie tore out her ponytail after clearing another patch of flooring. Then she raked her sore fingers through the tangles. A matted mess resulted. A bird could build a nest and raise a family in it. Those mice Goldie had set out those sticky pads for sure could too. Lexie trashed those pads on day one. Not that she wanted to see little mice crawling around her while she tortured her hands in staple pulling, but she didn't want to see them die. They had a right to be there as much as any of them did. When they hung the open sign on the door, then she'd figure out a humane way to deter them from entering. Until then, she agreed to commune with them.

A funny thing happened when she submitted like that. The things she feared most, in that case, mice crawling up her back and landing on her shoulder, never happened. She hadn't seen one mouse.

She knotted her hair on top of her head and tied an elastic band around it. Sweat dripped down her neck and across her chest. She pulled a wad of tissues from her front pocket and wiped her forehead first, then caught the beads rolling down the side of her neck.

Taylor had stopped taping and glanced at her.

Lexie fumbled with the tissues, then they fell to the ground. She leaned over to grab them, and her boobs practically popped out of her baggy scoop necked t-shirt.

She placed a hand to her chest and climbed to her feet.

A daze glossed over Taylor's eyes, like she had stepped out in front of a bus traveling eighty miles an hour and froze. She shook her head when Lexie caught her staring at the scooped opening to her shirt.

Well, hot damn. Her boobs had stunned Taylor.

Taylor's eyes broke out into a blinking frenzy and her cheeks blotched bright red. "Do you want to use my handkerchief?" She pulled one out of her pocket, and her keys fell to the floor.

As she bent to the grab them, Cashmere landed by her side in a flash.

"Someone thinks she's going for a ride," Lexie said.

Taylor giggled.

Ah, she has emotions.

Lexie reached for Taylor's handkerchief. "Thanks." She darted away before she did something embarrassing like blush, too.

Once they dug back into their projects, Lexie asked her, "So a writer, huh?"

"Not lately." Taylor fondled a tall piece of molding, sliding her long fingers up and down the length of it. "I have a severe case of writer's block. Hence why I'm trying hard to focus on the work here. It helped the last time writer's block struck."

A naughty tease embedded itself in Lexie's mind while she watched Taylor massage that molding. She imagined Taylor fondling her body with the same affectionate trace, sliding her fingers up and down the length of her torso, hips, legs, and beyond.

She usually preferred femmes to sporty women. Cute sundresses, long stylish hair, eyelashes extended and curled with mascara, and shiny glossed kissable lips caused her head to swirl and her tummy to flip. Taylor sported more of a casual style. Her cargo pants rode her hips, and fringes from her ponytail stuck out the side of her baseball cap. She was messy, and Lexie preferred stylish. Though, as the minutes extended and the room heated up more, the sporty, messy style grew on Lexie.

"Is the work helping so far?"

"Not yet." Taylor sighed and looked around the room. "Though, the possibilities are endless."

"Is your writing project boring? Is that why you're having a hard time writing it?"

"I've written myself into a corner." She cleared her throat. "The beginning flowed. Then I hit the dreaded middle. It's sagging. Somehow, the story died and now it reeks like week-old garbage left outside in a summer heat wave."

"It can't be that bad." Lexie sat back on her folded knees.

"It is. My characters flatlined on me." Taylor raised her eyebrows. "One minute they're there, the next they skipped town. Now, I type a sentence and erase it." She wiggled her free fingers to illustrate. "Over and over again. Each sentence gets worse than the one before it. Pretty much, every word is drowning in a sea of nothingness."

"No wonder you said yes to my aunt."

Taylor regarded her. "Well, it's not easy to say no to her. At least for me. She looks at me with those pouty eyes and I clam up. Kind of like my words on paper."

"Yeah, Auntie Maya has used that same power over me." Lexie wrinkled her nose and stared up at the ceiling. "This place smells. I would never choose to hang out here otherwise."

"I love the way it smells in here." Taylor lifted her nose. "It's earthy."

"It's pungent, like cat pee."

"Spoken like a writer," Taylor laughed.

Lexie sucked at writing, but enjoyed a good book. "Do ideas ping around your brain all day? Well, when you're not suffering from writer's block, that is?"

"Usually they do."

Lexie wanted to open her up even more. "What kinds of ideas?"

Taylor looked past her and out the front window. "I love dreaming up exciting lives of powerful women." She squinted, concentrating on something beyond the rundown room. "They speak to me all the time when I'm in the writing zone. Often at the worst times, actually. No invite. They roll on in and start feeding my mind with ideas." She picked up a chisel from the floor. "I eventually got smart and planted notepads all over the place. In each room, in my car, in a waterproof box in my garden.

I never leave the house without one." She fingered her back pocket and pulled out a worn-looking notepad. "See?"

"Did it go through the washing machine?"

She stuffed it back in her pocket. "Once or twice." She grinned, and tightened her grip around the chisel. "It gets used. When my characters speak, I listen."

"It's like having a set of friends around all the time, huh?"

"Yeah, I suppose it is." She adjusted her baseball cap. "They talk to me when I shower, drive, shop for groceries, hell even on the rare occasions when I exercise."

"Fascinating." Lexie unfolded her numb legs and spread them out in front of her, leaning back on her hands. "And now, they took off on vacation somewhere?"

She tapped the chisel against her palm. "Yep. They packed up and left." She laughed, then dropped to her knees and stuck the chisel in between the molding and wall. She slapped the handle of it, wedging it for leverage.

"Has my aunt been editing for you since you began writing?"

"Just about."

Taylor focused in on the work, removing the molding with great ease.

"You know what's amazing?" Lexie asked, cocking her head and gazing across the exposed subflooring before her.

Taylor slapped the chisel handle again. "What's that?"

"Your entire body relaxed once you began talking about writing. One minute your shoulders were scrunched way up to your ears, and now they're down where they belong."

"What can I say?" Taylor shrugged. "Writing has a way of tenderizing me, I suppose."

Lexie liked Taylor's way with words.

As always, curiosity poked at her. So she dropped another line to fish for details. "You should write a story about a woman who finds herself again by losing herself in a rehab project."

Taylor stopped tapping the handle of her chisel and stared up at her from under the rim of her baseball cap. "Oh, I'm not lost."

"I'm not suggesting an autobiographical piece. Purely fiction, of course."

There went Taylor's shoulders again, inching up to her ears.

"I'll consider it." She offered her a sidelong glance before continuing to work that chisel. "But right now, we should keep working."

Lexie sipped some water, and then she leaned back, supporting herself with her sore hands. "Ah, so you're one of those?"

Taylor looked up at her again with a blank stare.

"The kind who can't walk and chew gum at the same time or sing and cook."

She twisted her mouth. "Your aunt is counting on me. The more distracted I am, the—"

"The less you'll write," Lexie interrupted.

Taylor surrendered to the floor, dropping her chisel and sprawling flat, legs and arms extended in a snow angel pose. She stretched, and her body cracked. "Is this better?"

Lexie loved toying with her. She swallowed her chuckle before launching her next question. "So tell me about the character who ran away from your brain. What is she like?"

Taylor sat up, straightened her legs, and stretched her body forward. She regarded Lexie with a new set of eyes, more playful, flirty even, and that caused Lexie's skin to prickle.

"She's a nice person who lives a simple life and wants to make a difference in the world. She and her boyfriend are having issues. They're bored with each other."

Lexie exaggerated a yawn. "I'd probably run away, too."

Cashmere, sprawled out on her favorite spot in the boutique, on her blankie by the front corner, yawned too, seemingly bored as well. She stood and wandered over to the front window. Then she climbed up on the wide sill of the now clean window and escaped into the more interesting sights of tourists passing by.

"Do you have a dog in the book?"

"A dog? No. The woman is a detective. She doesn't have time for a dog."

"That's your problem right there. No dog. Mystery solved. Add a dog, the story comes alive." And for kicks, Lexie tossed in another suggestion. "Add in a female love interest, and bam, sizzle factor ignites and you've got a better story to tell."

Taylor's face reddened.

Lexie sipped some water, concentrating her gaze on Taylor to stoke that blush even more.

"Time for me to ask a question," Taylor said.

"Go ahead. I'm an open book." Except if she asked about her cooking skills. She hadn't picked up a spatula or bulb of garlic since her first week living with Christine. Her stomach didn't have the patience to wait for the food to cook. She'd start nibbling and drinking wine, and before long, her appetite vanished in the wake of her bloated belly from too many chips dunked in salsa.

"Why a pet boutique?"

Ah. Innocent question, of course. She perked up on her knees. "Well, that's easy. My aunt asked me to. She loves dogs as much as I do." She waved to Cashmere now pressing her nose against the window and snorting.

Taylor matched her gaze for a long moment. A shimmer flickered in the lighter golden spokes of her eyes. "She's a great dog." She stood back up, gripping her chisel.

The woman intrigued Lexie. She had an amiable side. She wore that amiability like a hat, tipped up at a slight angle to reveal just enough to tease.

"She is. We rescued her two years ago from a friend who traveled too much for work. Ironically, a few months after that, Christine began traveling too much, as well."

"Christine? The woman who you broke up with at Pusser's?"

Lexie bit the inside of her cheek to take away the sting of embarrassment. "The breakup was long overdue."

Empathy filled Taylor's eyes. "How she treated you when she moved to Miami was crappy. Your aunt filled me in on the details."

Alarm bells rung in Lexie's head. "What kind of details?"

"That she ghosted you since you moved here and that you deserved better than that."

69

Lexie didn't enjoy the spotlight on her at that moment. "Christine's a complicated person who is like your character who ran away. A workaholic." She flipped her hands in the air. "No mystery. Boring story. Doesn't end well." She paused a beat. "You need someone more fun to fill your pages. People like Christine are focused on work and nothing else."

Taylor considered her advice with knitted brows. "I'm sorry if she hurt you."

Lexie would not be pitied. "Christine was comfort food. I enjoyed having her around, but now I'm happier on my own."

Taylor adjusted her baseball cap again. "Good for you. Nice people always deserve to be happy."

Lexie picked up her tool again and massaged it between her fingers, lingering on the nicety. "What about you? Any Christine's or more considerate people in your life?"

"I'm at peace on my own." She smiled the kind of smile one would share to shut down a conversation. Pleasant. Short. Accentuated with a period at the end.

Lexie dug her tool under a new staple. "So we're back to short answers so soon?"

Taylor examined the molding. Rusted nails stuck out of it. "I don't have a lot I want to say on the subject."

"Okay. Got it."

Lexie took to her staple pulling instead. Dig. Yank. Twist. Pull. Repeat.

At least she uncovered a few details. Taylor was a writer with a boring character. She didn't want to disappoint Auntie Maya. She found peace on her own. If Taylor kept handing off information like that, she'd eventually get down to the details that coworkers shared like what kind of lunch she preferred and whether she took cream in her coffee.

About five minutes into the unbearable silence, Lexie pulled up on a staple and it flew. "It's too quiet in here," she said.

"Play some music, then." Taylor grazed her over with another playful glance. "Just not country."

Lexie enjoyed when Taylor's shoulders relaxed and face softened.

She stood. "Fine." She walked over to her cellphone on the folding table. Disco it would be, then. She clicked onto her Pandora station and turned up the volume to the sultry tune of Donna Summer's "Dim All the Lights."

Perfect song to fill in the silent gaps. The song waved from a mellow introduction to a full out head-swinging beat.

"Disco?"

"Yup." Lexie could answer in one-syllable words, too.

Taylor watched her dance past, then she darted her eyes back to her piece of rusty-nailed wood.

Lexie swayed back to her small patch of flooring, lowering herself to the ground on a four-beat move. She dug her tool under a new staple and bobbed her head along with the beat, whispering the lyrics.

Taylor's gaze warmed on her.

"You've got a pretty voice," Taylor said.

That's all Lexie needed to boost her levels. "Thanks."

Pop. The staple released its grip from the floorboard.

"Let's hear yours," Lexie said.

Taylor wagged her head. "No."

"Why not?"

Taylor flashed her a wicked grin. "We need the window glass to stay intact. Your aunt hasn't budgeted for a new one."

Lexie popped up another staple with ease. "You can't be that bad." She dropped back on her heels.

"I make noise. Lots of noise. Trust me." Taylor's face turned bright red the second her mouth closed. The sexual play plopped itself front and center, as did Taylor's discomfort with it.

"I've been told the same thing. What's noise to someone is beautiful music to another."

Taylor's face turned an even more alarming shade of red, and Lexie relished in that.

Taylor tossed her chisel back and forth between her hands. "Right then." Her cheeks shined and lit up her whole face. "I'll let you get back to orchestrating more beautiful music, then."

"Right then." Now Lexie's face blushed. She turned back to her patch of flooring and continued to sing along with Donna Summer and enjoy the tingles pulsing throughout her body.

By the time the next song ended, she had pulled up a pile of staples. With enough furtive glances from Taylor, she might very well complete the entire floor that afternoon.

~ ~

Later that night, Taylor balanced her laptop on her legs and stared at the empty screen.

Pretty much, a good writing session resembled great sex. It left her panting and heated. It had been months since she last had one and a couple of years since she reveled in a kiss, let alone sex.

After the day she spent in that hot storefront next to Lexie nurturing those staples up and out of their groove to the sexy tunes of Donna Summer, some thoughts brewed.

She began writing. Her words raced out of her fingers like they had little engines attached to them and competed with the words preceding and following them.

With her mind honed in on an alluring new character, Taylor followed her lead.

To Taylor's surprise, the slender, blonde woman took a turn and headed in a different direction than Taylor anticipated.

Every writer desired to be led off the projected path and onto one where surprises hid in the bushes, along the fences, and off in the distance where the green rolling hills met the bright blue hopeful sky.

Taylor went along for the journey, discovering an infatuation for that charming character.

After a few hours, Taylor stopped typing. She had written three chapters of a brand new book with a powerful lead character, bearing a striking resemblance to

Lexie.

Lexie danced around in her brain. She fed her hunger and helped her to liven up with fresh eyes. Thanks to a little provocative dancing and gestures by Lexie that day, and some good old-fashioned hard work, Taylor viewed the world differently from her typical perception of its flatness. A brand new three-dimensional dazzling display of literary inspiration appeared in its place.

She couldn't stop smiling.

Finally, the waters broke through the dam and flowed through her, cleansing her of all that grimy buildup from months of stagnation.

Something magical happened when sandpaper, chisels, and staples emerged. A prideful bond popped up, a pride born out of transformation. Fixing a broken building was therapeutic and better than any pill. It filled the mind with inspiration and offered a playground to create something out of nothing.

In Taylor's case, that something also took the form of a story with potential.

Taylor had to go cool herself off in a cold shower after that long and enjoyable writing session.

She stood underneath the stinging pellets of her shower massager and savored the goodness of the day. The words had flowed again thanks to an unknowing Lexie. Taylor twirled under the stream.

Taylor had always been attracted to woman like Lexie, fun, flirty, open. She and Nate would often sit in crowded malls and people watch together, pointing out women who caught their attention. They shared a commonality. They both adored women with ponytails and perky attitudes like Lexie.

Nate encouraged Taylor to explore her bisexuality by sharing fantasies over strangers in crowded malls. For sure, Nate would've encouraged her to talk with him about any brewing fantasies of Lexie.

Taylor relaxed under the warm water, enjoying the tickle of it on her breasts.

What would it be like to climb into the shower with Lexie?

She'd take the loofa sponge and dab some of that fresh-smelling lilac body wash onto it. Then she'd take her time smoothing it across her shoulder blades and down her spine, across her hip and to her navel. She had a sexy navel. Taylor got a good glimpse of it when Lexie flung off her shirt because of her spider freak-out.

Thank goodness for spiders!

Taylor would definitely spend some extra time on Lexie's navel while she explored the rest of her. She'd tease her by placing her lips on her neck and coaxing her into a moan with supple slips of her tongue to match the slow pace of her travels toward her earlobe. Taylor closed her eyes and bowed her head. Her body twitched in delight, intoxicated by the thought of Lexie's scent and smooth skin, and her desire to continue her travels with that loofa sponge.

By the time Taylor settled out of her fantasy, she sat on the tub's edge and panted, overcome by Lexie Tanner.

After a few minutes, reality began to snap back into place. Taylor didn't want reality knocking her from her high perch. From there, she enjoyed seeing the world in a brighter shade of green for once. From atop, things appeared less dingy and more alive.

Her writing mojo soared as a result of spending a few hours being aerated by Lexie. She was hot. She was flirty. And she was nice. But engaging in anything beyond fantasy could do some serious damage if things went south.

Taylor didn't even mean to flirt. It just happened. Then the lame innuendo about orchestrating beautiful music from noise. Argh. Lexie teetered on the edge of rebound. She was vulnerable. Taylor should've kept a clear distance. Kept the conversation superficial. Shared fewer suggestive smiles.

She'd tried.

Lexie pushed, though. She kept tilting her head back on a seductive swig of water. Then she'd sway her hips every time she dug into those staples. What the hell? How could Taylor not notice? She was overheated and lonely. Two major destructive forces.

Taylor climbed off the tub's edge and headed over to the steamy mirror. She wiped it with a washcloth and stared at her flushed face, the result of Lexie Tanner.

All afternoon, in her peripheral view, she'd catch Lexie's elegant fingers tracing the side of her cheek in long, graceful sweeps, causing Taylor to question if Lexie enjoyed teasing her or reveled in the touch of her own fingers along her silky skin. Either way, Taylor's head swirled, caught up in a euphoric ride of sensual possibilities.

Taylor put her bathrobe on and headed to her living room couch.

She plopped down on it, sighing.

Lexie was a flirt. Her sultry, teasing gazes spoke some truths about her sensuality. The way she batted her eyelashes when she'd scope out the massive floorboards in front of her. Then she kept pulling at her scooped-neck shirt, exposing her cleavage.

How could Taylor concentrate under those kinds of theatrics? Her tangled ponytail also took the stage one too many times that day. She kept running her fingers through it, causing wisps to feather her neck in sexy sweeps. She played with her, causing Taylor to have to sneak a glance in her direction. Why else would she run her fingers down her bare neck and pout her lips as she landed her baby blue eyes on her? Those weren't the moves of a woman disinterested in some serious attention. Lexie needed validation. Her lover broke up with her.

Well Taylor couldn't emotionally afford to become her validator.

No way. Off limits. Finish the project and get back to writing. That was the plan, and Taylor would stick to it. Her future depended on her being focused. She wanted to have her life back in order by the time she met her daughter. Once her daughter got her birth certificate, they'd be ready to sit across from each other and have a cup of coffee and a serious conversation about life.

Did her daughter even drink coffee? Maybe she preferred milk or orange juice.

Taylor had so much to learn. Like her name, for starters.

Well, she had the rest of her life, hopefully, to get to know her. But for now, she'd continue to live life one day at a time.

She'd start with getting dressed and then opening her mail.

So a few minutes later, sporting sweats and a t-shirt, she opened her door and reached into her mailbox. A pile had added up. She needed to be better at collecting it. The sun began to set and the sky took on a pink and magenta hue. It would be a nice night to sit out on her back patio, sip some wine, and open her mail.

So she drew open her slider and slipped outside into the balmy summer night. She sat on the yellow Adirondack chair, Nate's favorite. She thumbed through her mail, still a favorite activity of hers. Back in the days when she'd sent snail mail to agencies and publishing houses, she'd walk to the mailbox, hopeful of finding a surprise when she opened it—one of her self-addressed stamped envelopes coming back to her with good news.

Even though she'd already established her writing career, the familiar trace of hope lingered. Like the scent of a favorite bath soap from a good time in the past, it remained in that beloved place reserved to bring a person into a good vibe, regardless of what circled around her. Those moments washed away the past and helped lift her to catch a new perspective of herself, of someone who might deserve another chance at happiness.

All in all, it was a good day. A smile spread across her face, and for the first time since Oscar passed, she didn't wipe it away with her guilt for living while he had died.

Despite death being a natural part of life, it never fit. It poked and pinched and tormented the heart. Living in the past offered relief. When she tiptoed too closely to the edge of the present moment, she'd stop short to avoid falling too far away from what she'd grown to love and depend upon—that beautiful furry friend with his chubby legs and penchant for belly rubs.

But in that moment, under the bright stars and half-moon, Oscar's gentle spirit nudged her forward and he whispered his approval. She livened, smelling the damp night air and tasting sprinkles of joy. Tears rolled down her cheeks as she smiled even wider.

Oscar's and Nate's spirits swirled, nestling in beside her.

She picked up her notepad and pen, and jotted down her feelings.

I'm laughing. I'm joyful. I'm clear-headed. I'm free to bask in happy things again. Today, for the first time, I'm no longer bowing my head, shameful of laughter in the sorrow of your passing. You've both offered me your blessings. You're nudging me, directing me to lighten up and have some fun. A gate has opened and we're running, my dear Nate and gentle Oscar. Running together, Momma and Daddy with our arms wide, and you, Oscar, with your tail wagging, and the wind as our companion.

Sealing her eyes closed, Taylor placed her hand over her heart. "I mean it, Oscar and Nate. Every word."

She settled into the comforting memories that before used to create sad tears.

She'd had a good, purposeful day.

Her writing had finally come back from the dead.

Yeah, a good day, indeed.

Okay, and the flirting didn't hurt.

It felt pretty fucking amazing.

So did eating a tub of Ben and Jerry's ice cream, though. The after effect of it all was what raised concerns, she thought on a chuckle.

Taylor flipped the mail onto her lap one piece at a time. Subscription to *Literary World*, vendor letters promoting keychains and other giveaways, a notice about an upcoming conference in Boston, and a handwritten letter addressed to her.

"Uh." She slid her finger under the seal. Inside sat a note.

Dear Ms. Taylor,

The lady at the adoption center gave me your mailing address and suggested I begin by writing you a letter. I'm Stephanie, Stephanie Hunter, and I'm your biological daughter. I want to meet. Not because I expect you to be my mother. I'm eighteen, but I suppose you already know that about me. There's a lot you don't know. Well everything else really. I'm not mad at you. Honestly, I'm not. I would just like to ask you a few questions. Questions that may help me to understand my origins. Like do we have any health things I need to worry about? Do I have any biological siblings? Is my father a nice man? Things like that.

Taylor covered her mouth. She looked up from the letter and the stillness of the space choked off her air, causing her to swallow harder. She darted her eyes around her patio, trying to focus on something, anything to calm her rapid heartbeat. After a few tries, she steadied herself enough to continue reading.

You're a writer. I looked you up. You're kind of famous. At least in the book world. Do you get stopped at restaurants for your autograph? Do you need to wear sunglasses and a hat when out in public? Maybe not. I love reading Judy Blume, and she's famous. But if I sat next to her at a train station, I wouldn't imagine her to be anyone other than a stranger taking the same train as me. So that's good for you, I suppose. Have you planted me into any of your stories?

Lol. Don't worry, I've only wondered this for one day. You see, I got your contact info yesterday after I submitted my new birth certificate copy.

I'm not desperate. I swear. Just curious. Are you?

Would you like to meet? I love photographing flowers and there's this amazing botanical garden in D.C. I live a short distance from there. I'm minoring in photography and also speech communications, and majoring in psychology. More so because my parents are making me. They want me to follow in their footsteps as psychologists. Well, my gramma doesn't like psychology. It freaks her out. Hence the second minor of speech communications. She wants me to stand at the front of a church and minister the good word of God. I want to take pictures. Lol. I don't want to preach, and I don't care to hear about people's problems all day long either. My best friend, Amy, tells me enough of hers. Lol. My gramma would only pay for my college and apartment at George Mason University if I went the speech route. I'll be in college forever. But Gramma is paying, so I won't end up broke! Anyway, it would be cool if you ever want to meet at the botanical gardens and take photos with me.

Do you?

My number is 555-435-6798. Text me any time.

Sincerely yours,

Stephanie

With her hand still covering her mouth, Taylor leaned back against her chair. She clutched the letter to her chest with her free hand as her eyes filled with tears.

Her daughter was a photographer.

Her daughter didn't hate her.

Her parents were psychologists, which meant they could treat her and help her through the abandonment issues she likely suffered.

Her daughter wanted to meet her.

She let that marinate for a long time.

Then, as the stars popped up and the sky transitioned into a midnight blue, Taylor texted her daughter, Stephanie.

Hi, it's Taylor Henshaw. I got your letter. I'd love to photograph the botanical gardens in D.C. with you. When?

A moment later, Taylor's phone beeped.

Hi! Great. How about in the next few weeks? I'm taking an online summer class and need to build a blog with photos. So the timing is perfect. Do you like photography?

Taylor had no clue how to operate a camera. But they needed something to bond over. She'd figure it out. *I love it.*

Awesome. I'll send you a few dates and times, and you can tell me when is best. Talk to you later.

Taylor sat for a while, rereading the string of messages and enjoying the happiness it created in her heart. Then she thumbed through the rest of her mail and discovered a letter from the adoption agency sharing the good news and Stephanie's contact info with her.

So much excitement stirred within her.

She couldn't wait to tell Maya. But she knew Maya was with her son Rex and his girlfriend for the evening. She could leave her a voice message, but something so important needed better presentation than that. So Taylor would enjoy the evening, allowing her good news to marinate, and then she'd fill Maya in the next morning at their editorial meeting.

~ ~

The next day, Taylor arrived at Maya's house to share her good news and to declare victory over her writer's block. She'd start with her writing.

"I've got a new idea for a story." Taylor dropped her book bag on the floor near Maya's leather couch.

Maya eyed her bag, picked it up, and placed it on the coffee table. "A brand new idea?"

"Yes. Brand spanking new." Taylor had already written fifteen thousand words of it the day before. "It's flowing."

"Am I going to like it?" Maya lifted her eyeglasses off her face, exposing a set of hopeful eyes.

"I love it. I didn't even have to force it. I sat and the words came out of me. It's like a word goddess tossed them down from my brain, one after the other. I can barely keep up. The ideas are coming faster than I can type them."

Maya pulled her in her arms. "Oh, thank God. The Pet Boutique is working for you!" She squeezed her and stepped backward. "Honestly, your other one sucked. I lost sleep at night. I couldn't decide how you would turn it around. I couldn't see how you could. I fell asleep each time I read it. My snoring woke me up. Tell me about this one," she said on the same breath. "Please tell me there's sex, flirting, something to keep me excited."

"Much more than usual." Of course, the muse who whispered it into her ear would remain a secret. Thankfully, she had her great news to share to change the subject. "I got a letter from my daughter."

Maya's hands flew up to her face. "Tell me everything. Every single word."

Chapter Eight

"I'm not stepping through that mud." Ally crossed her arms over her chest and glared at the giant muddy hole smack dab in the center of the pathway.

"Well, I'm not going to hoist you over my shoulders and carry you through it." Jack mirrored his sister's stance. Nico fidgeted with the handle of his over-sized cooler.

Auntie Maya took off her sandals, rolled up her pink cotton pants, and walked through it. She raised her chin and swung her elbows on a mission to salvage her plans for a beautiful family picnic.

"Your father loved this place. We came here on our first date to hunt for shark teeth." She stepped up out of the muck and lowered her pants, covering up her mud-dipped feet. "It's going to be cold and frozen before we know it, the way time flies. So today we do this. We hike the trail to the water." She raised her arms to the sunny canopy of trees and spun. "It's majestic." She stopped spinning and glared at them all. "Now, get over yourselves. It's a little mud. So what?"

"Did you find any shark teeth?" Rex asked.

"Yes," Auntie Maya said. "Well, we didn't. A nice park ranger did and he gave it to us."

Lexie had visited Calvert Cliffs State Park with her aunt a while ago. The two-mile stretch across the swamp lands of the inner basin, linked together by foot bridges, took hikers and seekers of fossils and dolphin and shark teeth to the sandy beach front. Hikers could wade in the water and dig for novelties left behind some twenty million years ago or they could picnic and enjoy the beautiful open water scene with two enormous cliffs on either side. The park showcased the archeological layers of a time when the sea filled the beach and housed all sorts of sea creatures.

Lexie hadn't been as excited about something since, well, she supposed since working on The Pet Boutique with Taylor.

Rex unbuttoned his tight jeans and lowered them to the ground.

"What are you doing?" Jack whimpered like he'd never seen a man in biker shorts before.

"These are vintage, man." Rex rolled them up into a ball and handed them to his pregnant girlfriend, Wini, a shy and unassuming young twenty-something-year-old with a dainty smile and friendly eyes. Then he scooped her up and carried her across. "You heard Mom," he yelled over his shoulder as he lowered her to the ground. "Get over yourself and get in."

Lexie didn't like her bright white sneakers anyway. A little mud would darken them so they could blend in with her gray ankle socks. Cashmere sniffed the air, not so sure. Lexie pulled on her leash. "Come on, baby girl. If Momma can, you can." Lexie trudged right through the mud without lacing her sneakers tighter. Rookie hiking mistake. They got stuck while Lexie fell forward, face first into the mud.

"Oh my God," Auntie Maya screamed. "Someone help her."

Rex broke out into hysterical laughter.

Cashmere dug at the mud, flinging it everywhere. She yipped and tossed her chest up into the air in between thrusts, panic-stricken. Mud splattered across her pretty bright yellow life jacket harness.

"Well, let go of her leash," Jack said, jumping in to her rescue. He lent her a hand.

Lexie let go of her leash and climbed to her feet. She glanced down at her muddy front. "Well, at least the rest of my clothes will match my muddy sneakers now."

Jack stretched his eyes. "Well, that's one way to take the plunge." A small whimper of a laugh leaked out the side of his mouth.

A few minutes later, once Jack and Tom helped Nico tote the cooler over the mud, they took off down the trail. Everyone laughed at Lexie's muddy mishap as they followed the red-dotted trees toward the water.

Roots jutted up through the caked dirt, tripping up Cashmere under her clumsy lanky legs. They walked in comfortable silence, a rare oddity for the Merkel family. The echo of their relaxed pace lulled Lexie into a peaceful gait of her own. Cashmere stopped tripping and learned to adjust to the bumpy and twisting path.

Dragonflies accompanied them, zigzagging through the air. Cicadas sang and birds chirped. The air smelled like damp soil and health, vibrating around them and cocooning them into an oasis where tranquility thrived. The leaves waved and the grasses swayed. As they neared their destination, the mosquitoes began their curious investigation, humming around their heads and ears, escorting them through the swampy parts of the trail.

At one point, Jack hummed a Billy Joel song, "Uptown Girl." Nico chimed in after three stanzas.

Lexie kept her eyes peeled for the open water.

Forty minutes after they began, they walked around a spread of low-lying bushes and spotted it.

Cashmere yanked Lexie toward the water's edge. Lexie let her go. She charged toward it and landed on a splash, lapping up water and flapping her ears.

"You're going to let her swim by herself?" Jack asked, shading the sun from his dark eyes.

"She loves the water. She's wearing a doggy life jacket. It helps her stay afloat."

"How far will she swim?"

"She'll stay where people are."

Nico, the level-headed of the two, held his wrist. "Honey, she's fine. Lexie's not worried. You shouldn't be either."

Jack braced against his husband, fear trickling from his crooked brow down to his feet.

"Relax," Lexie said, patting him on the back as she passed him. "I'm going in too. Care to join me?"

His face contorted. "In that bacteria cesspool?" He lay his hand across his muddy heart.

Lexie handed her backpack off to Rex, who then handed it off to his timid girlfriend. Poor girl wouldn't stand a chance with the Merkel's.

"I love a good dip in bacteria." Rex scooped up Lexie and ran with her toward the water's edge. He hooted and she giggled over each bump until they landed in the water; their shirts, shorts, and everything else in between became soaked and clean.

She splashed around in cool knee-deep water to get rid of the rest of the caked-on mud. Cashmere paddled toward her and spun in a small circle while lapping more water.

Lexie grabbed her, and Cashmere wiggled out of her arms and headed over to a group of teens at the shore passing a ball back and forth. When it dropped, she latched onto it with her teeth and splashed back toward Lexie and Rex. The teens laughed and chased after her. She sped up, eyes bulging, ears bright pink.

"Between you and me," Rex said, "that ex-girlfriend of yours has no idea what she lost with you."

Cashmere dropped the ball in Lexie's opened hands and bobbed her head front and back, demanding a toss. So Lexie flung it back to one of the teens, giving Cashmere more reason to keep running and splashing.

"I'm happy I ended it. I'm pretty sure Cashmere is too."

Rex called out to Wini who stood alone on the shore. "Come in."

Lexie punched his arm. "She's pregnant. What if there *is* bacteria in here?"

"On second thought, we'll come to you." They trudged out of the knee deep water and plopped onto the shore instead so they could dig in the sand and search for shark teeth.

Lexie sifted through the wet sand, searching for fossilized treasure. "Are there still some in here?"

Rex sifted through a handful, scrutinizing it one small rock at a time. "Of course. This whole beach used to be underwater millions of years ago. Dolphins and sharks raised their families here, long before us humans messed with them. So I'm guessing they thrived, and at some point died. Their teeth had to go someplace, right?" Rex held up a fragment and squinted at it. He twisted his mouth and tossed it back in the water with a pout.

A few seconds later, Cashmere bolted toward them and dropped a large stick at Rex's feet. He stood and waved the stick in front of her face, then tossed it into the water. She cleared the stretch of rocks and shells that lined the immediate shore in one enormous leap.

She paddled toward the stick, grabbed it, and headed back to them with it lodged between her jaws.

She pounced around it like a baby goat, full of life and exuberance.

Then, she spotted another thrill.

She bolted and skidded to a halt behind a terrier mix and crammed her nose in between its trembling legs. She examined her toes, her legs, her crotch, her belly, and her playful side when she bowed low and barked. The terrier lunged at Cashmere with the might of a Great Dane, and Cashmere jumped backward and fell flat to the rocky sand in an odd moment of submissiveness. The terrier lifted her nose and waddled away.

Cashmere panted and cast the last bark before crawling to her feet and catching her second wind. She frolicked along the shore, sniffing the rocks and barging up in between people digging for shark teeth. By the time she landed by Lexie's side, she shook and flung wet sand all over them.

Lexie glanced at her. "You, Ms. Queen Cashmere, live life with gusto." Another shake and more wet sand stung her face.

"She sure does," Wini said.

Lexie petted her. "She's the best thing that's happened in my life, like ever."

Rex nodded in quiet understanding. Then he picked up a rock that formed a spiral. "I found a fossil."

Wini leaned in and kissed his cheek. "Save it. I'll polish it up and we can use it in the mobile I'm crafting for the baby."

"How many months pregnant are you?" Lexie asked.

She rubbed her belly. "Four."

Wini's face glowed. She looked young. Too young. "You have a pretty glow about you. Pregnancy is serving you well."

Wini blushed and raked her fingers through her pink-streaked hair, pausing at the end of it with a twist.

Out of the corner of her eye, Lexie caught her aunt waving them over to a spot near the cliffs. "Let's do our prayer and chat," she yelled through cupped hands.

Their prayer chat; when her cousins honored their late father, Lexie's Uncle Skip, with some prayers and recaps on their month.

As they headed toward the blanket, Lexie tapped Rex and mouthed, *she's adorable.*

To that, Rex beamed.

So that's what love looked like.

As the sun rose higher above their heads, Auntie Maya filled them in on the successful weeks of rehab at The Pet Boutique. Jack drew lines in the sand, pursing his lips the entire time. Nico occasionally patted his back and checked in with him. He'd offer Nico a conciliatory shrug.

"Lexie, it's your turn to share a recap with your Uncle Skip. Fill him in on something he's missed while in heaven. Maybe you can tell him the good news." Her aunt flexed her eyebrows.

Lexie frowned at her. "I have good news?"

"Of course you do." Auntie Maya laughed. "Come on. Don't be shy."

Ally flipped her long hair over her golden shoulder. "I know what it is." She bounced on her knees like a girl who needed to pee. "Let me tell everyone."

"Please do," Lexie said with curiosity. She hated that part, being the center of attention. Get the show over with already. Pass the baton on to Jack or someone who wanted to show off his life. "I don't have a clue what you're both referring to anyway."

"Christine, silly." Ally hoisted herself up to her feet and grabbed a water out of the alarmingly large cooler. "Lexie broke it off with her on the phone while at Pusser's!"

"Which means…" Auntie Maya presented her words in a drumroll.

"Which means what?" Lexie asked with a lot more grouchy flair than intended.

Auntie Maya sported an instant pout.

"Which means what?" Lexie asked again, gentler that time.

"You're single," she said flatly, like Lexie had stolen her thunder.

"Tom, what about your friend at the attorney's office on the corner of Arnold and Lexington?" Ally asked with great seriousness. "Didn't she get divorced?"

Tom eyed Ally, flicking her a warning to stop.

"Well, even if it's not her, I'm sure we have other people to set you up with."

Mr. and Mrs. Popularity. Of course, Lexie thought.

"I'm not on the market."

Jack perked up. "Honey, at thirty-five you better learn to cut your losses and get fishing fast if you want someone to bite."

"If you're referring to babies, I've got Cashmere." She tossed her arm around Cashmere's soggy back and hugged her. Cashmere sneezed in response.

"I'm referring to fun while you're young." Jack dangled a vine of grapes and bit into one.

"I have plenty of things to keep my fun intact." Besides Cashmere, Auntie Maya's peculiarity entertained her.

"You have Taylor." Auntie Maya winked.

"Who's Taylor?" Ally asked.

"She's into Lexie," Rex answered for her.

"Do you think so?" Auntie Maya asked.

Rex nodded.

"You should ask her on a date." Auntie Maya flung her hand up for all to join her. "Right? You're single. She's single."

"Are we sure she's into women?" Jack flung his question into the mix.

"She is." Auntie Maya nodded.

"Okay, excuse me." Lexie stood. "Before you all start making party favors for our wedding and little bootie socks for our eventual children, could we first finish eating our lunch?"

Nico leaned forward and grabbed a sandwich. "Yes, I agree."

Lexie sat back down and resumed normal breathing. She did enjoy a little crush on Taylor, but her family didn't need her to calculate to what extent. She enjoyed tossing personal questions at Taylor to see how red she could turn her face. It became a sort of hobby the other day, one that reminded her of those times when she would build a house of cards with Ally when younger. When Ally would turn to take a sip of lemonade, Lexie would topple it over.

She didn't want to topple Taylor's house of cards. But she'd like to catch a peek inside.

~ ~

Taylor and Lexie worked together for the next few weeks, enjoying some good laughs at Cashmere's and Maya's expense. A month and a half had gone by already since they first began work on the boutique, and things were falling into place on a good schedule. They worked well together. They often shared snack and lunch breaks sitting on the dusty floor, swapping turkey sandwiches for Reuben's and potato chips for Doritos.

They learned to navigate each other's moves and anticipate needs, like when Lexie needed a screwdriver or hammer because she often forgot to bring them with her to her corner of the storefront.

Each night, Taylor went home and wrote a few scenes. Scenes that included her new entertaining character and a dog she named Baby Cakes, a white boxer with the same adorable freckles as Cashmere.

Lexie even stopped asking so many questions. It seemed they had gotten to a point where the silence comforted. Taylor also enjoyed listening to Lexie hum and sing.

"I have to run to the hardware store, again," Taylor said, climbing off the ladder. She rubbed her dusty hands on her jeans and coughed. "This dust always causes me to cough."

"I can go to the store if you need me to." Lexie unscrewed the cap off a fresh water bottle and handed it to Taylor.

"You just want to get out of sweeping and cleaning the wall."

Lexie wiped her forehead with the back of her hand. "True. I hate cleaning. When I lived with Christine, I hired someone to clean for us. She didn't care if dust settled onto the furniture. She spent all her time working."

"What does she do for a living that had her working so much?"

"Sales." Lexie sighed heavily. "She loved to busy herself, working by day, tinkering around her office until the wee hours of the night. Not exactly the building blocks to a relationship, though."

"More like stumbling blocks."

Lexie opened her mouth to speak, and then hesitated. She settled on a shrug instead, but still clung to an unstated sentence or two. That much Taylor could tell. Even in the short amount of time they had spent together on the project, Taylor began to read the small clues when Lexie was hungry, bored, tired, and cranky. Working in a small, confined space helped with that.

Now it was her turn to ask some questions.

"How are you doing since the breakup?"

Lexie took out her ponytail and smoothed her shiny blonde hair back up into a neater one at her nape. "I'm doing okay. I know it's for the best. Now I get to live life on my own terms." She inhaled a sharp breath and then her chin began to quiver.

Taylor braced against the potential outcome of that chin quiver. "That's a good thing."

"Yes it is." Lexie stooped to pick up a nail. "I spent the past three years of my life tangled up in the whims of Christine's needs. When Christine was happy, I was too. When Christine had a bad day, I did too. I'm an empath like that."

Taylor studied her chin like it was a ticking bomb, careful not to disturb it. "That's a good quality."

Lexie pulled in her bottom lip and wavered for a moment before speaking. "She had it good with me. I offered her a happy life."

Taylor shuffled her feet, spreading dust. "It sounds like Christine will have many regrets once she slows down and considers everything."

"Not Christine. She'll never slow down. She got promoted last year and began to travel a lot. So our gap widened to the size of the Grand Canyon."

Lexie's cheek creased as she forced a smile.

"That happens," Taylor reassured. "Couples forget to do things together while they're busy pursuing their goals."

"Well, I'm glad we didn't get any further into our relationship before it took a nosedive. I have no desire to live my life in the shadows anymore."

"I don't blame you." Taylor had it so good with Nate. She never had to worry about his disinterest in her. "Just think, you can do anything now."

"Yes. I have my whole life ahead of me. I can do with it what I want now. I can hike the Appalachian Trail for six months, sleeping in a tent on top of the pebbly ground. I can take up wine tasting. I can learn Aikido." Lexie's chin began to quiver again, and tears now threatened her blue eyes.

"And you can renovate a pet boutique," Taylor added with a joyful ring.

Lexie bit down on her lower lip and took a deep restorative breath. "Yes. I can renovate a pet boutique."

They shared a smile. In that smile, Lexie's gratitude shone. A gratitude for Taylor helping to prevent an emotional meltdown over her ex-girlfriend, a woman who didn't love her as much as Lexie desired her to.

~ ~

While Taylor shopped at the hardware store, Goldie, Rex, and Wini, arrived to help in whatever way they could.

"Can you hand me the broom," Lexie asked Rex, ensuring Cashmere didn't drop and roll in the dust pile.

"Sweetheart," he asked Wini, "can you hand it to her?" Rex carried a bucket of plaster toward the front window.

Wini stood from the folding chair. "Sure." The pink stripe in her dark hair bounced along with her steps. "Here you go." She smiled demurely. "I can help if you want."

Lexie took the broom and scanned the storefront. "I could use help with washing the wall. The mural artist is coming to size it up."

"She's pregnant," Rex said.

"Pregnant," Wini said. "Not dead."

"You shouldn't be over-exerting yourself."

"How far along are you?" Goldie asked, coming in from the back.

"Almost five months," Rex answered for her.

Goldie scoffed. "I was eight months pregnant and mowing my grass." She tossed Wini a rag. "Here you go kiddo. Your baby is going to be fine. I'm highly intuitive about things like this."

Wini twisted the rag in her hands.

Lexie noticed two women fall in behind Goldie from the backroom. "Don't listen to anything this woman tells you," the dark-haired woman said. "She'll convince you that it's okay to run a half-marathon without a single dose of training."

"Yet your wife and son cheered you on from the finish line. Thank you very much." Goldie flicked her arm.

"She's got a point," the blonde woman said, kissing her cheek.

Goldie tapped the tip of the blonde's nose. "Emma, call your dad and remind him to bring ice cream later."

The dark-haired woman searched for the blonde woman's hand and lifted it to her lips. "She's already on it."

The blonde leaned into her, cradling her chin on the woman's well-defined shoulder. "Absolutely." Sprinkles of laughter dazzled her cheeks. She raised her hand to her chest. "I'm Emma," she said to Lexie, as if she needed that guidance. "This is my wife, Haley."

"The artist and her wife. A pleasure." Just like with Jack and Nico, a delightful surge always pulsed through Lexie whenever in the company of another same-sex couple. Her limbs lightened and the air flowed.

"So this is going to be a pet boutique," Emma said with awe as she stepped past

91

Lexie and into the vacant room. "Where is my canvas wall?"

Lexie pointed to it. "I need to wash it still. It should be ready to go by tomorrow." She turned to Wini. "Can you wash it or would you rather rest?"

Goldie pointed her eyes at Wini. "At five months, you can run a half-marathon, too. Hell, some women don't even know they're pregnant at this point. You can climb a stepstool and rub a rag up and down the wall. The baby is well-protected in your womb. He won't remember a thing."

"We're having a boy?" Rex asked.

Lexie tossed him a lip curl.

"Hey, she connects with these things. She's a psychic." Rex pointed a serious glance at Goldie. "Well?"

Haley placed her hands on the back of Goldie's shoulders. "I do need to warn you," she said to Rex and Wini. "The biological mother of our baby was expecting a girl, according to Goldie's intuition." Haley used air quotes. "We painted the nursery pink. Yeah, I know...terrible gender biasing. I get it. But hey, we were all goo goo gaa gaa over being new parents. Anyway, we were stuck with pink everything. My boy was two and still wearing pink outfits that we received at the shower. So grain of salt moment." She squeezed Goldie's shoulders and kissed her cheek. "We love Goldie anyway."

Goldie snickered and shooed her away. "So where are Maya and Taylor? And your dog?" she asked Lexie.

"Shopping for supplies. Again," Lexie added. "Second trip of the day."

"Not anymore." Auntie Maya pushed through the front door and held it open with her hip for Taylor and Cashmere. "We have fresh paint. Lots and lots of fresh paint. Oh, and rollers for everyone. It's going to be a paint party." Overstuffed plastic bags dangled from her arms.

Next, in walked Taylor, balancing a large ladder on top of her head. Cashmere pounced around at her feet, regaling the crowded space to clear a path for her new best friend.

Rex helped Taylor lower the ladder to the ground and prop it up against the wall.

"Oh, not that wall." Lexie butted in. "That's the wall we still need to wash and prep for Emma."

"Emma?" Taylor asked.

She turned and Emma stepped forward. "I'm Emma. Nice to meet you."

They shook hands.

"Oh, and I'm Haley."

Taylor extended her hand to her as well, and then turned over her shoulder, searching for more.

Rex urged Wini forward. "This is my girlfriend, Wini."

Taylor shook her hand, then noticed her pregnant belly. Taylor flinched, like she'd seen Jesus resurrect from the dead. Her eyes did some weird dance between narrowing and growing oddly large.

"Nice to meet you," Wini said in her faint voice.

Taylor's hand limped in Wini's. She withdrew it and stretched her lips thin. "Sorry, I felt a little dizzy for a second." She blinked and shook her head. "Allergies." She chuckled and exaggerated a sigh before swiping her hands together. Looking down at Cashmere, she asked, "What do you say we find those wrenches in my toolbox out back?"

Cashmere did a little flip in the air and barked.

Everyone laughed.

Except Taylor. Her face turned a pale shade of green.

Chapter Nine

Taylor balled herself up under a blanket in her dark, empty bedroom. She eventually drifted off to sleep after five hours of staring up at her ceiling fan. Then she woke hours later. Her heart pounded from the fragments of a dream with Oscar, a melancholy one about a night spent nursing him back to his feet after suffering a seizure.

That day marked four months since his passing.

Four months.

She sprang up and ran into the bathroom to splash water on her face. The further away from his death Taylor got, the heavier the lump in her throat became. He was everywhere and nowhere all at once.

Taylor stared at her tired complexion. The longer she stared, the more her emotions tumbled every which way. One second, she mourned Oscar, the next she desired Lexie, and still the next, her stomach dropped from the terrifying possibility of meeting her daughter and failing to impress her.

Seeing that young woman with a baby bump caused Taylor to second-guess her decision to contact Stephanie in the first place.

How would she explain her choice back then to Stephanie?

I was young?

So were many women. Like Wini.

Tension knotted in her shoulders. She needed to untangle.

So a few minutes later, she turned on the shower and eased under the hot stream.

She drifted away from thoughts of Oscar and of her daughter and landed back on Lexie. To Lexie's delicate contours, dimples, and gregarious personality.

Lexie was a good person. A talkative person. A nosy person. Mostly a pleasant person with a special way about her.

And Lexie had witnessed the mental war brewing in her head. She'd likely ask her all about it. Taylor didn't want her past to soil the new friendship before it had a chance to build momentum.

Taylor bowed her head under the stream.

Lexie.

Her timing sucked. Taylor faced a major shift in her life. She needed to prep for it. Not fantasize about the way Lexie's hair tangled up on top of her head in a sexy ponytail. Or the way her skin glistened when she pulled up staples. Or her vulnerable side. Her sweet, innocent, vulnerability.

Taylor's emotions took her on a ride. Up, down, backward, forward, and sideways. First things first. She needed to stop thinking of Lexie and start planning her first meeting with her daughter.

What would she say? *Sorry I gave you up. I got knocked up accidentally. I didn't abort you. That's something, right?*

Argh.

She wished she could reseal the records. Take back her consent. Save the young woman from learning that her mother couldn't handle a little life pressure.

She had quit on her daughter without even trying.

She would not quit on Maya.

She would show up at the boutique, lay the subflooring now that they delivered the plywood, and focus.

Period.

She shut off the water. Yes, that was a good solid plan.

Then an hour later, her plan fell like a poorly-designed house built on a sand dune. She spotted Lexie bent over a bucket, her ass perked up in the air in a set of tight blue jeans. And that fucking ponytail with the cute wisps flying all about. Lexie was rinsing her paintbrush, and water splattered all over the floor that she planned to work on that day.

"No, no, no," Taylor yelled and ran over to her. "Water's getting everywhere. The floor needs to be bone dry for me to lay the subflooring."

"Sorry. I needed to clean the brushes, and the sink clogged in the backroom. And another spider is staring at me from its massive web. What else did you want me to do? Let the paint cake up on the brush and ruin it?"

Taylor shrugged.

Lexie placed the sopping brush into a rag. "I suppose it's a good thing you showed up when you did. I can have you grab some more rags from the back and free Mr. Spider from his web at the same time." She handed the rag over to Taylor with a smile.

Her smile charmed through Taylor's resolve to stay focused.

Taylor no longer wanted to lay subflooring.

And she certainly didn't want to deal with Mr. Spider.

She wanted to kiss Lexie. Forget everything else and escape into her world for the time being.

But on the other hand, the practical side of her also wanted to stay mad at Lexie for ruining her floorboards, even though it wasn't her fault. Lexie didn't know she'd be laying the floors that day.

Then, more kinks in the plan got in her way when Cashmere took a drink from her bowl and sloshed water all over the place. When Taylor chased her away from the water, she sprinted toward the back doggy door that she had installed at Lexie's request, head first, legs flying behind her.

Taylor followed Cashmere's path of wet destruction with a rag, wiping up the puddles left behind. "Come with me," she said over her shoulder.

"I'm not going back there."

"I won't bite."

"Mr. Spider might."

"If we're going to work together on a rehab project in an old building, you need to learn a few things." Taylor stretched her hand out behind her. "Come on, I'll protect you from Mr. Spider."

Lexie's hand folded into Taylor's. As they walked forward, Lexie squeezed her fingers. "I'm not touching it. That's not happening."

Taylor led her into the backroom. A fluorescent bulb fixture with one working bulb hummed. She searched the far corners for the web. "Where is it?"

"Above the bathroom door." Lexie whimpered.

Taylor turned to Lexie who craned her neck away, toward the front of the store. "We're not diffusing a bomb here, Lexie. Ease up. You're stopping the blood flow to my fingertips." She tried to pull her hand free, but Lexie continued her death grip. So Taylor lifted Lexie's chin with her free hand. "You're being a wimp."

Lexie released Taylor's hand, but kept her chin propped on Taylor's finger. "I once read about a woman who died from a spider bite. One minute she's picnicking in the park with her family, the next, she's gasping. I'm not wimpy. I'm practical." The delicate skin around her eyes pinched.

"Practically unreasonable," she said with a tone much sharper than she meant to use.

"You're grumpy today," Lexie said, her chin still propped on Taylor's finger.

Taylor stared at her and attempted to soften her tension with a long exhale. "And you're being irrational."

"Human beings are hard-wired with innate fears to things that might kill them."

Taylor lowered her finger and crossed her arms. "How did smacking yourself upside the head that day work for you?"

Lexie leaned in and now propped Taylor's chin up with her finger. "That's a low-ball tactic." She darted her stare from one eye to the other, searching for a sympathy Taylor could not offer. After a long beat, she tightened her lips. "Fine, I call truce." She huffed backward. "So what's your plan? Are you going to ask me to face my fear and pluck the spider from its web? Because I'm telling you right now. Ain't gonna happen." She bobbed her head side-to-side like an indolent teenager refusing to take out the trash.

Taylor didn't want to freak her out or cause her to have a panic attack. She wanted her to thrive, to be empowered. Fear snuffed life out of a person. Face the stupid spider. Big deal. Taylor used to play with them as a kid.

Lexie's chest puffed up and down and the sides of her delicate neck pulsed.

Even scared, a sexy vibe shined in her.

She wanted to kiss her even more. Pull her into her arms and get her heart pulsing for a good reason.

"You're panicking," Taylor took a step toward her.

"You panicked yesterday, too," she said at last.

And so the digging began.

But a trusting softness lay in Lexie's eyes. "Yes. I did panic."

Lexie stepped even closer, dragging concern with her.

Taylor instantly regretted her admission, supplementing it with a partial truth. "Wini reminded me of someone I knew a long time ago." Let Lexie chew on that instead.

"Someone who hurt you?"

"No, of course not." Taylor stole the broom from the corner, busying herself with something Lexie wanted no part of. She squared off with Mr. Spider, placing the broom brush into the web. The spider wound up into it. Taylor turned over her shoulder and handed the broom to Lexie.

"Absolutely not." Lexie scoffed, and crossed her arms over her chest.

"This is a small step. Take it." Taylor extended the broom closer.

Lexie labored for a breath.

Taylor grabbed her hand and nursed it against the broom handle. She kept her hand cupped over Lexie's, and led her toward the back door. Once Taylor pushed open the door, Lexie flicked her wrist and the broom flew across the grass. Cashmere, standing by the back fence, spotted them. She tossed her orange duck up in the air as if celebrating their arrival. Then she pounced toward them and pressed her front paws on Lexie, knocking her backward. Her ankle twisted around Taylor's, and there went Taylor, landing on top of Lexie. Cashmere claimed the top spot, balancing a front paw on each one of them.

Laughter bubbled from Taylor as she managed to climb out of the pile. She offered Lexie a hand and pulled her up. Meanwhile Cashmere excitedly barked at them and danced in a circle.

A second later, one of the workers from a few storefronts over walked past the back fence, and Cashmere went berserk, breaking into a series of pirouettes in his direction.

Lexie wiped her hands on her jeans. "I can't believe you made me take out that spider." She flung her hands in the air and bowed on a cry. "Argh. You're terrible." She rose. She braced her hands against her cheeks and stared at Taylor. "Terrible. Terrible."

She looked adorable with her messy ponytail and dirty cheeks.

"You claimed the power seat. It's over," Taylor said loudly over Cashmere's barks. "The spider is free. You're free. Win-win."

Taylor picked up the broom from where Lexie had flung it. Then she leaned it against the back of the store and walked inside.

"Back to my earlier question that you never answered." Lexie marched in behind her. "Who did Wini remind you of from your past?"

Taylor grabbed a bucket of rags and headed over to the wet mess Lexie left behind. She tossed a few down and moved them around with her foot. "It's not important. The past is the past."

Lexie placed her hands on her hips. "Well, that's not a good enough answer."

"Since when is my life any of your business?" Her harsh tone, completely unintentional, echoed against the tall ceilings.

Lexie's face flinched. The spider might've hurt less.

"I'm sorry," Taylor said softly.

She didn't want to hurt anyone. But she also didn't want to hang her dreadful past out on the line for everyone to pick apart. She still couldn't grasp what she had done eighteen years ago. How could she expect someone as innocent and friendly as Lexie to grasp it?

She clenched her jaw, not sure where to go with the conversation from there. "It's probably best not to try and figure me out. I'm complicated," she said, sadly.

~ ~

After completing the removal of the old tile from the bathroom, Lexie took a seat against the back wall. Cashmere curled up into a ball by Lexie's side and snored gently. Taylor banged around in the front room, cleaning up after hammering the last of the plywood into place.

All day long, Lexie worked in silence, bothered by Taylor's firm reaction to her line of questioning. Taylor's life was none of her business, true. But they had been working together for almost two months by then, and that had to mean something. Or did it? Maybe she did annoy Taylor.

Or maybe Taylor trusted her with a paintbrush and chisel, but not enough to provide the necessary context to pull together the personal tidbits she had shared thus far.

Fair enough.

It still hurt, though. She hated the awkward tension. They hadn't even shared a proper meal together, yet they suffered through their first argument.

She and Christine had never argued in the three years they'd dated. She spent a couple of months with this woman and she snapped.

They had at least met their construction goal for the day. So at least they made a good team.

While Lexie contemplated their quibble some more, Emma had arrived and Taylor helped her spread drop cloths on the floor and raise the stepladder.

Then, Taylor turned the corner and spotted Lexie on the floor. "Not afraid of a new spider crawling on you?" A sheepish grin spread across her face.

"I already scanned for spiders. We're all set." Lexie pointed to the fridge. "I've got beer. You're welcome to join me and Cashmere." She then patted the space next to them.

Taylor headed to the fridge and fished out the beers. Using the edge of the counter as leverage, with a single pound from her palm, she popped the tops off.

Lexie wrapped her hand around the cool, wet bottle. "Thanks."

Taylor swigged some, eyeing her from above. "I'm sorry, Lexie. I didn't mean to snap earlier. I'm a private person with a lot of ugly baggage."

Lexie peeled the tip of the label on her bottle, an act she started back in her college days. "It's okay. I shouldn't have dug."

Taylor laughed. "You do dig."

"I do. It's the curious side of me." She paused for a beat. "You know, I'm a great sounding board. If something's bothering you, I can listen about as good as I dig."

Taylor tipped the bottle to her cheek. "Should I need a sounding board, you'll be my go-to."

Lexie looked down at Cashmere. She was a cute ball of perfection, curled up and snoring. "Please sit with us."

Taylor's forehead creases relaxed, creating the illusion of a woman at peace. "Okay. For a few minutes. But only to let Emma work her magic on the mural."

"Of course." Lexie patted the floor next to Cashmere.

"Again, I'm sorry I snapped earlier. I guess I am grumpy."

Lexie pointed to herself. "Again. Great sounding board. I'm nonjudgmental, and am good at figuring out everyone else's moves. Just not my own."

Taylor eased into a gentle smile. "I'll definitely keep that in mind."

"Good." Lexie nudged her with her elbow.

Taylor reached down and pet Cashmere's head. She fingered the space between her eyes with short strokes. "Dogs are amazing. I used to have one."

"What was your dog's name?"

"His name was Oscar. He was a Maltese and poodle mix, and he was the best cuddler. He died four months ago today, and I haven't taken a full breath since then."

Taylor's cheek flinched. Her strokes between Cashmere's eyes increased in length and quantity.

Lexie couldn't imagine losing Cashmere. "I'm so sorry. And I'm sorry I called you grumpy. Of course, you're grumpy. You deserve to be grumpy. Be grumpy all you want."

"You dig and you ramble." Taylor's eyes filled with laughter.

"It's a side effect of always trying to fit in."

"I hear you on that."

"But you're a world-class author. You fit in naturally. It comes with the territory, doesn't it?"

Taylor tipped her head back on a laugh. "Not in the least bit. Your aunt glamorizes me on jacket copy and press releases. The real me is quiet and contemplative."

"And heartbroken," Lexie stated rather than asked.

"And heartbroken. Yes." Taylor massaged Cashmere's ears. A sadness trickled down her face. "Oscar was my sidekick. We did everything together."

"That's got to be rough."

She smiled weakly. "He looked like a cream-colored teddy bear with his fur and dark, playful eyes." She continued to knead Cashmere's ears with a loving touch, causing her to snore. "He would curl up into a ball on my lap and feed me good juju. And God forbid Maya and I had an argument on the phone over something to do with editing. He'd pounce between my feet and demand I scoop him up and bathe him in kisses and high inflection compliments. Which I did." She paused and pain spread across her face. "And which I miss doing so much," she whispered with a shake to her voice.

Instantly, sorrow pooled in between them.

In the silence that followed, tears began to sting Lexie's eyes.

Taylor's cheek flinched. "Everything changed when Oscar passed."

"I'm sure it did."

"No more walks around the neighborhood. So no more keeping the neighborhood clean of litter from the Seven Eleven store on the corner entrance to my subdivision. I used to stuff two trash bags every morning on our thirty minute walk around the streets."

"Two?"

Taylor laughed, which dislodged a few tears from her wet eyes. "I'm having a hard time writing because everywhere I turn there he is in spirit but not in physical reality where I want him to be."

The sorrow etched in Taylor's words. Lexie swallowed hard.

"I can't bring myself to remove his bowl yet. Or his crate of squeaky toys. Or his pillows in the front window and near the fireplace. They're sacred, you know?"

Lexie nodded, taking on the full brunt of Taylor's sadness.

"How can I stuff them away in a closet and pretend they no longer matter?"

Lexie took a deep breath. "You need more time."

Taylor remained silent for a moment as her fingers trailed Cashmere's neck. "I know that in order to move forward and ever be able to write from a happy place again, I'm going to have to begin the process of storing away his things. I'm not there, yet. But I'm getting there. This place is helping." She leaned down and kissed Cashmere's head. "She's helping, too."

Lexie wanted to hug her. But settled on an arm pat. "All in good time."

Taylor released a tense breath. "Yes. All in good time." She climbed up to her feet, and pet Cashmere again. "Enjoy her as much as possible. The time flies by faster than you can imagine."

Lexie cocked her head and smiled up at her. "Sage advice. Thank you. And thanks for sharing that with me."

Taylor tipped her still full bottle of beer to the air. "I'm going to watch the artist at work. Care to join me?"

"She won't mind?"

Taylor smiled. "She's a talker, too."

Lexie eased Cashmere's head off her leg. She opened her sleepy eyes and popped up on her feet. The three of them joined Emma as she sketched a dog next to a tree with the edge of a flat paintbrush. "Oh hello," she said, glancing at them over her shoulder.

"How do you know where to place things?" Lexie asked. "Aren't you afraid to mess that part up?"

"Nah, everything's temporary." Emma stepped down from the ladder and scanned her sketch. "Besides, the best art is imperfect anyway."

"Hmm. Even with writing?" Taylor challenged her.

"Of course." Emma's cheeks rose in delight. "Imperfect stories are my favorite. They're raw and real."

Taylor cupped her chin. "I like that. Takes a bit of the pressure off trying to be perfect."

Emma flitted a glance between Lexie and Taylor, as if trying to size them up. "Absolutely. Imperfections keep a pulse on reality and intrigue." She turned back to her sketch. "Perfection is boring. It's the conflicts in between the lines that grab a person and cause her to see things for what they are."

"Which is?" Taylor asked.

"Possibilities of course." On that, Emma climbed up two steps of the ladder and drew a giant, black swoosh through her tree. Taylor gazed at it through engaged eyes, mesmerized by it.

What they saw in that mark, Lexie hadn't a clue. Though, it impacted Taylor. Her eyes twinkled. Yes, twinkled like little gems finding light at the end of a dark tunnel.

Chapter Ten

Stephanie had only texted Taylor twice since the adoption records were unsealed. Her initial text and the one with dates for photographing the botanical gardens. Then out of the blue, a new text arrived to Taylor's delight.

Do you have any tips on how to write a blog?

Taylor panicked for a moment. What if she didn't advise her correctly? What if she messed up her blogging process by giving her the wrong tips? She steadied her breathing, staring at the text message.

Her daughter asked her for advice. She let that sink in for a good long moment. Then her heart leaped and washed away the panic. *I have a few I can share. Where in the process are you in need of help?*

The entire process. Lol

Three little dots appeared.

Just kidding. I struggle with what to write about.

Ah, writer's block. My specialty.

You get writer's block?

Absolutely. It's important not to get down on yourself over it because then you'll end up more stuck. Taylor needed to take her own advice.

Oh, so like quicksand?

Exactly. Relax and let go. Have you ever tried freewriting?

Explain please!

Taylor loved her exclamation point. *Okay, well, set a timer for ten minutes, then type. Don't stop typing until the timer goes off.*

What do I type, though?

Pick an object in the room. A lamp. A blanket. Anything. And write about it. Describe it in great detail. Write about how the color affects you. What it reminds you of. Things like that.

Will people want to read about a lamp, though?

No. Well maybe. Ha ha. The point is once you begin to write about it, your mind will relax and will surprise you by taking you on a creative ride. When the timer goes off, you'll have written about far more than the lamp. And that will be your guide and your idea. Taylor couldn't bring herself to do that herself while suffering from her block. Sometimes life blocked more than words. Hopefully, it would actually work for Stephanie.

I like that idea.

You'll be amazed. You'll start off talking about a lamp and end up turning over a topic about friendship, creativity, or civic engagement by the end. It's a cool process.

I have a lot to learn.

Don't we all?

Lol. Okay, I'm off to write. Thanks for the advice! I figured you were the right person to ask.

Taylor wanted more than anything to continue being the right person for her to ask. She'd give up chocolate, sleep on the ground without a tent, walk cross-country, anything to be that right person. *Good luck!*

Thanks! Oh, and thank you for confirming the botanical garden date. I'll see you soon!

~ ~

"Do you miss Christine?" Auntie Maya asked Lexie as they unpacked shelving from boxes.

Her question threatened Lexie's good mood. She didn't want to talk about Christine. She had already packaged her up. She had no place in the present. She wanted to move forward. But her aunt liked mulling around the past, rummaging through memories like they were rusted trinkets in bins at an antique shop. Kind of like she did herself with Taylor about Wini and her panic face. "No, I don't miss her. I've moved on."

"I don't believe you."

She wouldn't get into it with her aunt. Yes, Christine's abrupt silence still hurt her. It bruised her ego more than her heart, though. And the fact that Taylor had been there to witness the showdown on the phone that day at Pusser's pierced her bubble even more.

She didn't miss her. She missed someone. She missed having someone to go home to. Not that she spent any time at home. She didn't have one anymore. But still. She would eventually. And when it grew cold, she would enjoy cuddling up to someone. The lack of companionship left her empty. Not Christine.

Recovering her ego from the breakup resembled the days following a kettlebell workout, only a tad bit more drawn out. It hurt to climb stairs, to get up off the couch, and to walk at a pace faster than an elderly person pushing a cart around Walmart. Eventually, the pain subsided to a dull throb. A few stretches and Epsom salt baths eased the soreness out of its tight grip. That soak allowed freedom from the splinters of disappointment.

A month into the breakup and Lexie started to believe that the past belonged in the past.

They had a full day ahead of them organizing their shelves. She wanted to laugh, not launch a defense to take away the sting of her injured ego.

Thankfully, Taylor drifted through the front door carrying laminate flooring boxes. She was a strong woman with a knack for hard work. She had committed to Auntie Maya and followed through—an admirable quality.

That quality drew Lexie in. Like with any good television series, she *had* to binge watch.

They shared a sweet smile as Taylor walked past her.

It had been three days since Lexie and Taylor tabled their quibble and Taylor had apologized to Lexie for being short with her. Call it an unstated rule. Lexie stopped being so nosy, and Taylor didn't snap at her. Problem solved.

Today was a new day. She'd be in control of her emotions. She showed up to help. So help she would. First, Cashmere needed to eat. So she prepped her food and placed her bowl down.

In her typical frenzied state when food appeared, Cashmere catapulted toward the bowl and barked, lunging at it. Bark. Lunge. Stomp. Repeat a few dozen times.

"Eat," Lexie said in a high-pitched voice.

She barked, lunged, and stomped again.

"Eat! We're watching. Everyone is watching."

She perked her ears as if the attention finally dawned on her, then bowed her head and chowed like a starving dog who hadn't seen food in months.

That crazy antic earned her some hearty awes.

"Okay, ladies. Now that Queen Cashmere has eaten, I must go," Auntie Maya said. "I have my weekly appointment with Goldie now. I'll be back in an hour or so. Depends on how much comes through for her."

"Does that really work?" Taylor asked as she approached the folding table full of brass door handle hardware.

"Sure does. That's how I learned about this place."

Lexie chuckled at her aunt's naivety. "Didn't have anything to do with the fact that Goldie owns the place?" she asked.

Her aunt's cheeks dropped. "Goldie would never feed me stuff to suit her own needs. She's not like that."

Taylor sorted through some loose screws and nails on the table. "Can she tell if the new front door is going to deliver on time?"

Auntie Maya tossed her hands up. "Now you're both poking fun at her. I don't like it. Not a bit. She happens to be the one police call on to solve supposed unsolvable cases. She pointed to the exact position of a missing police detective's car when someone drove off with it during an investigation at Centennial Park. She doesn't just solve official stuff. She also chats with pets who have passed. They relay messages to her that they can't get across to their owners."

She waited on some reaction, staring wide-eyed at them. "It's true. Once my little Toby stressed out about some construction in the kitchen and he visited Goldie in a dream to ask her why her momma had moved his food bowl. I had indeed moved it," she accentuated that last part.

"I asked her about Oscar," Taylor said. "He didn't come through. She told me to wait for a sign." She continued to mess with the screws and nails. "I'm still waiting."

"He'll show you a sign one day," Auntie Maya said.

Lexie turned her focus on the wall mural Emma had painted a few days before. "She did an amazing job."

"Goldie predicted Emma and Haley," her aunt said. "She saw the sun shining all over their relationship. Look at them. Happily together for over a decade now. And they have a son!" Auntie Maya moved to the mural and leaned in closer to the white boxer with a freckle on her chest. "That's Cashmere." She turned to Lexie. "She painted your Cashmere."

Cashmere bolted through the doggy door toward them. She landed on an excited thud in front of Auntie Maya. "Cashmere, you're going to be famous here. Forever the baby girl to The Pet Boutique." Auntie Maya bent and kissed Cashmere in between her eyes before bowing her forehead to meet hers. They stared at each other, Cashmere wagging her nub, waiting on something to happen. "Do you want to come see Ms. Goldie with me?"

Cashmere's big expressive eyes wandered left to right.

"Is that a yes?"

Cashmere bounced back and yipped.

"Very well. You two don't get into too much trouble while we're gone. Toodles." She walked toward the front door with her typical sing-song vibe, and Cashmere strutted behind her.

When they cleared the store, Taylor asked, "Do you believe in all that stuff?"

She wished she could. She wished she could pay someone to tell her where her life headed. That'd be a hell of a lot easier than winging it as she had for the past thirty-five years. "There's a lot of stuff in this world I don't understand. Doesn't mean it isn't real. Just because I can't hear a dog whistle, doesn't mean the sound doesn't exist."

"Hmm." Taylor hesitated. Her dark mocha shadowed eyes shimmered in a relaxed, soothing manner. Then she braced her hands on her hips. "So you mentioned at lunch that day at Pusser's that you're a photographer."

"I can work my way around a camera. Not sure my former boss would agree." She twisted her smile. "I asked for a leave of absence, and he denied it. He didn't exactly fight for me to stay."

Taylor ignored that part, walked over to a set of folding chairs near the new mural and sat on a tired thump.

Lexie sat with more grace on the seat next to her. "Do you want to hire me?" She chuckled.

Taylor didn't laugh. Instead, she took off her baseball cap and raked her fingers through her tangled hair. "Okay, here's the thing. I don't like to talk about this because it's uncomfortable for me. But I need to ask for your help if I'm going to get through it."

Lexie braced herself. "Go on."

Taylor's breaths quickened like she labored for them. "I have a daughter." She gulped with great effort. "And she wants to take me along on a photography trip to the botanical gardens in D.C." She exhaled rapidly and rubbed her forehead. "I have no clue how to even hold a camera."

Another shared personal fact. Lexie's heart twirled, despite Taylor's mounting meltdown over breathing. "She's your daughter. Surely she won't be surprised about that?"

Her forehead creased into a frown.

Lexie nudged her with her elbow. "It's not that difficult a question, is it?"

Taylor stretched her gaze up to the ceiling. "We don't know each other."

"Oh, come on, that's ridiculous. You're being a little hard on yourself, no? Kids are tough, but my aunt survived. So anyone can."

"It's not that easy," Taylor said, lowering her gaze back down to meet Lexie's.

"Okay, help me out here..." Lexie steadied for a better view on the situation so she could help her. It's what she did when curiosity plopped her in the front seat of a mystery she wanted to solve. "You're her mother. She's your daughter. Granted kids don't always click with their parents, but surely you're connected enough to know her deep down." Then it dawned on Lexie. "Oh no. Does she do drugs?"

"What?" Taylor scoffed. "God. No." Taylor flexed her jawline. "Then again, I can't be sure."

Lexie sat back and resisted more questions. "You're confusing me."

She regarded Lexie for a moment, biting her trembling lip. "She, um," Taylor cleared her throat and touched the front of it, stretching. "I gave her up for adoption." Her eyes pinched upwards. "I was eighteen and now she's an adult. She just turned eighteen and approved to unseal the adoption records recently."

"Why did you give her up for adoption?" The judgment landed in a heap between them before she could analyze it and stop its harshness.

Taylor bit into her fist, and rocked back and forth. "This was a bad idea."

Lexie leaned into her and lowered Taylor's fist, placing it in her lap. "No, no, no. Please no. I didn't mean to ask why."

Taylor didn't pull her hand back. It relaxed under Lexie's caress. "What if she reacts the same way?"

Lexie leaned in even more. "She won't. She reached out to you. She invited you to the botanical gardens. She wouldn't do that if she didn't want to spend quality time together."

"I hope you're right. I was young. I had no support. She deserved better than a life with no resources."

"I'm sure you did the right thing."

"I hope so. I have to say that I still kick myself for wimping out on motherhood."

"Oh, come on. You didn't wimp out. You chose in the best way you could under the circumstances, I'm sure."

Taylor leveled a gaze on her. "I never wanted to hurt her by my decision. But what if I did?"

Lexie understood her concern on some level. After all, her parents chose to leave her every summer when she was a kid to pursue things other than her. Of course, the older she got, the more she forgave them. They may have fallen short in the parenting realm, but redeemed themselves by giving their time to pursuits that went beyond Lexie to communities in need of their help. Her parents hadn't set out to hurt her. They probably assumed they hurt her less by not bringing her along. Lexie had to agree. Summering in malaria-infested communities, digging wells, and sleeping in straw houses didn't sound like fun. She much preferred Auntie Maya's comfortable home and fun-filled, albeit wacky at times, family.

"Time is a great equalizer. It offers insights you can only gain through the passage of it. You can't predict how she'll be, but the fact she reached out tells me she's going to understand." Lexie tightened her other hand over Taylor's. "You choose to give her a chance. That's a lot of love and responsibility. You did it for selfless not selfish reasons. That's a big difference that doesn't go unnoticed."

Gratitude washed over Taylor's face. "No one's ever put it like that. I could've used that insight eighteen years ago." She chuckled, softly. "The second the bus took off down the interstate away from the halfway house, I suffered severe regret."

"A halfway house?"

"My parents assumed I took a gap year between high school and college."

Acting on a nurturing instinct, Lexie reached up and cradled Taylor's cheek. "That must've been a lot to sift through at such a young age."

Taylor's eyes carried a sadness that Lexie wanted to take away.

"When I met Wini that day, you were right. I did panic. She reminded me of that time in life when everything changed. In a flash, the familiar stench of inadequacy clung to me all over again."

Lexie lowered her hand from Taylor's cheek and rested it on her hand again. "Inadequacy?"

"Well, you know, Wini, she has it all together. A full support system. An extended family who cares about her. Family who will host birthday parties, dress up for Halloween, and toss themselves in the cold to create snow angels for her baby.

114

She's protected, nurtured, and better equipped to bring a baby into the world than I ever was. And that made me sad. Which is why I clammed up."

She squeezed Taylor's hand. "Your daughter will understand."

"I also feel guilty because I never gave my parents the chance to decide if they would've provided me that support system. What if they would've understood and accepted my pregnancy? They still don't know, and that also brings a lot of guilt. I need to tell them. I also need to tell my daughter that she has grandparents. What if they don't want to meet her? A lot of what-ifs are running through my mind."

"Everything will work out." Lexie kept her hand over Taylor's.

Keeping her voice to a whisper, Taylor said, "You were right about something, Lexie."

"I'm right about a lot of things." She offered her a sidelong glance, enjoying the growing trust they shared. "But what thing in particular are you referring to? Because I kind of want to do more of it."

"You're easy to talk with. Getting some of this out helps clear up space in my mind." She lowered her eyes and glanced around the laminate flooring boxes at their feet. "I've told three people in my life about the baby. Well four, if you count Stephanie. That's her name. Stephanie."

"It's a pretty name." Lexie kept her hands laced over Taylor's.

"Maya knows, of course, and my late husband, Nate, and now you."

Late husband? Lexie thought. "You had a husband?" Lexie whispered the question.

"I'm a widower. Yes." Taylor lowered her shoulders.

Lexie's breath hitched. "Wow. You've had a rough go at life."

Taylor blew off the pity with a quick click to her tongue. "Which is why I'm hoping the next few decades are kinder." She winked.

Lexie paused to catch her bearings, and then joined Taylor's sweep to hopefulness. "Well, let's see to it that it is. What can I do to help?"

"I need a few pointers so I don't show up like a total dweeb."

Render a few pointers? Taylor, the woman who likely first assumed Lexie was nothing more than a prissy, spoiled brat prancing around in flimsy sandals, whacking spiders out of her hair now asked her for a few pointers. "I'll do you better than that. I'll even trust you with one of my cameras."

"Really?"

"Yes." Pride filled Lexie. That kind of pride lifted her. She had value to offer and Taylor wanted to accept it.

~ ~

When Taylor asked for a few pointers, she meant point her in the direction of a few resources, like YouTube videos. She didn't expect Lexie to drop everything and take her offsite that very night.

But she did, and that thrilled Taylor.

She enjoyed Lexie's company, and trusted in the friendship that began to blossom between them.

They headed to Lake Kittamaqundi with Lexie's camera.

A three-man band played rich rock tunes from the seventies on the outdoor pavilion stage while families, friends, and dogs peppered the grassy hill in front of it. Cashmere darted to every shrub and blade of grass in her path, tugging Lexie like a rag doll. Taylor grew concerned for her camera because it dangled from her shoulder and kept bouncing against Lexie's perky ass.

"Let me take Cashmere's leash," Taylor offered.

"For now." Lexie beamed. "Once we get to the clearing around the other side of the lake, I'm going to have you take pictures of her.

So they headed to an isolated area with trees and bushes as their only companion. Without the distraction of others, Cashmere relaxed and eased up on the yanking.

Lexie stood in the middle of the grass and stretched her neck to peek at the cloudless summer sky. "I love this weather." She released a laugh that landed in Taylor's ears like a wind chime, peaceful and gentle. She radiated gratitude, staring out at the lake as if none of the floating plastic water bottles and bags existed.

She was a beautiful woman.

116

A beautiful distraction and muse all wrapped up into one tempting package.

Lexie had jumpstarted her writing again with her sexy and nurturing ways. She didn't expect that benefit.

Taylor typically shied away from benefits because they always came crashing down on her in the end. They lulled her into their cocoon and bathed her in comfort and blessings, then fell apart and tossed her to the ground on a hard thud. Next thing, she had to scramble, gather what little possessions remained, and run for cover, promising herself never to let that happen again.

Until the next welcoming cocoon appeared.

What could she say? She was a sucker for hope.

"Okay, teach me something." Taylor shaded the setting sun with her hand.

"Okay." Lexie's lips twitched, and the red hue of her cheeks showed a nervous side of her. "Where to even start?"

"Is this going to be complicated?"

She bobbled her head back and forth. "You probably have plans, right? It's Friday. I'm sorry. I'll keep it very simple so you can go do whatever it is you do on Friday nights."

Drink two Miller Lights, eat a bowl of air-popped popcorn with butter and salt, and watch NCIS until my eyes grow too heavy.

"I'm not in a rush. I'm wondering if I should take notes."

Lexie looked at her butt. "Where's your trusted notepad?"

Taylor blushed. "You remembered that tidbit of info?"

"I told you that I'm a good listener." Her voice carried a flirt to it.

"With my nerves all over the place lately, I've forgotten about my notepad."

"Well, that's okay. You know where to find me if you have more questions after our lesson." Lexie offered her a wink that sent Taylor flying.

"Okay, so," Lexie began fiddling with the settings on the camera. "Knowledge is power. So what do you say we power you up with some?" Lexie's question cradled a sultry whisper.

"I love that idea," she whispered back.

Lexie offered Taylor a quick tutorial on things like how to hold the camera, set up a good composite using the rule of thirds and the on-camera grid system, focus, and use the settings. "If you're shooting flowers, you're going to want to use a macro lens." She handed the camera to her.

"It all seems pretty easy." Taylor steadied the camera in her hands.

"Okay, then hotshot." Lexie folded her hands across her chest and tossed her hair over her shoulder. "Go ahead and snap away."

Taylor positioned herself in front of Lexie and took a few shots.

"I'm getting the hang of it."

"What is your aperture set to?"

"What's that?"

Lexie released another one of her alluring chiming laughs. "Come here. Bring it on over. Let me show you."

She walked her through more settings that meant nothing to Taylor. They went in one ear and out the other not because Lexie bored her with details. No, because Lexie's hair had brushed against Taylor's arm again and blocked any other logic from entering.

"Okay, now to get a good portrait of anything in nature, you're going to want to capture it from unique angles. She plopped on the grass, belly down, ass perked up to the sky. "Come down here with me."

"You're bossy."

"Just get down here."

Taylor obliged.

"Grab it." Lexie handed the camera over to her.

Taylor balanced on her elbows, pointing the camera at Cashmere. She posed naturally as she sniffed the fragrant meadow air.

Lexie leaned in close and whispered, "Use the grid by lining Cashmere up along one of the intersections."

Her breath tickled the side of Taylor's face. "Got it."

"Take it."

Taylor depressed the shutter button and snapped several in a row.

Lexie scooted even closer. "Let's see how you did."

They scanned the pictures.

"See that blurred greenery behind her ears," Lexie asked, pointing to the camera screen with the tip of her dainty finger. "That's a hell of a shot."

Taylor beamed. "Really?"

Lexie tapped Taylor's forearm. "You have nothing to worry about. She'll be impressed. She's going to like you."

Her confidence was a platform that aided Taylor to stand taller and face the sea of uncertainty that had waterlogged her for so long.

Lexie remained close, supporting her against the fears that once derailed her. Something in the depth of her stare lulled her into blurting out a fact that had eaten away at her since getting pregnant. "I had a blind date that turned into a one-night stand. I never got to tell the man that he was a father."

~ ~

Lexie groaned, in response. She needed to control that stupid, insensitive reflex. At least she didn't have an eye roll issue like her cousins. She twisted her mouth, bracing to see Taylor's reaction to her groan. She fidgeted with the camera strap instead.

Lexie rose, walked over to Cashmere, and fastened the leash on her collar. "Those things happen," she said in her most nurturing of voices.

She'd slept with three people in her entire life, and each one took her months to get up the courage. She persevered and carried on with her act to show Taylor she could open up to her if need be. "Don't be so hard on yourself. She won't be. By the time you meet her, you'll kick yourself in the ass for wasting all that time worrying about how to break that to her."

Taylor handed the camera back to Lexie and took Cashmere's leash. She led forward, away from the direction of the crowded grassy hill and toward the one-mile length of the lake loop. "I've looked forward to this for many years, and now that it's coming up, I've never been more scared."

"You can take Cashmere with you. She loves flowers." Lexie scooped her head under the camera strap. "As long as you have treats, she'll do whatever you tell her." As if on cue, Cashmere stopped and looked up at Lexie. "Aw, you little stinker. You're too smart." She dipped into her pocketbook and pulled out a treat. Cashmere didn't blink. She didn't move. She stared at that cookie like it was a juicy steak.

"Toss her the cookie," Taylor said. "She's drooling."

Lexie popped it in the air and Cashmere caught it on a graceful leap, smacking her lips together and moseying on her way. Cashmere snorted at the ground and sneezed three times in a row.

Taylor laughed and gazed at Cashmere with a motherly type love, the kind a parent displayed when a kid learned to ride a bike for the first time or painted something ugly with finger paints but she loved anyway.

"I bet you'd be a good mom," Lexie said. "Would you ever consider having another child or adopting one?"

Taylor cocked her head. "It's not something I gave much thought to after everything I went through. Besides, Nate couldn't have children, so we adopted our dog, Oscar, instead. I wouldn't say no to a child if the right circumstance presented itself. But the older I get, dog adoptions appeal more to me."

Lexie snuck in a playful blow. "True. I guess being fifty starts to wear you down." She continued staring at the ground, watching Cashmere's feet prance in her lopsided gait.

Taylor laughed. Then it fizzled out like a dying engine. She stopped walking and Cashmere looked back at her with that *what the hell are you doing* face. "I don't even have a gray hair on my head." Her eyes stretched open wider. "Now granted, I'm not the fittest person on the planet. I do aerobics sometimes. It may take me a second longer to jump out of bed in the morning, but my bones aren't breaking. Fifty? Seriously?"

Lexie allowed the laughter to exit. "You walked right into it, *Ms. the older I get, dog adoptions appeal more to me.*"

Her eyes sparkled back to life.

Lexie nudged her. "You might be a decade and a half younger than I just accused you of being, but your memory sucks. You did tell me Stephanie's age already. Remember? And you also told me your age when you gave birth. It's simple math. Eighteen and eighteen has never added up to fifty for me. And I suck at math."

Taylor chuckled.

Cashmere bounced and stuck her butt up in the air, obviously impatient with their slow crawl.

They walked part of the loop in silence, both taking in the balmy evening and the chirps of tree frogs filling the peaceful trail with their songs.

The more their silence carried on, the more curious Lexie grew about Taylor. Curiosity had a way of sneaking in and taking over all sense of politeness for Lexie. She couldn't help herself sometimes. Like in that moment, a question dangled itself before her and teased her. If she didn't quench curiosity's thirst, it would continue to tickle her until she caved. "What was your husband like?"

Taylor's cheek flinched. "Kind. Nate was kind."

"How long were you together?"

"We became good friends in the ninth grade." Taylor's eyes remained glued on Cashmere.

"You loved him, huh?"

"Yeah. We grew up together." A melancholy haze took over her face. "We learned how to drive stick shifts in a cemetery together, of all places. Our families vacationed in Ocean City together. We started dating, and then broke up for a while starting in our senior year of high school. He dated the captain of the cheerleading squad, and that killed me. We eventually got back together again after life had tumbled us around a bit." She paused as the apprehension bubbled. "After the whole *got pregnant on a blind date, had a baby, gave her up, and headed home on a bus seated next to a nice man named Roger Lyles* thing."

Hearing about her relationship stirred up an odd sludge at the bottom of their new paradigm. It coiled up around her and forced her to reality's surface. *We grew up together. Our families spent vacations in Ocean City.*

She kept poking out of habit. "How long ago did he pass?"

"About four years ago. Motorcycle accident."

Lexie's stomach turned. "Oh geez. That's terrible. I'm so sorry."

"We fought most about that damned motorcycle. I questioned why the obsession with riding it, and he questioned why the obsession with finding my daughter."

"He didn't want you to find her?"

Taylor hesitated, biting her lip. "It wasn't so much that. He worried that my daughter wouldn't want me to find her. He didn't want me to get hurt. That's all."

The mood dropped, and Lexie's shoulders grew heavy.

Lexie's life was complicated, too, sort of. Nothing like Taylor's. Sure, she had to file for unemployment benefits. At least she could go get a job cleaning toilets any day if she wanted to remain officially employed. Taylor couldn't take back the past eighteen years. That had to hurt in ways Lexie would never understand.

"Can I ask you a very personal question?"

"More digging, huh?" Taylor nudged her side, lifting the mood back to something more playful.

"I'm going to assume something here, so please forgive me if I'm wrong, but did Nate know you were attracted to females?"

Taylor held Lexie's stare, and in the passing moments, an understanding surfaced. "Yes. He knew that I'm bisexual." Her eyes twinkled and continued to wrap Lexie in a warm embrace, one that turned her knees to jelly.

They both chuckled, kicking up stones with their sneakers and skipping over the unnecessary words to fill in the space. "I could sort of tell. You know?" Lexie tilted her head. "By the way you smile and stuff."

Taylor bowed her head. Her face blotched.

Lexie continued anyway. "I've always been curious how that works for a bisexual being married and whether you have to cut off one part of yourself to feed the other."

Taylor's ears turned red. "No. We rocked our relationship. I loved him, and he

122

fulfilled me in life, love, and sex. Of course, if he wasn't open and nurturing to my sexuality, I may have had a different answer for you."

Their hands brushed against each other as they walked.

"Have you ever had a girlfriend?" Lexie asked.

"For a short while." Taylor kicked a small stone with her toe. "Once before I started to officially date Nate. And again, after I returned from that long bus ride. But I wasn't in the right frame of mind for that one, so it didn't work. The sex was great, though." Taylor laughed and elbowed Lexie, blushing more.

They shared a few extended giggles, and then Taylor continued. "After I told Nate about giving up my daughter for adoption, he took care of me and my heart. And he did until the day he passed."

Lexie's heart melted. "I've never heard anyone say anything more beautiful than that."

Taylor nodded and rested on an easy smile. "I do wish he could be here for the visit."

"He will be."

Taylor released her breath on a gasp. "Yeah. You're right." She bit down on her lower lip. "I'm still going to freak out."

"Seriously, take Cashmere with you. She'll be a good ice-breaker."

"What if she's afraid of dogs?"

"I can go with you if you want. Pretend I'm an old friend who likes flowers, too."

"I don't want to start off with lies telling her we're old friends."

Lexie flinched backward, not expecting the blow.

Taylor laughed hard.

"Why are you laughing at me?"

"You wear your emotions all over your face." She wrinkled up her nose in exaggeration. "And I like that."

That little move and Taylor's laughter caused Lexie's heart to thump.

"I meant I should tell her the truth. That you're a friend. Not an *old* friend, but a friend. Why do we need to shove adjectives like 'old' in front of it? Didn't we already have this discussion about old stuff?"

"You're something else, Taylor Henshaw."

Taylor smiled. "That was sweet of you to offer to come with me. Even though I'll be anxious, it's probably best if I meet her on my own this first time."

"I agree. And you'll do great."

Taylor leaned in and traced her finger along Lexie's cheek. "You have a little black fleck." Taylor worked her finger against her cheek in slow, careful rotations.

A tingle sprouted and traveled all the way south.

"Ah, there," Taylor stepped back and examined her finger. "See, a little black fleck."

Lexie's mind tangled in a goo of sexual pleasure, imagining Taylor's fingers working their magic on her. Sex with Taylor would be incredible, life-altering, and euphoric. The heat caused her inner thighs to become hot and wet. Imagine the touch of her tongue?

It would be amazing. But the wrong choice at that point in time. Taylor had a lot to sort through in life. Way more than Lexie, and Lexie could barely handle the sorting. Imagine tossing a kid she never met and the death of a partner on top of the pile? Taylor was off the table for the time being.

Still, even just kissing her would be amazing.

Chapter Eleven

The big day arrived—the day Taylor would meet Stephanie at the botanical gardens in Washington, D.C.

She woke to a tight chest. Not heart-attack tightness. More like a shackled tightness.

The panic set in, taking a sharp stab at her senses.

Everything in her told her to hit the pause button and take a little more time to prep emotionally for what could happen. In that moment, the ground sucked her in, tensing her muscles and cutting off vital circulation.

She couldn't take a full breath.

How would she be able to click a camera or say anything intelligent?

Her throat swelled and the room spun. Everything turned blurry and the air thickened, causing Taylor to gasp.

Her heart galloped, leaving her behind in a chokehold of dust.

"Panic attack," she managed to say aloud. "It's just a panic attack."

Taylor dropped her head between her knees and exhaled five sharp breaths. Then she tensed her toes and fingers for five seconds and released them. She did that until her mind cleared and her breath caught back up to her.

When she sustained a normal, albeit shaky, breath, finally, she picked up her phone and texted Stephanie.

Hi there, I have to cancel today. I'm so sorry. Can we do it again another time?

She hovered above the send button.

She could've folded a dryer full of clothes during her contemplation. She'd already waited eighteen years, she couldn't chicken out.

She erased the text and sent her a positive one instead. *Hey, just confirming today. Let me know if all is still a go.*

Then she showered, steadying for the day ahead and whatever it might bring.

When she finished drying her hair and getting dressed, she checked her cell. A text from Stephanie waited for her.

Hi, there. I'm sorry, but I need to cancel today. I could lie and tell you something came up. I know better than to lie. So I'll tell you the truth. My gramma would prefer if I got to know you through more letters first. She's a bit overprotective. And maybe she's right. I do love writing letters. It's easier to say what you want. I promise, I'll write a letter soon. You have my address from the letter I wrote you? Writing letters is better. My words come out better when I use a pen against paper. It's always been the case. Now I know that's probably because you're a writer and most writers enjoy that kind of stuff. Anyway, I hope it's not a big deal to cancel. I'll write to you soon and we can reschedule some other time.

P.S. The freewriting helped. I've written five blog entries already! Thanks for the tips.

Taylor sat on the edge of her bed and released a big sigh of relief. Then she texted Stephanie back.

No worries. I completely understand. Writing letters sounds like fun until we can one day meet. I do love the feel of pen against paper. I am so happy the freewriting helped!

~ ~

Lexie unlocked the front door to The Pet Boutique to grab her aunt's sweater for her. She promised her aunt she'd be in and out so she wouldn't be late for bagels and muffins at the cemetery.

She looked forward to being with the Merkel gang. They had grown on her since she returned from New Hampshire. Even Jack. Nico helped soften his snobby side with his down-to-earth personality. Jack even warmed up to Cashmere.

Lexie nudged the door open with her hip.

Once inside, she noticed the lights in the backroom and the familiar curvy outline pacing. "Taylor?"

Taylor let a little scream escape and jumped a few inches. "Geez, Lexie. You scared me."

"What are you doing here? Today is the big day."

Taylor walked toward her, carrying a heavy load of concern on her shoulders.

"It's canceled. So I came here to work, and realized I had my good clothes on. So instead, I'm checking inventory on our supplies."

"Why is it canceled?"

Hesitation pooled in her eyes and her chin quivered. "Her grandmother freaked out. She's overprotective. Anyway, she asked if we could reschedule later once we got to know each other through letters." She groaned and ran her fingers through her hair.

Sounded like the grandmother could be a potential problem down the road if Taylor didn't keep a careful eye on her. Lexie couldn't stand to see her upset. "That settles it, then." She approached her, then looped her elbow in hers. "You're coming with me."

"Where?" Taylor didn't resist her lead.

"Breakfast at the cemetery. A cure all for any and all stress and sad moods."

~ ~

"I'm so happy you could join us," Maya leaped to her feet when they arrived. She wrapped herself in Taylor's arms and whispered. "Why are you here?"

"We had to reschedule. No biggie. So Lexie invited me."

Maya and Lexie exchanged smirks.

Taylor would fill Maya in later. She gripped a bottle of orange juice and ground her teeth. How she wished she could transport herself back in time to a few months ago when life bored her. That boredom simplified things like a good routine often did. No erratic heartbeats. No disappointment. Just a steady stream of familiar dull thumping on her brain, instead of the discomfort from planting herself in the middle of a family's sacred time together.

Taylor had never met Maya's kids and spouses, except for Rex and Wini.

On the drive over, Lexie had filled her in on everyone in a way that Maya never would. She expected greetings of eye rolls, awkward handshakes, and stares, but instead received warm smiles and muffins. Lots of muffins. How many could those people eat in one sitting?

Jack, the one Taylor feared the most, offered his tripod chair up to her. Apparently, he loved her books. "I've read them all," he gushed, welcoming Taylor in like she was the Queen of England there for tea and biscuits. "Your use of sensory details is exquisite." A giggle traced the edge of his sentences.

Ally, the most complex of the bunch, according to Lexie, wore happiness like an accessory. "So are you two dating?" she asked.

Lexie choked on her muffin.

Taylor's face burned hot.

Maya dribbled her coffee down the front of her silk blouse.

"No," Taylor said. "We're working together on The Pet Boutique."

Jack leaned forward and petted the top of Cashmere's head. *Pat. Pat. Pat.* Cashmere flinched each time. "Aren't you supposed to be working on your next book?"

"Writer's slump, Jack," Lexie said matter-of-factly. "Ease up on her. She's enjoying herself on the rehab project. Aren't you?" she asked Taylor.

Before she could answer, the loud muffler of a motorcycle broke through the morning peace.

Cashmere jumped to her feet and wagged her nub, whining in the motorcycle's direction.

Taylor noticed that Lexie had tightened her grip on the leash.

That sound killed Taylor every time. She bit down on her cheek waiting for it to pass. It grew louder and more ferocious. It stabbed at her, twisting and jabbing.

Lexie placed her free hand on hers without a word. It comforted Taylor, bringing her back to focus.

"Ah-ha," Maya clapped. "Rex is here."

"Without his pregnant bride I see," Jack muttered.

There the judgment lurked. The critical flair Lexie went on and on about on the drive over. Cold and icy. Jealous over the adoptive son. The tension rode in like a tidal wave—strong, fierce, and unforgiving. A new panic about Stephanie's well-being set in. Did Stephanie have siblings who despised her, too?

"Rex doesn't want her on a motorcycle, remember?" Nico pursed his lips together. "Now, behave."

Taylor liked Nico instantly.

Once Rex cut the engine, Lexie let go of Cashmere's leash. Then Cashmere bolted toward Rex and greeted him with an exuberant series of hops. After their loving reunion, Cashmere followed him toward the family. He walked into their circle with an easy-going swagger. "Hey, nice," he said, taking in the sight of Taylor sitting on Jack's tripod chair. "Another welcome guest to the Merkel family."

Taylor extended her hand, and he bypassed it, pulling her into a tight hug, complete with a pat on the back. "They don't bite. They eye roll a lot. But no bite," he whispered, then released her. "Oh, hey, weren't you photographing the botanical gardens today, though?"

Taylor froze.

Lexie stirred next to her, narrowing in on her aunt.

Maya swiped her hands together and chuckled nervously. "Oh dear, you need more coffee Jack."

Taylor smiled down at her feet when Lexie's hand brushed against hers. "I didn't say anything," she leaned in and whispered. "I swear I didn't."

~ ~

"Here you are, cousin," Rex handed Lexie a small blue foiled gift-wrapped box with a white bow. "Happy birthday."

"It's your birthday?" Taylor asked.

Lexie offered her a coy grin.

Rex hugged her and kissed the top of her head. "You might be older than me, but I'm still taller."

That wouldn't be hard to conquer with Lexie's five-foot, two-inch frame. "You didn't have to get me anything."

"It's small. Much better than forgetting it like that idiot ex-girlfriend of yours."

"Open it," Auntie Maya cheered, then lifted a bigger box wrapped in colorful comic strip newspaper from behind the cooler. "Then, open mine."

"Your girlfriend forgot your birthday?" Taylor asked.

"In her defense, Christine needed to prep for a new client that day." Lexie smiled weakly.

Taylor arched her eyebrow.

"A big client," Lexie added. "Like so big, it landed her a big promotion."

"If you ever forget my birthday, I'll drown myself in a bath," Jack said, fingering Nico's cheek with a lazy touch.

"I know, sweetheart." Nico tapped Jack's wrist, and spoke to Taylor. "Anything short of a two-day trip to a swanky spa, Godiva chocolates, champagne, and new silky pajamas would crush him." Nico shrugged with a smile. "I need him to sing me 'Happy Birthday' and I'm set."

It didn't surprise Lexie that Jack didn't counter that. Auntie Maya spoiled her first born, and poor Nico had to pay the price. God love his patience.

Lexie unwrapped the gift and opened the box. Inside lay a magnet that read Proud Godmother in a pretty scroll writing. Lexie placed her hand over her heart while gazing at it. "Me?"

Rex lay his head on her shoulder. "Wini decided on you over her sister. She chose you because I adore and trust you."

Everyone, even Jack and Ally, cupped their hands over their faces to contain their joy. A new family member, untarnished and ready to be loved would soon fill in those awkward moments and hidden jealous vibes amongst them all.

"I'm honored."

Rex lifted his head and scanned the spread of food. "Okay, did someone bring cake?"

Ally elbowed her husband, Tom, who then rose on command, fully trained and housebroken to Ally's pedigree standards. He headed over to the cooler, opened it, and pulled out Lexie's favorite—strawberry cheesecake.

"Aw you guys." Lexie hugged her aunt.

Her aunt pulled away and handed over her gift. "Every thirty-six-year-old should have one of these." She winked.

"Should I open it here?" Lexie feared her aunt's bold side in such times. It wouldn't surprise her to find a dildo in the box.

Her aunt helped herself to the gift wrapping, sliding her finger under the seam. "Come on, help me."

Lexie exchanged a smirk with Taylor who gazed at her with a sultry hint, subtle, but still there. She flirted with her gaze for a moment longer, enjoying the pull it had on her heart before joining her aunt in tearing open the comic strip newspaper.

Lexie stared down at the picture on the box. "A bonsai tree?"

"No, a money tree."

Taylor laughed. "It helps you to nurture." Her mouth twisted up at the corner. "She got me one too. Right before asking me to take on The Pet Boutique project. Surprisingly, it's thriving."

"That's right. Look at the success it's churning in you." Auntie Maya opened her eyes wide. "Your latest chapters are amazing."

Taylor beamed. "Seems the painting and hammering have worked again."

"Working with your hands takes the sorrow away," Auntie Maya chimed. "Now Oscar can rest in peace. His momma will be all right. You see, the money tree and The Pet Boutique have healed you." Auntie Maya squeezed Taylor's cheek. "Okay, let's eat cheesecake."

As Auntie Maya danced toward Tom and the cheesecake, Lexie stole a glance at Taylor.

Taylor folded her arms over her chest, taking it all in. She caught Lexie's glance. Her eyes twinkled in the sunlight as she leaned into her and whispered, "Your ex forgot your birthday? Really?"

"She never did excel in the memory department."

"Neither did she excel in common decency."

Her kindness curled up around Lexie like a shawl. The lingering tingle remained in Lexie for the rest of their breakfast.

Chapter Twelve

Later on, as Taylor drove with her and Cashmere back to the boutique, that tingling pulsed its way deeper in her when Taylor asked, "So what will you do with the rest of your birthday?"

She'd love to spend it with her. Get lost somewhere in the woods. Giggle about their money trees and the funny things Cashmere would do to get their attention should they stop and share more of those long gazes.

Tiny butterflies fluttered about her belly and up into the back of her throat. She lifted her shoulders, pulled in her bottom lip, and gripped her steering wheel tighter. "I'll be taking Cashmere to the park. She has a favorite watering hole."

Cashmere popped her head in between the two seats. She darted her eyes back and forth, and then she licked Taylor's face.

Taylor laughed.

"You could come along. Cashmere would be happy about that."

They drove silently for a moment. Lexie began to turn her wheel to the left to go back to the boutique then Taylor spoke up. "Fuck it. Let's go. It's your birthday. We could all use a break from the boutique for a few hours."

Lexie didn't need any massaging to get her to turn right instead. "You heard her Cashmere. We're going to the park!"

Cashmere's perked ears bathed Lexie in joy. Well, okay, Taylor's light vanilla musk fragrance filling her car might've had a little something to do with the happiness, too.

A short while later, they climbed out of the car. Cashmere bolted toward the path, jerking Lexie before she could shut her door.

Taylor grabbed for the leash. "I got her."

They followed an excited Cashmere who had to stop and sniff every last twig and weed. By the time they got to the entrance of her favorite path that led to her watering hole, Lexie had already snapped close to fifty pictures of Cashmere leading a patient Taylor.

She would secretly study each one later in the privacy of her room at Auntie Maya's. By study, she meant adjust the settings, as any professional photographer would ordinarily do, of course.

Taylor's ponytail bobbed up and down. She wore dark blue jeans that sculpted her curves and a matching jean jacket with a white button down. The style complimented her. She typically wore her beat up cargo pants and stained t-shirts spackled with primer, paint, and sawdust. She had cleaned up nice for her missed daughter reunion.

Cashmere took the lead, pulling Taylor down the narrow wooded path that Lexie named "Narnia." The secluded path would filter them to a pond. The trail wound around a stream and transported Lexie to another place in the world—a place where nature sang and filled in the gaps.

When within sight of the watering hole, Cashmere bolted ahead. Taylor gripped the leash tighter. So Cashmere lunged ahead harder, yipping and panting. Finally, Taylor wised and let go of the leash, and Cashmere leaped into the shallow water.

Taylor was stylish *and* smart.

"Should I jump in after her to get a hold of her leash?"

Lexie chuckled. "The leash is for looks only in the park. I typically let her trot beside me without holding it. If the park rangers appear or someone fears her, then I pick it up. Now, if motorcycles were allowed on the trails, this would not be the case. She chases them. It happened once up in New Hampshire, and I nearly had a heart attack."

Taylor laughed.

As the leaves swayed, so too did Lexie's soul. The breeze blew her hair in gentle waves and carried with it the scent of pine and honeysuckle that she loved so much.

It reminded her of picnic lunches as a kid when she'd eat on the flat rocks overlooking the forest and adjacent wildflower field that accompanied it. Her aunt and uncle used to take them to hike there as kids, and Lexie continued the tradition with Cashmere now.

"I love it here," Lexie said. "It's the one place in the world where I don't worry about anything."

"The trees add a magical touch," Taylor said, staring up at the leaves.

Lexie moved closer to Taylor. "The trees filter out the negative."

Taylor stared at her, her face half in shadow and half in dappled sunlight.

Lexie's heart reverberated against her lungs.

"Can I tell you what else takes away the negative?" Taylor asked in a husky tone, a slight trepidation resting on her lips.

The sun poked through the canopy of trees and cast a brilliant ray pointing down on them. The cicadas' song brightened. Cashmere paddled and splashed, entertaining herself just fine on her own. The air swaddled them into a cozy bubble. "Tell me," Lexie whispered.

Taylor bit the bottom corner of her lip and stepped closer. "You."

~ ~

Lexie's hand found its way in Taylor's. The air stirred with intense temptation.

Taylor wanted a kiss. A simple kiss. To touch her soothing lips. To enjoy the warm space between them.

Lexie's longing gaze hinted her heart fluttered in the same realm.

Taylor gazed back into her trusting eyes. Acceptance and desire pooled in them. Lexie had no idea what kind of complexities Taylor faced from guilt to pain, and everything in between that spectrum.

Or maybe she did. Lexie dug, and Taylor handed information over to her like passing the salt at dinner or the remote control during a commercial. Taylor had already fleshed out her past, present, and potential future for Lexie. None of her circumstances seemed to bother Lexie. What more could scare her away?

Lexie moved her hand away from Taylor's and brought it up to her cheek. She nurtured it, feathering her fingers up and down the side of her face, neck, and collarbone. Taylor's heartbeat quickened, sending a jolt straight down to her instant wetness.

Lexie leaned in close to her, keeping her eyes fixed. Taylor met her halfway, aching to be even closer. She released Lexie's tight ponytail and ran her fingers through the fluid, silky waves. Lexie leaned in closer still, and in the space of that peaceful oasis, Lexie kissed her. Slow but intentional. Then she cupped her hands around Taylor's face and waited on her to decide where to go from there.

Taylor kissed her back, leaving nothing to guess about her desire. She bypassed all the silent alarms warning her of a potential crash somewhere down the road. She'd deal with it when it came upon her. For now, she ignored everything else to rollick in the passion and heat.

They were the wind, flowing together and fed by the currents of a powerful desire. Under that sunny sky, with Cashmere blissfully paddling and floating in the watering hole beside them, Taylor discovered a different bliss than she'd experienced in the past. Its succulent taste melted within her where it swirled together like cream in coffee, smooth and bold, a nirvana combination.

Crunch. Snap. Crash.

"Jerry, get back here," a man yelled from the path.

Lexie jumped backward, her face flushing.

The leaves rustled, and Taylor expected a black bear to come charging through the woods at them. She grabbed Lexie's hand. Then a white puffball of a dog, the size of her Oscar, no bigger than a large housecat, sprang out of the path with all fours in the air, and in two giant bouncing leaps, landed on a splash next to Cashmere.

Cashmere splashed with her mouth hanging open, tongue flapping to the side, bright eyes bulging. She even managed to get enough lift to twirl.

She was a hot mess.

A man wearing hiking boots and a flannel-padded shirt ran toward the water. "Jerry, come on. You can't do that." His thick eyebrows furrowed together. "I'm sorry

136

if we frightened you. He loves this spot."

Lexie wiped her forehead like she'd seen Bigfoot cross the water and scale up the other side of the hill. Frenzied and red, Lexie pointed her eyes at Cashmere, who continued to paddle with frantic strokes, chasing the now drenched and muddy little dog in circles.

~ ~

Several minutes and a few chuckles later, they headed back up the path to the car. The whole time, Lexie wrestled with how to reignite the passion of moments before. Taylor walked rigidly, hands in her pockets and eyes pointed straight at Cashmere.

As they stepped onto the open grassy field off the parking lot, Lexie stopped Taylor. "About that."

"That? You mean our kiss?"

Our kiss. The intimacy of that phrase sent Lexie's heart back into overdrive. "Yes," she said, enraptured by Taylor's innocent bewilderment. "I want more of it."

Taylor glanced around. "Right here?"

Lexie loved how linear Taylor could be at times. "Someplace with a bit more privacy." She pulled on the bottom of Taylor's jean jacket. "That is if you're into that."

Taylor puffed out small, intoxicating doses of desire, tickling Lexie's face. She placed her finger on Lexie's bottom lip and stroked it.

"I take that as a yes." Lexie offered her a sugary smile and skipped up to the car, wanting to leave Taylor desiring more of where that came from.

She opened the door and let Cashmere in. "Okay stinky, guess who's getting a bath in a few minutes." She bent over and pulled out her pocketbook. "The passenger door is unlocked," she said to Taylor without looking up at her. Instead she glanced at her phone. Her forehead creased. "Uh. Rex called." She held the phone up to her ear. "Let me see what he has to say. Probably wants me to go hang out at a biker bar with him. His preggo girlfriend can't, so the birthday girl is the next best thing."

Lexie's lightness faded the second Rex's voice panicked. She bowed her head and covered her other ear.

"Lexie it's my mother. She's had a heart attack. This time for real. We're at St. Agnes."

Lexie's hands and arms trembled. She couldn't find the home button on her phone to shut it off.

Taylor took her phone. "I heard him. I'll drive." Taylor plucked the keys from her fingers.

"What about Cashmere?" Panic trailed her question.

"I'll take care of Cashmere," Taylor said with more authority. "I'll drop you off and then hang with her."

Lexie surrendered without much pressing. She dropped into the passenger seat. "I hope it's just another panic attack."

Taylor grabbed her hand. "Me too."

Cashmere stared at them, back and forth, sensing the doom. Lexie turned inward toward Cashmere and pet her with her free hand. Cashmere bowed her head against Lexie's like she did the day Lexie sobbed when Christine suggested she go live in Maryland with her aunt and get settled there. Cashmere understood change intimately, and that familiarity with it concerned Lexie.

Lexie turned her head and stared up at Taylor, who shared her concern. They were connected through Auntie Maya, and Lexie appreciated that more than ever in that scary moment.

Chapter Thirteen

The waiting room at St. Agnes teemed with miserable sick faces. Old and young, whines sat on the verge of becoming full-blown tantrums if the doctors didn't get their asses in gear. How long did it take to get some news?

Lexie paced along with her cousins and their spouses. Wini offered her a cup of coffee. "It's not too bad, for hospital coffee. I've had a lot worse."

"You've spent time in hospitals?" Lexie asked, taking it from her.

"Both of my parents died of cancer when I was in high school. So I'm pretty familiar with the smells, food, and yes," she dipped her cup forward, "coffee. This time decaf."

"Gosh, I'm sorry."

Wini massaged her belly. "That's why this little one is so important to me. It's lonely without my parents."

Lexie's extended family blessed her with loyalty and love. They were rough around the edges with their occasional elitist acts and judgments, but they did open their arms to her ever since her childhood days when her parents would abandon her each summer vacation to do research. Where her parents still treated her like an inconvenience, Auntie Maya and the Merkel gang welcomed her in as an integral piece of their family unit. Sure, they razzed her and rolled their eyes at her once in a while, but they did that to their own mother and each other, too. So Lexie learned to flow with it.

Jack and Ally perched themselves on orange vinyl chairs, rocking back and forth and shaking their heads. Rex spoke with the front desk clerk again. But even his charm didn't win them any special rewards. They had to wait their turn like everyone else.

Lexie's phone chimed with a message from Taylor. *How is she?*

Stable. She's in with the doctor now.

I'm at the boutique with Cashmere. Do you want me to stay here with her or should I drop her at home?

Lexie wanted to see Taylor. *Bring her home, and then swing by the hospital.*

Are you sure? I don't want to intrude on your family.

Please come. And yes, please drop her off at home. The other dogs are used to her now. So you can let her roam free in the house with them. The front door key code is 1111.

How security conscious of you both.

Lexie laughed. *Just get here.*

~ ~

Taylor drove Cashmere back to Maya and Lexie's. She let Cashmere in, and Toby, Skittles, Rudy, and Snowball bolted toward her. Cashmere uncharacteristically bowed her head into a submissive pose as they sniffed and shoved their noses in between her trembling legs. Once the investigation ended, Cashmere pounced on her front paws over and over, riling up the others to follow her in circular dashes around the staircase. Their barks echoed and their paws slid. They played in total bliss, not knowing that their momma lay in a hospital bed.

One minute Taylor laughed at their fun antics and the next a surprise assault of tears shattered the mood when she remembered Oscar and his goofball ways. Then she pictured Maya lying in a hospital bed, hooked up to wires and monitors.

Taylor sat in the foyer with her back against the wall and took a ride with the emotions to the soundtrack of five dogs at play.

She dropped her head into her hands and ran her fingers over her tired temples. She couldn't bear another loss in life. Anytime she handed her heart over to someone she cared about, bad things like death happened.

~ ~

Taylor finally arrived. By then, the doctor had allowed them to visit Auntie Maya, two at a time. Lexie hung back with Taylor while Rex and Wini took their ten-minute turn.

"She's going to be all right, then?" Taylor asked.

"After surgery tomorrow, she'll be good to go. She won't be running any marathons in the coming weeks. But sure enough, she'll be bossing us around at the boutique before long."

Taylor eased up on her tense mood. "The Pet Boutique. It won't be long now. I just have a few more rehab things to do. Next thing after that is shelving and merchandise."

"And marketing. And PR. And live videos. And the grand opening. And Shelter Days," Lexie added.

"It's a good thing she has you. You're going to have your work cut out for you."

Lexie laughed. "She planned all along to put me to work so I would stay here." She lolled her head to the side. "This neck of mine can't wait to soak in a hot bath later on."

Taylor rested her head back against the wall. "I'm glad everything is going to be okay. Life is full of surprises, isn't it? You never know from one minute to the next what it'll throw at you."

Lexie placed her hand on Taylor's. "The day didn't exactly end as we expected, did it?"

Taylor sat up and took her hand back. She ran it through her hair. "Not really. I'm happy she's okay, though." She stood and smiled down at her. Not the warm smile from earlier that day. Rather, one Lexie might toss at a colleague after a long day of running an event or photographing the mayor's ball. One that signaled she had finished her job and began to pack it in. The remnants of it lodged itself in her throat, forming a lump that displaced her breath and caused it to rattle.

Taylor stood before her, tired and weary.

"Is everything okay?" Lexie rose and met her face-to-face.

"I'm a bit overwhelmed by everything. Stephanie, writing, and now this scare with Maya."

Lexie bucked her head back. "You do have a lot on your plate."

Taylor shouldered the weight of her life. "I'm all over the place, Lexie."

Lexie's chest tightened.

Taylor scanned the waiting room with great concern. "I'm going to head out."

"Without seeing my aunt?"

Taylor's forehead creased in painful folds.

"Hey, guess what?" Rex's voice bounced off the beige walls in a high soprano ring. "She's joking around. Which means, she's going to be fine." He turned to Taylor. "Let's grab some juices in the cafeteria. Mom wants to say hi to you. She's charmed that you're here." He elbowed Taylor like they were old pals.

Taylor stepped back from both of them, and the space sucked the life right out of Lexie's chest, rendering her heart damaged, too.

"I have to go." Taylor said to Rex. "Please say hi to your mom and tell her I'll say a few prayers."

"Oh, of course," Rex said, patting her upper arm. "I'll see you around."

He turned to Lexie, "Come on. She's expecting cranberry juice, but she's getting water. I'll let you break that news to her. You're the one she wants to see right now."

Lexie swallowed the sadness on her tongue. "Fine, let's go."

~ ~

Taylor sat on her back patio regretting her reaction. She texted Lexie.

I'm sorry I left the way I did.

Why did you leave so abruptly?

Hospitals freak me out, Lexie.

I'm sure they do. Is that the only reason you left?

I've got a lot on my mind and I'm not sure what to do with everything. I need a little time to get through it all.

I understand. Take as much time as you need. I'll give you some space.

Taylor stared at the string of messages for half an hour trying to come up with a way to respond. Nothing she typed worked. She settled on a simple thank you.

A little while later, she opened a notepad. She had promised to write Stephanie a letter, so she would.

Dear Stephanie,

Today is a special day. It happens to be the day I met Ms. Peabody. She's a remarkable lady who opened her home to me eighteen years ago. She fed me greens and yogurts and once in a while a piece of carrot cake. She took care of me while I was pregnant with you. A lady at the abortion clinic handed me Ms. Peabody's number. She told me Ms. Peabody could help me. You see, back then, my mother would've kicked me to the curbside had she discovered my pregnancy. How would I nurse a healthy baby to life while sleeping on a park bench and eating out of garbage cans? My mother had a zero-tolerance policy—I'd been told that since the first day I started my period. I didn't see any other choice but abortion, until that nice lady handed me Ms. Peabody's phone number and urged me to call her. If after a week I still thought abortion to be my only choice, then I could come back to her and sign the papers. Well, the fact I am writing this letter means I didn't sign those papers. A different set, yes. A set that offered life. A set that lifted you into a beautiful life with understanding and loving parents.

I figured I'd start there so you'd know I loved you.

I have from the moment of my positive pregnancy test result.

That's it for now.

Write back soon!

Taylor lingered over the letter.

Stupidest letter ever.

She crumpled it up and tossed it on the ground next to her water glass. She began a fresh one.

Dear Stephanie,

143

So here's a question for you—do you have any pets? I'd love to tell you about one named Cashmere. She's a nut, and I adore her. She's not mine. She belongs to a friend. She does this crazy thing with a stuffed duck. She treats it like a pet of her own. She carries it everywhere. It's orange and has stuffing seeping out its seams. I've sewed it a few times, but I'm a writer, not a seamstress. So you can imagine how that's been working out! Well, she loves it still anyway. It's the simple joys, isn't it? Oh and speaking of simple joys…the other day I had to pry open her jaw because she loves to eat things she finds on the street more than the home-cooked food my friend, Lexie, prepares for her. Simple joys, right? Nothing says simple like a chicken bone from the street corner. Yup, that's what I discovered when I pried open her jaw. A chicken bone lodged in between her back teeth! Crazy girl. God love her!

Have an awesome day, and hope to get a letter back from you soon.

P.S. I'm so happy your blog is going well. Let me know if I can help with any other writing questions.

She pointed her pen to the blank spot where she should write her name. What should she call herself? Taylor like in her initial introductory text? Or T?

Yes. Maybe T. That had a friendly kick to it.

Take care,

T

She reread it a few times, and stuffed it into an envelope. She'd mail it the next day.

It read well enough. Maybe too inflated though. She had to borrow a happy story from Lexie's life. She didn't have a good enough story of her own to share. She had to rely on someone else to fill in the cracks of her life. Whenever she relied on anyone else, she'd always come up short. They eventually went away and left her clinging to an empty should've or could've.

~ ~

Two weeks had passed since Maya's heart attack. In those two weeks, Taylor spent her time completing most of the rehab on The Pet Boutique. Lexie hadn't shown up, and only shared small text messages to check on things. At night, Taylor tried to write more successful chapters and failed to produce the same sizzle factor as her previous ones.

Maya showed up at her front door with Cashmere in tow. "Okay, so are you going to tell me what the hell is wrong with you? When you didn't call me back after my last two messages, I called an Uber. So start talking." Maya charged through her front door. Cashmere broke out with a random burst of energy, tearing through the living room like an out-of-control windup toy.

Once she circled the room ten times, she stopped in front of Taylor and planted a big, wet, sloppy lick on her nose. "You're a silly girl." She scratched behind her ears.

"Lexie is working a freelance gig today. So I'm pet-sitting. None of my kids know this, though. Lexie's the only one who realizes I'm not some weak, feeble old woman who can't be alone for an hour."

"But you had heart surgery."

"And I'm fine. The doctor cautioned against driving, but not living, for crying out loud." She handed Taylor a travel mug. "I brewed extra decaf coffee today and don't want it to go to waste. You're welcome." She strolled into the living room and plopped down on the couch.

Taylor gulped the bitter coffee. Bits of coffee grinds floated around her tongue. "You ought to use a filter."

"Fuck that." Maya waved her off and swung the arm of her funky, chunky reading glasses. "When I speak with my children or niece, I use filters. Not with you or any of my other clients. I speak my mind. That's why you keep coming back, isn't it?"

"I was talking about the coffee."

Maya eased up on her eyeglass swinging. "Oh."

She was right about the straight talk, though. "I count on you to be honest with me."

Maya sat taller. "Great because I've got a lot to say."

Taylor braced for hell.

"Your chapter resembles a dried-up forest. There are so many potentials, and yet you didn't grab at any. What happened to the witty and sexy character from last chapter?"

"My creativity is dead again." Truth. Without Lexie as her muse the past two weeks, she lost her mojo. The reliance buried her in fear. The latest chapter showed it.

"Well, then, you need to reincarnate it. Honestly, I'd much rather be stuck in the middle of a desert with no water or sunscreen than in this last chapter."

"I don't believe in reincarnation." Sadness gripped her heart and twisted it. "There's a big, empty hole now." A round of emotions sat ready to launch. "It sucks the life right out of me."

"What's really going on?" Maya asked, softly.

Taylor wavered on keeping her truth hidden or allowing it space to breathe. She needed it to breathe. "I miss being Oscar's mom. I miss cooking him breakfast and dinner. I miss walking him. I hate not seeing his furry face in the front window when I get out of my car, and his pirouettes down the hall when I open the door."

Maya softened even more and came to her side. "Aw sweetie, it'll get easier."

Taylor teetered on that line between want and apprehension.

"It's not just Oscar."

"Was it my heart attack? Did I kill your creativity?"

"No, of course not."

She twirled her eyeglasses again. "Then what?"

"I'm all over the place with my feelings and I'm afraid to hurt people because of that."

"What people? Me? Stephanie?"

The emotions of everything caught up to her. She buried her face in her hands and fell into a heap of sobs. "I kissed Lexie."

The couch puffed up as Maya sat beside her and placed her hand on her wrist. Then, a second later, "Lexie? You kissed my Lexie?"

Taylor sobbed harder, letting all her emotions run free.

Maya comforted her, encouraging more tears to release. "Tell me what's going on."

Taylor wiped the tears from her face, sniffing back her cries.

Maya handed her a tissue. "Here, blow your nose."

Taylor followed her instruction and eased backward against the couch, staring at the tissue. "Where did this tissue come from? It's not used is it?"

Maya patted Taylor's arm. "You're a funny lady."

"I'm also a fucked-up lady."

"We all are." Maya leaned back and propped her feet up on the glass coffee table. "Put your feet up. It's full of smudges anyway. You ought to hire someone to clean for you."

Taylor raised her feet and blew her nose again before releasing another long storm of sobs over the next few minutes. In that time, Cashmere joined her on the couch, snuggling her snout under Taylor's leg.

"Why are you fucked up?"

Taylor paused, opening up space to search for the right way to explain. "Many reasons. Stephanie and I are both afraid to meet in person. I desire someone other than Nate, and he can't do anything about it from his grave. I haven't visited my mother in two years because my heart clutches every time she treats me like her angel. I miss Oscar so much still, that I turn to Cashmere to fill the void. And Cashmere's not my dog!"

Cashmere popped her head up.

"Hang on. Back up." Maya pointed to her thumb. "Number one, of course you're afraid. But Stephanie wrote you a letter, which proves she wants to try. So give her time." She pointed to her next finger in line. "Two, guilt is a natural progression in the grieving process. I still haven't dated a soul and it's been many long years." She pointed to her next finger. "Three, go visit your mother. Share a meal with her. It's

147

time to let her in on everything. You're both grownups. She'll get over it." She pointed to the last finger. "Lastly, Cashmere is happy to be everyone's dog. Oscar would approve."

Taylor shed more tears and smeared them as they stung her cheeks. Maya dug into her pocketbook and handed her a full packet of tissues.

"Do you want to know the truth about my stinky writing?"

"Please, fill me in."

"Part of me is afraid to write something good enough for publication because I've never done that without Oscar. He's been there for every book. He is as much a part of my writing as I am. He's on my website, blog, ads, posts, back of book copy, and in every acknowledgement. How can I cut him out of all that? In my mind, he'll die all over again."

"Why do you have to cut him out?"

Taylor sniffed and rubbed her nose with the back of her hand. "It's misleading. New readers who don't know he died will see his picture and my notes about him being my sidekick and talk about him as though he still lives. That'll kill me because he doesn't." She wailed, unable to stop the flood of sadness.

Maya rubbed her back. "Keep his spirit in there, as it always has been. Simply change the words to reflect his spirit on your journey. He'll live forever like that. Why do you think I bothered with The Pet Boutique?"

Taylor stopped wailing long enough to shrug. "Why?"

"I'll tell you why. When we lose someone, we want to keep their spirit alive. We do this by honoring their legacy. My kids won't be able to cut me out of their lives any more than you can cut out Nate or Oscar. The Pet Boutique will keep my family together. Shelter Days will become our new family day, and I hope they carry that on when I die."

Taylor lingered on that, allowing it its rightful spot in the silence for a moment. "That's beautiful."

"I agree." She paused. "When life needs tinkering, I tinker. When it needs pizzazz injected into it, I inject it. Simple. Get in, get it done, and get out."

148

"You make everything sound so normal." Taylor blew her nose.

Maya sat up. "No. I don't like normal. Since when have I ever been normal? Don't squish me into the same sentence as that word. I prefer if you say I make everything sound possible. Without it what the hell would we be?"

"Possible is scary."

She rested her chin in her hand. "Good. It should be."

Kissing Lexie reminded Taylor of life's possibilities. No brakes, just pedal to the metal and go. She needed to refuel before taking off at that kind of breakneck speed. That was Nate's department. Helmet on, rev the engine, and speed off to possible trouble. The endless possibilities in life wreaked a havoc that bucked her heart. It confused her, freaking her out and exhilarating her all at the same time.

Tell that to someone as quintessential as Maya though and Taylor might end up on her own couch for the rest of the morning. Maya's unplanned visit had turned into a shrink appointment. Taylor revealed secrets she didn't have the full rights to disclose.

"Lexie is good for you. You needn't fear her. She's as loyal and fun as they come. She takes after me in that department." Maya bopped her head proudly.

"My emotions are messed up. I don't want to shovel that onto someone as nice as Lexie. Besides, I need to focus on one thing at a time." She pointed to the manuscript. "Writing for starters. And then, my next priority has to be Stephanie. I need to focus on building that relationship first before I can consider building a love one, too."

"Love isn't like a single-dose eye-drop packet. It doesn't tap out on one use. Building a relationship with Stephanie is going to take time." She sat up taller. "Please don't spend too much time worrying. When you worry, you write garbage. You're capable of much more than that."

She wanted to be a good, responsible person who decided things critically. "I don't want to screw anything else up in my life."

"As far as I see it, you are if you keep fearing the things that can bring out the best version of you."

149

"By that you mean Lexie?"

"By that I mean every aspect of your life. Stop bracing for impact. You're not in a road race or on a collision course. Take your foot off the brake and ease into the life you deserve."

"I don't deserve to live with such ease."

Maya shook her head, misting her with pity. "You can't see the goodness in yourself because you don't trust yourself to choose decisions you can live with. Am I right?"

Taylor nodded.

"Because of one decision you made so long ago," Maya stated with her wise voice.

"That was a pretty major decision."

"It was best."

Taylor fiddled with her fingers, afraid to meet her friend's eyes.

"My own mother would disown me for that decision. My grandparents too. I would disgust them if they ever found out I gave up my baby."

"How do you feel about that choice?"

"Like a quitter."

"You were eighteen."

"Eighteen, not eight."

Maya paused. "You've got to be willing to cut yourself some slack. You see it as failure. I don't. You can never label yourself a quitter when you make a choice and follow through with it, no matter the choice. And my opinion or anyone else's on the choices you make in life shouldn't matter."

Taylor met her eye then. "You're not bothered by people's judgments?"

She batted her long eyelashes. "I don't give a fuck." She stretched the word out, along with her neck for emphasis. "Let's say for shits and giggles, you failed. So what? Failing is part of life. Get comfortable with it. Embrace it. It's what brings you insights. What's life without insights? Dead. That's what it is."

Taylor sat back and lingered on the truth. Being a writer required that she dig deep into the soul, into places too scary for most. She had to uncover unpleasant truths and expose them because any other way would come across shallow. The reader would not buy into the words of the characters. They'd roll their eyes and slam the book shut.

Maya picked up the manuscript. "This is you ignoring insights. Set your fears and sadness free. The literary world needs you to step it up and get out of your own way."

She gripped Taylor's shoulders. "Fuck. Stop being so afraid to feel something."

Taylor cried again.

"Stop crying." Maya wiped the tears from her cheeks.

"These aren't sad tears anymore." Taylor sniffled.

"Well then, what the hell are they?"

Taylor smiled and stared at Maya for an extended moment. "They're tears of acceptance."

Maya pulled her into a tight hug.

"Thank you for that," Taylor mumbled into her shoulder.

"You're welcome." Maya continued to hug her. "Now don't you dare break Lexie's heart."

"I would never intentionally break anyone's heart."

"Good girl. Now, I think Cashmere would like a walk."

Cashmere sat tall, staring at them with her big, eager eyes. She whined and readjusted her straddle over a pillow.

Taylor pulled out of Maya's hug. "I suppose you're right."

She petted the back of Cashmere's neck, and then Cashmere licked Taylor's cheek in response. "Is she right, sweet girl?"

Cashmere lowered her head to rest on Taylor's shoulder.

Taylor melted, leaning into the embrace. "You are a sweet one." She stroked her fur.

Cashmere stretched away and jumped off the couch. She stared at Taylor, and then she barked. Not a cute little bark, but a sharp, high-pitched one. The kind she used when she wanted all attention focused on her when she ate.

"What?"

Bark.

"What do you want?"

Bark.

Circle.

Bark.

"A walk?"

Bark.

Twirl.

Bark.

Pounce.

Taylor lifted off the couch. "Okay then. Walk it is."

"I'm going to relax and watch some television," Maya said, already reclining backward.

Cashmere didn't care. She trotted over to the door.

A few minutes later, they set off down the street. Cashmere walked a few brisk steps ahead, curious with the leaves, sidewalk, and squirrels, completely oblivious to anything not filled with glee.

As life should be.

Chapter Fourteen

Since her aunt's surgery, Lexie had spent the next few weeks with her. She wanted to offer Taylor space. So she avoided The Pet Boutique and shared short texts with Taylor about shipments and shelving plans.

She missed Taylor. Terribly. She missed joking with her. She missed seeing her eyebrows knit together when Lexie succeeded at confusing her with some oddball statement. She missed toying with her. Most of all, she missed the moment they shared. Lexie tried not to dwell, but lost that pursuit. She caved and journeyed on the memory of Taylor's lips on hers. The passion in her kiss had circulated through her on that day, feeding her a new tempting possibility to explore life's generous spread of euphoria.

She didn't want to stay away too long. So when her aunt asked her to drive her to the boutique to check on Taylor's progress, Lexie agreed. "Sure, I'll drive you. Let me grab Cashmere's leash."

~ ~

Lexie entered behind Cashmere and Auntie Maya. Taylor was bent over a shelf, screwing in a bolt. Her heart thumped at the sight of her hair cascading over her toned shoulders.

"Oh, be still my heart." Auntie Maya paused and took in the storefront. "The shelves are amazing."

As is Taylor's perky ass from this angle, Lexie thought.

Taylor smiled at them as any good professional with a screwdriver and tool belt slung around her waist would.

153

"I thought you'd be happy," Taylor said to Auntie Maya. She stepped back and admired her work. Surety sat on the curve of her cheek. "I had an idea on how to secure that mosaic mirror you picked up at the thrift store." She lifted the sagging tool belt and stole a concerned glance at Lexie as she waved at Auntie Maya to follow.

Taylor led them to the new curved reception counter that had been delivered earlier in the week. Its autumn-colored inlaid stained wood panels and brushed steel frame complemented the colorful merchandise they had planned to purchase.

"I found these screw inserts at the hardware store. They hold up to three hundred pounds. It'll be simple. Hardest part is deciding where you want it because once it goes up, it stays up. Unless you have someone else to patch and paint." She smirked.

The massive four-foot, melon-bronze mirror shone with its Moroccan style and hand-sketched mirror tiles. Auntie Maya walked past it against the wall and over to the bathroom. "I need to tinkle before I can decide anything that serious."

Cashmere flung a piece of paper up in the air with her nose and barked at it. Her bark echoed slightly less than when the store had no shelves or desk. Still though, it pierced Lexie's ears.

Taylor fidgeted with the plastic pieces in her hand, gathering them back into their plastic holders.

"So," Lexie started.

"So," Taylor followed her suit. "She's getting stronger, huh?"

"Yes. She's still stubborn, though."

Taylor glanced down at her feet and back up at her. "I'm sorry again for the way I left things at the hospital."

"I understand. Do you feel a little less jumbled?"

A sheepish glaze came across her face. "I do. Thank you for being so understanding and not getting upset with me."

Taylor's gaze lowered to her lips and lingered for a moment, touching Lexie where she didn't expect to be touched after the space she created over the past few weeks.

"I missed you," Taylor said. "And I'd like to explain better what—"

A loud shriek came from the bathroom, followed by a loud thump and silence.

They locked stares before bolting into action, leaping over empty shelving boxes to get to Auntie Maya. Taylor tapped on the door, and Lexie pushed her aside and kicked it open to find her aunt standing on the toilet seat, fright trickling around the wrinkles lining the edges of her jaw. "Watch out! It's getting away," she screamed.

Running at them, a mouse darted side-to-side and flicked its whiskers at Lexie. It took off between her feet. Lexie placed her hand on her heart, afraid that time she'd be shoved off into the back of an ambulance.

"You're killing me," Taylor said. Annoyance filled in the gaps where her softness from moments before sat. She tore away, muttering something about her own heart.

"What's up her butt?" Auntie Maya climbed down and lost her balance, landing in Lexie's arms.

"You're killing us both." She helped her aunt to stand tall. "You just had surgery. You have no idea how to chill out. I'll tell you what I'd be doing right now if I had heart surgery a few weeks ago."

Auntie Maya tossed her a questionable eyebrow arch.

"I'd be eating ice cream and binge watching *The X-Files*."

"Well, I don't care much for television."

"You're missing the point entirely." Lexie huffed away and found Taylor staring blankly out the front window.

Lexie sauntered over to her. With each step grew a quiet understanding of the nightmares that plagued Taylor. Losing out on her daughter due to bad timing. Losing out on a relationship with her parents out of fear of being rejected. Losing her husband in an accident. Losing her dog. Then losing her writing mojo because life had tossed her too many blockages. Misfortune had scarred her, its patterns too complex to explain or understand.

Life scared her. She didn't want to lose anyone or anything else.

No wonder she needed space.

Lexie came and stood by her side. She leaned in close and whispered. "I'm sorry, too."

155

Taylor matched her gaze. "For what?"

"For all your losses."

A hint of a gracious tune played in her brown eyes, and Lexie spotted the shedding of her tough exterior.

Taylor squeezed Lexie's hand.

"It's been a tough few weeks, Lexie. Sitting in that hospital waiting room reminded me of how fragile life can be. It brought me right back to those dark days in my past. I didn't expect the same blow, but it knocked me over. I'm not sure where I'm headed, and that scares me." She released Lexie, and their hands brushed together before Taylor turned to tend to her job.

Meanwhile Cashmere found something in the corner that got her hopping and yipping. She danced around a wad of duct tape, pinging it back and forth between her two front paws, pausing to verify that Taylor and Lexie paid attention.

Taylor went over to her, bent, and grabbed the duct tape wad. She tossed it at Lexie's feet.

Cashmere dashed at her with all four paws in the air, tongue hanging out the side of her mouth, eyes wide as silver dollars.

"You're ridiculous," Lexie said to Cashmere, bending down to hug her. "But I adore you anyway." She nuzzled her face in Cashmere's fur.

"The day you freelanced, your aunt brought her by my house," Taylor said. "I took her on a walk and she led me down streets I didn't even know existed in my neighborhood."

Lexie buried her face deeper into Cashmere's squishy fur. "You must have loved that, sweet girl."

"She did. I did, too. Bring Cashmere by and we can all go on a walk together. You know, discover all the great grassy spots while she reads her p-mail."

Lexie giggled, her face still buried against Cashmere. "We'd both love that." She squeezed her. "Wouldn't we?"

Cashmere responded with a snort before rising on all fours and taking her excitement to the front window. She barked, likely at a leaf blowing by, and then ran circles around the boxes and shelves.

"Let's make it happen soon, then," Taylor said on a whisper, then focused back on her task.

Lexie admired her profile for a moment longer before glancing back out the window that once disgusted her. Free of grime, she now enjoyed the view of a café across the way with its bright blue and white checkered awnings.

In the span of a few weeks, they went from hot and heavy in the park with Cashmere darting between them, to Auntie Maya suffering a heart attack, to apprehensions, to Auntie Maya once again pushing their hearts into overdrive, and back to Cashmere once again darting around in between them all.

Taylor's lingering touch had warmed Lexie. She caught a glimpse of the affectionate side Taylor had revealed in the park, a side Lexie liked and wanted to embrace.

In good time, hopefully.

She headed over to the bathroom and let her be.

After a few minutes, when Lexie came out of the bathroom, she halted. Taylor sat with her legs folded and Cashmere stood in between them resting her forehead against Taylor's, eyes soulful and kind, searching upwards to meet her human friend. Taylor rubbed the squishy fur on the back of Cashmere's neck and released a low whimper. Cashmere remained still as Taylor massaged and sought comfort in her. Next thing, Cashmere curled up in between Taylor's legs and rested her head on her thigh. Taylor rubbed between her eyes and in a moment, Cashmere snored.

Lexie tiptoed backward, practicing her patience by allowing them that private moment of reassurance and bonding.

~ ~

Being around Lexie electrified Taylor. Seeing her that day brought her back to life again. A few weeks ago, she feared getting too close because of the potential loss she might suffer once again. But after sharing space with her that day, Taylor opened up to the potential risk of future heartbreak to experience her joy.

She wanted to be with her. She enjoyed sharing time with her at The Pet Boutique and sneaking stealthy glances when Lexie worked. She wanted to spend days in the dappled sun under that tree with Cashmere darting between them as they kissed. She never laughed so much as she did the day she spent with Lexie and Maya's family around the headstone.

With Lexie, she caught a glimpse of a life she didn't want to escape. She wanted to plant herself in Lexie's warm and friendly world right then. She craved to be in that sweet spot where Cashmere stuck her head in between them as they drove to the park, and where she could share insecurities she had about Stephanie, and Lexie would soothe her nerves with that smile of hers.

Before any of that could happen, she needed to take care of a few things that Maya had brought up to her.

First, she had a good long heart-to-heart with Oscar about how much she loved him, and then when she was ready, she did something she'd been afraid to do since he passed. She picked up his toys and beds from the various rooms and placed them in the back of her walk-in closet for safekeeping.

Then, she called her parents to tell them she'd be coming by for an overnight visit the next day.

~ ~

When Taylor arrived at her parent's home, she trembled when she stood in the middle of her old bedroom. She folded her arms around herself.

Her father struggled to secure the new mini-blinds in the window.

"I don't need them. Let them be."

Her mother Edina scowled at her. "We're not going to let you sleep in here without blinds. Those teenaged boys who live in this neighborhood would love to snoop out those perky breasts." Her mother said this as if she didn't have a better body than Taylor herself did. Her mother, at sixty-two years of age still ran the Marine Corps 10K race in D.C. every October.

"It's not like I'm going to prance around the room naked, Mom."

"All right, hang on." Her father clicked the blinds into place and raised his arms in victory. "There. You can prance around this room any old way you'd like now." He carried his tool bucket past them. "You're welcome."

"If we had more notice, he would've freshened up the wallpaper and hung a skylight for you," her mom joked.

"Dad, can you wait? I've got to talk with you both about something." Taylor squeezed her arms a little tighter around herself.

Her mom sat on the ivory eyeleted blanket on the king-size, pillow-crazed bed. "Tell us what's going on," she said, patting the bed next to her.

Like a refreshing spring rain after a long, dark winter, her mother's sincerity took away the anxiety that had built up since Taylor's life-long descent from her teenage self. Taylor eased into her mother's invite and rested her head on her shoulder.

Her father still gripped the metal handle of his bucket.

"You might want to put that down."

He didn't. "Tell us what's on your mind."

So she did. She took her foot off the brake pedal and accelerated toward the truth. And when she did, the love and compassion of her parents' responses helped set her free, free like a bird spreading her wings and charting a new course—one that buzzed her back to life. An authentic life.

Chapter Fifteen

Lexie tagged along with her aunt and the rest of the Merkel gang to the follow-up visit at the heart clinic.

"We'll need to clear some room around the patient so I can check her vitals." A stocky nurse with pokey dishwater-colored hair waited for the Merkel gang to move out of her way.

Rex circled to his mother's other side and continued to tease her white hair so he could smooth it into a side bang for her.

"He should've gone to barber school." Auntie Maya spoke to the disinterested nurse.

She grabbed her aunt's arm and secured the blood pressure cuff around it.

"Instead the kid grows medicinal marijuana," she whispered.

The nurse pumped the pressure gauge, staring at the instrument reading.

"Do you have an opinion on marijuana?" She continued to barrage the nurse because she had no clue how to stop when she started something.

The nurse removed the pressure cuff and folded it under her arm. "You might need some." She winked and walked out of the room.

"Did she insult me?" Auntie Maya stared at the door in shock.

Wini came up beside Rex and handed him a silver bobby pin. She wore a cute dress that bellowed out under her bra, accentuating her belly. She even waddled, gently pressing her hand against her baby bump.

He gripped the bobby pin between his teeth, securing his mother's bang.

"She was having fun with you," Wini said. "Not at your expense."

That answer satisfied Auntie Maya, but not Jack.

He ran his hands through his thick black hair. "She was rude."

Nico rubbed his arm. "Stop. She's tired. She works ridiculous hours and gets paid too little for what she does. Just relax."

Jack pulled his lips in tight. He turned on his heel and stared out the window.

"Honestly, you all didn't have to come for my follow-up," Auntie Maya said even though she had invited them all. Tom couldn't come because he had a boss to answer to. The rest of them, entrepreneurs at heart, could set their own rules. When Auntie Maya asked for support, they all ran and surrounded her like an elephant tribe did to protect a sick newborn.

The wait would be long. The last follow-up that Lexie took her aunt to lasted two hours. So she brought along some wholesale catalogues that a few vendors had left with Taylor at the boutique. "Let's go through these and start selecting the items we want to get."

Auntie Maya wiggled her bottom against the exam table. "This table is terrible. The first thing we need to order are comfortable chairs."

"It's a store, Mom," Ally said. "If you fill it with chairs, people are going to hang out and drive you batty."

"Who's driving whom batty?" The charming Dr. Champlain entered the room. He dipped past Ally and Wini and circled by Rex. "What a remarkable side bang."

Rex smoothed his palm over his mother's hair one last time. "She needs to look beautiful for the grand opening of her new pet boutique. So I'm practicing."

Dr. Champlain glanced at the chart. "Pet boutique, huh? That sounds like lots of lifting heavy bags of kibble and standing on your feet all day long."

Auntie Maya shifted again. "Well, that's what'll keep me young. I sit too much when editing. I need an excuse to stand up."

"Maya, we need to talk about a few things. We can do so in private, if you prefer?"

Her forehead wrinkled. "I want everyone here."

They all moved in like a synchronized team.

"As you know, we ran some additional tests."

Lexie's throat clammed shut. She couldn't swallow.

"Go on." Jack pushed his way closer to the exam table.

"You have signs of coronary microvascular disease. The walls of the heart's tiny arteries are damaged. It is largely caused by a drop in estrogen levels. This is why you're still experiencing pain."

"Pain?" Ally asked, sharply. "You're in pain?"

Auntie Maya clenched her jaw. "It's not that bad. Just a little twinge."

"It's treatable," the doctor said in a more cheerful tone. "I'm going to want you to cut down your stress level."

"The boutique." Jack's hands flew up. "I told you this was a bad idea." He pointed at Nico. "Right? Didn't I call this?"

Nico nodded like the good husband he was.

"Opening a business is stressful." The doctor pointed his eyes at Lexie's aunt. "I want you to promise me that you'll take it easy, take the medicine that I prescribe, and follow my instructions. The first one is I insist you take the month off from work. We need your stress levels way below where they are now."

Auntie Maya saluted him. "Right on, doc."

"He's serious," Jack whined, running his hand through his hair again. Jack needed to take his stress down a notch, too.

After the doctor left, the Merkel gang gathered their belongings and kissed their mother goodbye. Lexie waited behind the curtain for her aunt to get dressed. "The Pet Boutique is exactly what I need," she said with such strained force that the entire medical office suite must've perked their ears.

~ ~

Later on, once they returned to The Pet Boutique, Auntie Maya ripped the plastic wrapping off a new set of towels for the DIY pet washing stations. "Honestly, I'm fine. I'm not taking the month off. We'll just be getting started."

"You promised him!"

"I did so to shush your cousins. They're the stress producers." She wagged her head side-to-side. "Goldie didn't see this coming, I guess. None of it. She was vacationing in Denver with Emma, Haley, and their son. I suppose she had a right to take time off from the voices in her head. See what happens when someone takes time off? People have heart attacks. We have dogs to get adopted. Pets to get fed. Leashes to sell. I don't have time for a heart disease. Besides, I'm sure you need to get back to a serious job search. I've been working you so much you haven't had time to interview." She folded a towel. "I'm sorry about that."

Lexie still collected unemployment and her aunt paid her a stipend. So she'd rather keep busy. She had a bunch of ideas running through her mind about marketing and events they could run. And working alongside Taylor had been nice. The boutique transformed into a more beautiful place with each new day. It would turn a profit fast. She loved that Cashmere could hang with her all day long. "How about if I stay on and manage the place for a while?"

Auntie Maya raised her chin. "Well, that would take the stress away from having to explain to the kids why my business partner took a job photographing homes again."

"So you'd be okay with that?"

Tears pooled in her tired light blue eyes. "I hoped that you'd come to that conclusion." She glanced at Cashmere gnawing on a new chew toy next to her feet. Then she patted her chest. "Jump up, Cashmere."

Cashmere leaped to her feet, and Auntie Maya grabbed her front paws. "Your momma is a super momma. But you already knew that." They danced under the newly painted raftered ceiling, Cashmere balanced on her hind legs trying, with no success, to catch a lick of her face with her big wet tongue.

Lexie hugged herself. "I could offer pet photography portraits as a side gig. You could get a cut of it, seeing as I'd be drumming up clients while on duty. If Emma and Haley ever moved back East, Emma could be the resident painter of portraits. Think of the money!"

Auntie Maya lowered Cashmere's front paws to the floor. "Your money is not what I want."

"What do you want?"

"The gift of your company. The boutique would never be fun without you. Besides, who else is going to ensure that our Sunday family meetings stay intact if I croak?"

"Auntie. That's terrible. Stop it."

She looked deeply into her eyes. "I mean it Lexie. This place will be the safe home for my legacy. Something to keep all of you together when I die. Instead of meeting at the cemetery, you'll meet here. The Pet Boutique will ensure you all have a commonplace to be together as a family. You'll all come here to the café, bring your pets, and have a good time in my and your uncle's memory."

Lexie laughed. "You're so dramatic."

Her aunt grabbed her wrists and swung them. "Promise me."

Lexie laughed again, but the edginess to her eyes stopped it mid-way up her throat. "Okay. Yes. Of course. I promise. Though, who's going to listen to me?"

Her aunt squeezed her wrists. "Lexie, listen to me. They trust you. Every single last one of them. When you lived in New Hampshire, this family faded. Then you came back and they're back to being a family again. You bring that out by reminding them how important family is. You're the catalyst, Lexie. I expect you to remain that when I die one day." She loosened her grip.

Lexie blinked back tears. "You'd never believe me if I told you how much that meant to me."

She tightened her squeeze again. "Why didn't you tell me about the kiss?"

Lexie's mouth flew open.

"She's one of my best friends, Lexie. She had to tell someone."

Lexie chuckled. "What else did she tell you?"

Auntie Maya lifted her hand to Lexie's shoulder and gripped it. "She's got a lot on her plate." She narrowed her eyes and they twinkled. "She just needs some time to sort through a few things."

"Yeah. She does." Lexie inhaled a tight breath. "She told you that?"

A flicker of regret flashed across her aunt's face. "Ah, don't listen to me." She waved her away. "I blow things out of proportion. Believe me, she likes you Lexie. She does." Her aunt bobbed her head a few times as if convincing herself of that fact. "Hell, maybe she'll even write you into one of her sex scenes in this latest book. She does write a sex scene like nobody's business."

"Auntie!" Lexie lifted her hand to slap her arm but remembered her heart disease.

Not only did she have to worry about that, but now a new concern planted itself on her heart. Had Taylor confessed some reservations about her to her aunt? Lexie didn't want to become another thing Taylor had to balance in her complicated life.

~ ~

The following week, Lexie was putting some touches on the front window display when Goldie opened the front door to The Pet Boutique.

"Hello there," she sang. She stopped short in front of the card rack display. "Oh, I love these." Then she walked past Lexie and toward the back of the boutique.

Emma, Haley, and a little boy trailed in behind her. The little boy let go of Emma's hand and darted toward the center of the storefront where some shelving units still sat in boxes. He stared up at the large ball lights hanging from the open rafter ceiling. His eyes grew large. "Wow!" He bounced. "Can you get one for me?"

Emma ran over to the boy and grabbed for his hand. "You can't run away like that, Billy. There's stuff everywhere and you can get hurt." Emma pulled him up into her arms. Haley kissed his cheek. The perfect family. They only needed a camera to capture the Hallmark moment.

"Those aren't toys, silly." Haley tickled his side, and he squirmed and squealed. His orange hair flamed out the top of his head and a large dimple sat on his cheek.

Haley turned to Lexie. "Our son has no fears." She glanced at the finished walls. "I like the color. Perfect choice."

"Thanks," Lexie said. "It's all coming together."

A lot more work still needed to be done for opening day, but they were closer than on day one. They still needed to order merchandise to fill the empty shelves and pick out furniture for their pet café.

166

"Oh my God," Haley said swinging toward the mural. "This is amazing."

Emma's rosy cheeks carried love. She shifted her toddler higher up her hip. "I'm happy with how it came out."

"We are, too." Lexie walked past the reception counter and toward them.

A second later, Cashmere bolted through the back doggy door and landed on a jiggle at their feet.

She lived for visitors. When someone entered, she sprinted from the front door to the back about ten times before she could contain herself and settle on her haunches long enough for the visitor to pet her head. The minute the pet happened, she shot to all fours and entertained with a few spins at varying heights.

The boy squealed again. "I want to see the doggy."

He wiggled, and Emma lowered him. "Be gentle." She guided him forward, and Cashmere lost it in a series of pirouettes.

Haley straddled Cashmere's back and massaged her shoulders. She stopped jumping and let the boy pet her freckled chest. She stared at the boy with her tender, curious eyes.

Lexie took in the beautiful family moment, and a strange twinge of jealousy twisted in her. Would she ever experience a happily ever after like they did?

She wrestled with that question for an extended moment before Goldie interrupted her train of thought with a loud cheer from the back where Charlie had installed the stainless steel DIY bath stations. "Amazing! My husband is a gem, that's for sure."

The three of them shared smiles.

"Charlie's going to be sad he'll miss the rest of the setup for opening day," Goldie said as she reentered the main space. "He's now stuck in Rhode Island, helping out his friend—a recent flood destroyed his restaurant."

Billy grew bored with Cashmere, and took off to the folding table, where Lexie had left a box of donuts. "Mommy, can I have the pink donut?" Billy's eyes grew wide as his little hands stretched toward the box.

Emma pulled his hands down. "You just had eggs."

Poor kid's mouth watered. Even Lexie wanted another donut, and she'd already had two. "How about for later? I can put one in a baggie for a yummy mid-morning snack."

His eyes danced between his mommies.

Haley waved to Emma. "It's Momma E's call."

"Haley, he has type one diabetes," Emma said in a sing-song voice.

Billy pulled his shoulders down and whined. "Please, Momma E. Sal said donuts won't hurt me."

Emma pursed her lips. "We'll take half a donut in the baggie for later."

Haley turned to Lexie. "He has an imaginary friend who tells him a lot of things lately. Things like he doesn't need to drink milk anymore and he doesn't need a lot of sleep."

Lexie chuckled, remembering her childhood imaginary friend, Malory. She'd tell her to do everything her parents told her not to do like slide down the stairs on her bum and eat all the cookies from the cookie jar.

"We had to become pseudo nutritionists recently," Haley said. "The doctor diagnosed him with diabetes a few months ago."

"His biological grandmother and uncle both have it, too," Emma said.

"Can I go say hi to Bella now?" Billy shifted on his little legs, bored with the adult talk.

"Bella?" Lexie asked.

"My little goofball cat," Goldie rejoined their circle.

Haley wrapped her arm around her son's bony shoulders. "Come on kiddo. Let's go see if we can play fort on Auntie Goldie's couch, then we'll invite Bella in to join us for some milk." She turned over her shoulder. "Goldie hates when we do that."

"We love it," Billy screamed out.

"It's a wonder the courts handed a kid over to us," Emma laughed.

"You seem like great parents," Lexie said.

"We hope we are." She squeezed herself in a hug.

"They are." Goldie swung an arm around Emma. "I saw it all unfold before they did, right?"

Emma chuckled. "You told us you saw a dog in our future. Not a kid."

"Close enough." Goldie shrugged. "You're not a paying customer, so you get the condensed version. I still see a dog in your future."

"Nice." Emma bobbed her head. "Easy to say standing in the middle of a future pet boutique." She glanced at the chalkboard sign above the colorful reception counter and the notice about Shelter Days. "Maybe one day we'll meet up with our future family addition right here on a Shelter Day."

"Don't you know it," Goldie said and strutted past.

Cashmere trotted toward them carrying her orange duck. Goldie bent to shake it from her, and Cashmere gripped it tighter.

"You do have your hands full enough with Billy, though," Goldie said.

"You think?" Emma sent a playful wink Lexie's way and shook her head.

"There's room in your family for a dog who's a bit more relaxed."

Lexie's curiosity piqued. As always. "Did you adopt Billy as a baby?"

"Yes. We adopted him from a teenage girl."

"Is she still involved?" Lexie asked.

"She's still a kid." Emma played with the fringe on her pocketbook strap. "We're open with her and Billy. We wanted to leave the door open so she could be a part of his life when she's ready. Right now, she lives with her parents in Connecticut. So she hasn't had any contact. She's a cheerleader and on the debate team from what we hear. She's a normal kid, like all kids should be."

Lexie loved her nonjudgmental attitude. "Like all kids should be," Lexie repeated.

"Well, I should check on Bella." Emma curtsied away. "You should consider having an artist on standby to paint portraits." She walked forward, turning over her shoulder. "Just a thought."

"That's exactly what I told my aunt!"

Emma winked. "We'll talk, then."

When Emma walked out, Lexie turned to Goldie. "What do you think of that idea?"

"It has the sun shining all over it."

"I bet you say that about everyone you care about."

Cashmere released her grip on the orange duck, and Goldie flung it across the room.

Cashmere leaped after it.

"They'd prefer moving back East to increase the frequency of Billy's visits with his biological mother. Also, Emma would prefer to live in Maryland again. Winters last too long in Denver for her taste."

Lexie understood.

"So your aunt…" Goldie examined the cream-colored ceiling rafters that Lexie had painstakingly painted. "She's doing better?"

"You're a psychic. You should know." Lexie joked, but it fell flat between them. Goldie's face contorted into concern.

"I had a vibe, but I thought it was about The Pet Boutique."

"She's going to be fine."

"I failed her. Things don't always come in defined. It's a lot like assembling the pieces of a jigsaw puzzle. Sometimes the pieces fit and other times they don't."

"No one expects complete accuracy."

Goldie chuckled. "Your aunt does. But she's hard to read these days."

"Why?"

"She's blocked. Hence, this place. A pet boutique. Of all things." Goldie walked over to the mural. "Ever since I told her I thought Ally and Tom were having some issues, she's been off."

"Why would you tell her that?"

"Because I sensed it. I thought Ally could use Maya's guidance. Then she shocked me when she asked to lease my empty storefront and open a pet boutique. She assumed The Pet Boutique would help serve as a distraction for Ally. Then Ally and Tom rekindled. I guess." She wrinkled her face. "Or they didn't have any issues to begin with. Sometimes these things come out weird, like I said."

"She said that you encouraged her."

"Ideas excite your aunt. Once an idea flirts with her, she's all in. I thought it would help her unblock. Then she got stressed with how much work needed to be done."

"Hence me."

"I don't know. Maybe." Goldie shrugged. "She begged me to let her lease it. That threw me. Then she signed the lease and suffered a heart attack. I didn't see that coming."

"None of us saw any of this coming."

Goldie sized up Lexie. "This has been good for you."

Lexie shrank back against the reception counter. "How do you mean?"

"You've got a certain aura about you. I say this a lot, but it's true. The sun is shining all over you right now."

Her skin prickled, replacing some of the doubt that had implanted itself in her heart. "Really?"

Goldie clicked her tongue. "Yep. I should go and confirm that Billy isn't pulling my cat's tail." She walked past Lexie and stopped in front of a pile of boxes stuffed with chew toys. She picked up Taylor's hat. "I love this hat." She smoothed her hand over it, then placed it back on the boxes. "There may be some clouds that skip by, Lexie. They clear eventually if you're patient enough to weather through them. Just remember that the sun always shines even behind those clouds."

Clouds? What happened to the sun? Lexie's heart clenched as Goldie waltzed out the front door.

She glanced back at Taylor's hat. The sun cascaded a beam of bright light right on the paw-print design.

She shrugged away the sense of foreboding and took a picture of the hat with the sunbeams dancing along its seams. Then she sent Taylor the picture and a message. *You forgot something at the boutique. I'm on my way home. Do you want me to drop it off?*

She responded a moment later. *That would be cool.*

~ ~

An hour later, Lexie pulled into the double driveway of Taylor's sprawling white rancher. An orange and red leafed wreath with sparkling brown and auburn balls hung from the center of a modest cream-colored front door.

Taylor opened the door wearing a navy blue Nike hoodie and a pair of jeans. "Hi," she said.

"Hello." Lexie dangled the hat by her finger. "Goldie loves your hat. She didn't wear it or anything like that. She just stated that she loves it. Those exact words." Lexie stopped rambling when Taylor leaned against the doorframe with a tease in her eyes.

"Did she tell you to bring it by?"

Her words lingered in the air, like a flirt beckoning for a response.

A tickle grew inside Lexie, replacing any hint of her earlier doubt. "Sort of. Yes."

"Let me guess…"

"The sun was shining all over it." They both said in unison, then fell into a laugh.

Lexie extended the hat. "Well, here you go."

Taylor stared at it, and then turned inward. "Come in."

Lexie followed her into her living room, a nice open space that filtered into a dining room and a small kitchen nook. The home had country-style appeal. Not at all what she'd expect from Taylor. With her sporty style, she'd peg her for more of a minimalistic, no frills, beige walls and counters, no pictures type of a person. Everywhere Lexie turned, she met up with cozy charm. Quotes about love, family, success, and dogs, hung in wooden picture frames of various sizes. Muted-colored pillows cozied a blue and cream plaid sofa and loveseat combination. A huge ottoman sprawled before a recliner that survived a lot of life.

They entered the kitchen nook.

Lexie spun the hat.

Taylor took it, and placed it on Lexie's head, securing the loose strands that always misbehaved behind her ears.

Lexie's breath hitched.

172

"I baked some banana bread." Taylor stepped back and pulled out a single fork. She dug into the bread, then in one slow and steady move, she slipped it onto Lexie's tongue.

"Delicious, isn't it?"

Lexie savored the sweetness, nodding.

"How's your aunt?"

"She told you the news of her heart disease?" Of course she did, Lexie thought before she could answer. They told each other everything important apparently. Important. Like their kiss. Which was fine by Lexie. The kiss meant something to Taylor. At least that's how Lexie chose to interpret it.

"She called me while I visited with my parents. She sounds optimistic."

"You visited your parents?"

Taylor forked a bite in between her lips. "Yep. I told them about their granddaughter."

"How did it go?"

"Better than I ever dreamed imaginable." Taylor lingered on the last bite.

Lexie was happy for her.

"I feel at peace. So much so that I'm ready to ask Stephanie if she wants to reschedule soon. Will the botanical gardens still have blooms and bees?"

"Sure. With global warming upon us, anything's possible."

"I need to practice with my camera more." She moved a step closer, not taking her eyes off Lexie.

The nook shrunk to half its size. "Sounds like you'll need additional lessons, then?"

"I will."

Her stomach took a flip toward hopeful.

"Fine, then we'll resume our lessons."

Taylor took another bold step closer, now staring at her lips. "Fine. I look forward to my next lesson."

The sultry haze taking over Taylor's eyes told Lexie their talks of photography had already ended. "How far do you want to take it this time?" Lexie asked.

Taylor dropped the fork on the counter and lifted the hat off Lexie's head. "Farther than last time."

She searched for her voice. "I might need some reminders of where we left off."

Taylor leaned in closer.

Lexie eased into Taylor's soothing affection.

Taylor cupped Lexie's face. Her thumb trailed the sides of her jaw. "I'm a complicated person, Lexie. I can't promise I'll be any less complicated going forward."

She coiled her fingers in Taylor's belt loops, pulling her in even closer. "I'm growing kind of fond of your complications. And I want to kiss you. Right now. Would that be okay with you?"

That twinkle Lexie enjoyed popped up again, shining brightly at her and sending her somersaulting into the unknown.

Taylor inched closer, hovering next to the corner of Lexie's lips. "We no longer have the possibility of a dog or stranger barging in to pull us away this time."

Her chest rose and fell without grace. "Well, thank God for that."

Taylor kissed her, more firmly than the first time. No skirting around insecurities and what-if questions. Just full-out, unbridled passion released in the insistent passes they shared. Her tongue fluttered through, and Lexie met it with matching finesse.

Taylor nudged her against the refrigerator. Magnets and loose papers fell at her ankles, tickling, teasing, and lapping to meet her heightened senses. Taylor was danger, excitement, and heat coiled before her, provoking her hips to rock and moans to escape. She tasted warm and intense. Her fingers pulled at Taylor's belt loops, craving to rip them and tear open her jeans. Her hips swayed in a provocative beat, urging Taylor to follow.

Follow she did. She matched her, sway for sway, rolling in the heat. Lexie ached to touch her skin.

Taylor edged forward, pushing pleasantries aside. She revealed a hunger for deeper, more intense pleasure.

"Are you sure about this?" Lexie asked.

"I want you, Lexie Tanner. I have from the very first day I met you."

Lexie responded with equal hunger, unhitching from the belt loops and attempting to unbutton Taylor's jeans. "Help me get these jeans out of the way."

Taylor's lips curved upwards against Lexie's as she unbuttoned her jeans then unzipped Lexie's hooded sweatshirt. Lexie wiggled out of it and threw it across the room. Then Taylor wrestled out of her sneakers and jeans, flicking them out of the way.

They undressed each other, throwing shirts, hoodies, undies, socks, bras in the air to find their own place to settle, far away from them.

Lexie took in the sight of Taylor's round breasts, toned abs, and curvy hips. "You're amazing." She ran her fingers in delicate circles down the length of her, starting at her neck, down to the sides of her breasts, the center of her abs and back out to explore the fullness of her hips.

Then, Taylor mirrored her move, only she stopped at the side of her breast and rested the tip of her finger on one of Lexie's sensitive, engorged nipples. Lexie's knees buckled.

Taylor caught her with strong arms. They closed the gap between them, their nipples gliding together with their sultry sways as they both ran their hands across their delicate, sizzling skin.

Lexie had entered nirvana, swept up in Taylor's delicious moves yet kept grounded by her sensual touch. She teased her tongue along the side of Taylor's neck as Taylor led her over to the couch.

A tease played out on Taylor's face as Lexie straddled her.

"Are *you* sure?" Taylor whispered, flirting with Lexie's lips.

She placed her finger against Taylor's trembling lips. Her eyes glittered in the sunny room. Lexie traced her finger down the side of Taylor's cheek, down her neck and on the side of her full breast once again, hungry for more of her. "I am a million-percent sure."

Lexie lowered herself and Taylor kissed her breast with slow, tender circles, bringing her nipple to new heightened pleasure. When she took it into her mouth, Lexie moaned above her.

Taylor placed her hands in Lexie's hair and massaged her scalp, tangling her fingers in it. They grinded together, as Lexie had to that Donna Summer song.

Taylor rose and took over the top position, now straddling Lexie. She explored her body with a nurturing touch. A deep moan crawled out of the back of Lexie's throat as Taylor treated the sensitive spot below her ear to kisses before moving to the crook of her neck, down the side of her breast, and toward her navel. Taylor stopped and admired her, viewing her skin as if it were precious and valuable, like expensive silk.

"Lexie, it's been a very long time since I've done this." That twinkle returned to her eye. "So you'll have to be patient with me."

"Cashmere is with my aunt. So I've no place to be."

Taylor teased her with small kisses, sprinkling them around her cheeks, in the hollow of her neck, around the beginning of her cleavage. She pressed against Lexie, cutting off her air supply. Lexie didn't care. That kind of loss was worth it. It caused her toes to curl and her inner thighs to pulse.

Lexie wrapped her legs around Taylor's waist, and their wetness blended as the space between them closed.

Taylor eased up by rolling on her side and propping her head with an elbow. She stared into Lexie's eyes as she massaged her belly. Then she traced her delicate nipple between two fingers. Lexie released a moan and arched her back.

Taylor leaned down and kissed the corner of her mouth—a thoughtful, delicate peck that sent flutters up her spine.

They sought each other out, and together explored each other's wetness. The silky touch intoxicated Lexie. Her fingers paused on Taylor's swollen and pulsing clit, circling it with the tip of her finger. Taylor groaned an affectionate, extended, low groan that drove Lexie wild. Her fingers entered Taylor. She was warm, wet, and smelled like earth after rain, delicate and fresh. They stared into each other's eyes. Then Taylor closed her lids as she rode out the ripples of ecstasy from Lexie's touch.

Lexie pleasured in Taylor's ravenous desire and flexed jaw until finally her sex pulsed against Lexie's fingers and she craned her neck backward in a state of intoxication.

Lexie pulled out of her, and involuntarily brought her fingers up to her mouth and tasted Taylor.

Taylor settled into an easy gaze, her heart slowing its beats.

Still hungry, Lexie couldn't take it. She wanted to press her pulsing body against Taylor's and release the pressure bubbling inside. So she sat up and pushed Taylor down against the couch, straddling her once again. She stared down at her, and the ends of her hair flirted with Taylor's nipples. "I've never experienced this level of intoxication before."

Taylor placed her finger on Lexie's lips and traced them. "I don't think a word exists to describe how I'm feeling right now."

Lexie released a chuckle and lowered her head to rest on Taylor's chest. Taylor brought her arms around Lexie and hugged her tightly, kissing her head. Taylor's heart thumped below her, and it comforted her. Within a few moments, their bodies united in a deep, pulsating dance. One breath. One heartbeat. In perfect sync.

"You're a beautiful woman," Taylor whispered. "And I want to take you to the edge and back."

For the first time in her life, Lexie felt beautiful inside and out. She kissed Taylor, pressing her lips firmly with confidence. Then Taylor retook the top position, and when she did, she showered Lexie with reverent passes of her tongue. Taylor moaned into her mouth, and lowered her body to greet her.

"Please," Lexie pleaded. "Please take me to that edge and back."

Taylor led Lexie on a journey as she traveled down the length of her and took her wetness into her warm mouth and gifted her with ultimate bliss. Her body lifted, floating on the edge of an intense wave that sent her reeling and flying toward the center of ecstasy. Taylor's tongue sent ripples through Lexie, freeing her from the ordinary, and transporting her to that delectable spot where purity and love blended and formed paradise. She floated high, way on top of that wave until it welcomed her to break free and enjoy the ride home.

Lexie landed at the shore of pleasure, breathless and trembling.

Taylor curled up next to her, staring at her with grace and appreciation.

Lexie brushed Taylor's cheek, amazed to be the receiver of one of nature's greatest gifts—an orgasm straight from nirvana itself.

~ ~

"The couch is comfortable," Lexie said, grunting slightly as she crawled to a sitting position. "But next time let's use the bed." She stroked Taylor's cheek before rising and heading to the bathroom.

Taylor admired her perky ass, naked and white.

Next time. Taylor could spend the next month tangled on the small couch with her.

Taylor stared up at the ceiling and exhaled a satisfied breath. At least one part of her life had shaped up. Now, if she could just get everything else to fall into place, she could finally settle into a comfortable trek with Lexie.

Peace flittered around her heart.

She needed to keep her concerns at bay. Yes, she still needed to work through meeting Stephanie. But suddenly courage took over.

They had written several letters, but they needed to meet each other. Pull off the bandage in a quick swipe and bare their souls to each other.

She pushed that thought aside for now, blowing it away like a dandelion puff. It floated past and landed somewhere else to wait until she was ready for it.

When Lexie returned, she brought two glasses of water.

Taylor sipped some. "I'm glad you're here." She lingered her gaze on Lexie's pink lips.

They sat in comfortable silence, holding hands and breathing in sync. After a few minutes, Lexie turned to her and asked, "Tell me what's on your mind."

Taylor wanted to share her vulnerability and not hide from it anymore. "I feel a little scared."

Lexie scooted on her butt, folding her legs underneath her. "About what?" Her worried eyes peeked at Taylor from above the rim of the glass.

"I worry that you'll be disappointed when you meet the real me."

"This wasn't the real you?" Lexie asked.

"No. Well, I mean yes. Yes, this is the real me. But there are other parts of me that I've tried hard to package away. I don't want you to be disappointed if a little of that person comes back out for a quick dip."

"You're being too hard on yourself."

"You sound like Maya now."

"Well, that's because we're smart ladies. What we see in you is the helper. The loving mother who wants to improve things. The friend willing to stack her goals off to the side to rehab a dream for someone else. All you see is the person who gave up her daughter."

Lexie stared at her with big, loving eyes and touched her cheek again, something Taylor enjoyed. "You are a good person who's done great things, so stop focusing on that one part of your life."

Taylor turned away and stared at a carpet stain in the corner that Oscar created in his last days. She couldn't bring herself to remove it. She bit her lip, blocking the small cry in the back of her throat. Her darned emotions always popped up without warning. She wanted to cry. She wanted to be vulnerable with Lexie. So she allowed the tears to fall.

Lexie placed her hand on her wrist.

Taylor released her emotions, unleashing the parts of herself that she wished didn't belong to her. The irresponsible side. The selfish side.

She began to learn that real progress happened not from ignoring her faults, but from accepting them and doing better from that point forward. That's all anyone could do. The fact that Lexie still kept her hand on her wrist, told her that Lexie cared and trusted that she could move past the blockages that had stopped her before.

"You have a way of simplifying things, Lexie."

"Life doesn't have to be so hard. I learned that a while back through my parents.

179

I always assumed they didn't love me as much as they loved their community work. They sacrificed time with me to bring much-needed aid to communities who suffered. But as I matured and learned about how their actions saved people, I began to realize that their choice to leave me safely behind with my aunt meant they did love me. They wrote me letters over the summers when they traveled, and if FaceTime had existed, they would've FaceTimed with me, too."

"That's why you and your aunt are so close."

"Yep. She's more like a mother to me than an aunt. And my mother resents her for that, even though she asked for her help. They barely see each other anymore. Just on the rare occasion my parents come to Maryland for a quick trip to see friends."

"And you?"

Lexie nodded. "Of course. We do lunch when they're in town. And I see them in their new retirement home in North Carolina at the holidays." Her voice lowered to reserved levels.

"You're sad about that." Taylor stroked the side of her face.

Lexie settled into one of her dazzling smiles. "I've learned to stop analyzing and accept who they are. They've never been any different. So expecting them to morph into parents like on *The Brady Bunch* is a big waste of my time."

"You're not only gorgeous, but you're so smart, too." Taylor nuzzled her nose against Lexie's.

"You're not too bad yourself," Lexie whispered, bathing her in warmth. "And just wait and see. Your daughter is going to adore you."

Taylor took in the compassion cradling the baby blue in Lexie's eyes. "You fill me with confidence. It's overflowing right now. So much so, that I'm deciding right now to text her tomorrow and reschedule our meeting."

Lexie cheered her on with a radiant smile. "You got this."

She leaned back toward Lexie, and kissed her, showing her without words how much her kindness and compassion meant to her.

After that, Taylor took her to her bedroom and made love to Lexie again, savoring the beauty and comfort of being in her arms. Afterwards, Lexie rolled over and propped herself on her elbow, staring down at Taylor with a satisfied glow. She ran her fingers through Taylor's hair. "I love your free-flowing waves. I do love your ponytail, too, but there's something about how these waves flirt with your face and neck that I find extremely sexy."

Taylor rolled onto her side and met Lexie's gaze. She had never felt quite as sexy before. A small piece of her hair tickled her forehead. It dangled around her eye. She blew at it, and it flopped. "Even that stubborn piece?"

Lexie twirled it. "Even this stubborn piece."

They stared at each other in the dimly lit room. Affection and playfulness swirled around them. "I'm starved," Taylor said.

Lexie scooted up to her knees on a single leap. "Me too. My tummy is growling."

Taylor moved in toward her belly, placing her ear against its supple nakedness. "Your belly wants a peanut butter and jelly sandwich."

Lexie giggled. "That hair of yours is not only sexy, but it tickles!"

She squirmed, and Taylor nuzzled her belly even more. "Oh, wait. There's more. Your belly is also asking for cheese doodles."

"Cheese doodles?" Lexie giggled some more, filling the room with a joy it hadn't experienced in years. "My belly is quite demanding."

Taylor inched up to Lexie's lips and kissed her. "I'm growing rather fond of its demands. What do you say we go meet those demands before we starve to death?"

Lexie leaped off the bed first and raced toward the door. "Last one to the kitchen has to make the sandwiches."

"Ah, the competitive type," Taylor said, chasing her through the doorway and down the hall. "A woman after my own heart."

Lexie turned over her shoulder and showered Taylor in a beautiful, seductive glance. "I hope so."

Chapter Sixteen

Taylor woke to the smell of brewed coffee. She opened her eyes and stretched. The night before, Lexie had helped her set the coffee maker to go off automatically at eight a.m. After that, they kissed each other on the front stoop before Lexie waved and headed back to be with Cashmere.

Standing in the middle of her sunny kitchen, renewed energy surfaced in Taylor. Its surge beckoned her to take a bold step and send Stephanie a text.

So she did.

Hey, it's me.

Stephanie texted right back.

Hey you.

Taylor responded.

Can we meet sometime soon?

The three little dots lasted forever.

Yeah, it's time.

Taylor's hand lifted to her heart. A moment later, she responded. *The botanical gardens this weekend?*

Again with the three little dots. They lasted double the time.

I'm in Baltimore today at Inner Harbor, researching for an article I'm writing for my blog. Want to meet?

Meet. Her heart wobbled around her chest. *Bite the bullet. Cut to the chase. Take your foot off the brake.* None of those phrases helped her any. Her three little dots must've concerned Stephanie.

Sure. I can meet you there at noon. She could write a scene. Meet her daughter.

Get to The Pet Boutique later on. *There's a lot of great places we can eat if you want to get lunch, too,* she added confidently, like she scheduled dates to see her abandoned children all the time.

I'd rather just chat this first time, if that's okay? Besides, I can't eat gluten and that makes eating out difficult. I have celiac disease. Wait, do you, too?

No. I don't.

Hmm. I guess I got it from my biological father.

Deep Sigh. Taylor tapped her fingers on her counter. How to respond but with the obvious.

It's possible.

She would meet Stephanie. Her stomach tumbled. *So I suppose we can meet in front of where they dock the Lady Baltimore. Sound good?*

Absolutely!

What will you be wearing so I know it's you?

Oh that's easy. I'll likely be the only one in a wheelchair.

Wheelchair? The fire. The birth certificate. My God, was she burned? Did she lose her legs to cancer? Did she have MS? She couldn't let those three little dots linger for too long following that declaration.

Perfect. I'll look out for you. See you soon.

Perfect? What the fuck did she say that for?

You bet.

~ ~

Taylor sat in her car and attempted to steady her breathing. But her breaths shook and her face blotched, nonetheless. A deafening buzz sounded in her ears and the air surrounding her took on a hazy spin.

What-ifs piled up in her mind. What if she had never said yes to a ride in Tim Flurry's red Camaro? What if he had come back to school the next day instead of running off to Michigan as others told her he had done?

If none of that happened, Stephanie Hunter would not be excited about her research in Baltimore because she wouldn't be alive. Stephanie Hunter was alive and doing well. Taylor said that to herself over and over again as she sat in her car by the American Visionary Art Museum.

Eventually, she summoned the courage to climb out, feed the parking meter, and walk the mile or so along the Inner Harbor dock toward where her daughter would be waiting for her.

Taylor walked and twisted her emerald ring, the engagement ring Nate had placed on her finger on their second Christmas living together.

She swallowed about a million times more than necessary. The veins in her neck throbbed. She should've told Maya. Maya would be angry that she didn't fill her in on the drive into the city. She could've helped her prep. Told her what to say, what not to say. She was a mother. She acquired such knowledge. With two minutes to spare, Taylor faced the challenge on her own. She recited the mantra, *Stephanie Hunter is alive.*

Taylor rounded the bend in the dock, and the crowded boardwalk sat in front of her like a plank off the side of a boat in the middle of the ocean. She wobbled forward, carrying her satchel of nerves over her shoulder and licking her lips until her lip balm disappeared.

She slowed her pace, trying unsuccessfully to calm her heartbeat. She squinted, scanning the distance for a wheelchair. Everything blurred. Her temples pounded, urging her to turn around and run. Run as fast as her feet would take her.

Then, the sun reflected off metal ahead. There, right in front of Lady Baltimore, a beautiful young woman with long brown hair sat in a wheelchair. Despite the knocking in her heart, she quickened her pace, now eager to rip off the bandage and start the healing.

As Taylor neared her, she glanced at Stephanie's legs. One was in a cast and her opposite arm in a sling. She had suffered a fall of some sort, likely. Relief pooled in Taylor, a relief born out of the notion that her daughter wasn't burned in a fire years ago, suffering from MS, or missing one or both of her legs. "Are you Stephanie?" she asked with a shaky voice.

"Yes, hi!" Stephanie extended her hand. Her eyes shimmered and dimples appeared in the apple of her happy, rosy cheeks. Happy. She looked happy. Unscarred by life's cruel hands. Bright-eyed and animated, and thankfully, all Taylor dreamed her to be since that dreaded day eighteen years ago.

Taylor shook her hand.

A nice firm, confident shake. She was a leader. Taylor could see it in the way she raised her chin and met her eyes. "I'm at a loss for words," Taylor said, laboring for composure.

Stephanie released her hand, and folded hers in her lap. A pretty diamond ring caught the sun and blinded Taylor. Stephanie noticed and covered it with her other hand. "You look like the picture on your book covers."

Taylor swallowed hard. "You've seen my book covers?"

"I read every one of your books over the last two months." Stephanie waved at her leg. "I have a lot of time on my hands."

Taylor flushed. Her books had been read by over a hundred thousand people, but none meant more than the one sitting before her. "Wow. Thanks."

"My mom bought them for me." She lingered on a blink. "She's always been a fan of yours. She has a thing for suspense. Of course, she can't tell my gramma that. Gramma is a hard-nosed Christian who believes any book that has any form of evil in it is, well, evil." She giggled.

Taylor knitted her eyebrows together, confused.

"Oh, my mother didn't connect you to me. She never knew your name. Then we got the birth certificate straightened out and she discovered you were my mother when the records were unsealed. As you can imagine, she was surprised."

Surprised. Surprised could mean a lot of things. Surprised that someone who wrote complex characters who always got their act together by the end of the story could dump their child into the arms of strangers? Surprised someone with her supposed resources could turn away from a child? Did she have the full story? Was that in the records?

"Sure." Taylor released a nervous chuckle, and looked at her feet before meeting her eyes again. "Have you been waiting long?"

"I've been people-watching in this spot for an hour. It's been interesting." She giggled again. "Very interesting."

"How so?"

"Most people never look up from their cellphones. Have you ever noticed that? It's like that on campus, too. That can be kind of dangerous when you're in a wheelchair."

Taylor scanned the crowd and, yeah, most people bowed their heads and walked while glancing at their phones.

"Come on," she said, advancing the motorized wheelchair forward with a joystick. "Let's find a place where you can sit."

"I don't mind standing." Taylor didn't want to be more difficult than she already had been for the past eighteen years.

"Let's walk, then. Well, I mean you walk, I'll ride." She set the course along the boardwalk. "Inner Harbor is a great place. So much to see. But not wheelchair-friendly. Way too many distracted people."

"How did you hurt yourself?"

"Climbing off my fiancé's motorcycle."

Taylor's heart thudded.

"Are you okay?" Stephanie asked. "Are you going to throw up?"

Taylor scratched the side of her neck. The sun burned it. "It's hot out here for October."

"That global warming. I tell you." She shook her head.

Remnants of Lexie's global warming comment rattled around her brain.

"So you mentioned your fiancé. You're getting married?" She doled out the question relaxed, like she was talking with a thirty-year-old and not someone who still couldn't legally drink.

"In a few years. We don't want to rush into it. Well, my gramma, especially. She asked us to wait until we're done with college. Then we'll have her blessing."

"Wise." Not that she could counsel her any better.

"Thank you so much for meeting me today. You're a busy writer with deadlines and a life. So I appreciate it."

"Oh, gosh. Are you kidding? It's a pleasure." Taylor glanced at a paw print tattoo on her wrist.

Stephanie caught her. "My dog Otis. He passed last January."

"Mine passed a few months ago. Oscar."

"You should get a tattoo of his paws."

"It's something I thought about doing."

"It doesn't hurt. I got mine when I turned eighteen. My mom wasn't happy."

Her mom.

How different would her life have gone had Taylor raised her? Would she be as sprightly and innocent? She never would've had her dog Otis. Or her dog tattoo. Or her fiancé. For that matter, she'd be walking because she wouldn't have broken her leg falling off a motorcycle.

She kicked her foot forward, whisking the what-ifs to the side.

Life had other plans.

Taylor admired her smile. Had she created it? Did she have anything to do with the deep dimple on her right cheek?

Taylor followed close beside her, warding off potential crashes with clueless cellphone abusers too busy to see her wheeling past. Her long brown hair swayed with each progression forward.

Taylor's greatest mystery sat right beside her. That sent a shiver through her. For all those years, she dreamed about that exact moment. There they were, talking like they'd picked up the conversation from the day before.

"I've jotted down enough notes to write a good blog post on technology and how it affects society."

She was smart. Studious. Industrious. Resourceful. A daughter anyone would be proud of.

They continued to stroll and roll for the next half hour, making small talk about the weather, school, and the beautiful Inner Harbor.

Once they got back to the same place they started, Stephanie smiled up at Taylor and asked, "I'd love to hear more about you. Can you tell me about your family?"

"Well, let's see, um, I'm the only child to a set of parents who always wanted the best for me. They'd rather I live closer to them than I do," Taylor said. "I moved away from home right after college, and over the years, our visits have grown further apart, despite being only two hours away from each other." She paused. "That's on me. Life gets busy. Before you know it, monthly visits turn into biannual ones, and then the space spans even wider until it turns into three hundred sixty-five days."

"Then into eighteen years," she finished for her.

"Yeah." Taylor tucked her hands into her jean pockets.

"So," she brightened. "Do you have any kids? Are you married? Boyfriend? Girlfriend? Alien? Anyone?"

Stephanie sure did have a light way about her. She didn't get that trait from her. She liked it. "I have a good friend. I'll leave it at that for now."

"We all need a good friend." Stephanie stretched her neck. She glanced around their spot, taking in the world with young eyes full of hope and questions.

"What about you? Tell me more. What do you like to do in your free time when you're not gathering research for a blog post?"

Stephanie grappled with the question for a moment, then said. "Well, I love being a Toastmaster."

"What's a Toastmaster?" She pictured Stephanie hovering above a stainless steel toaster, gripping a set of silicone thongs as she braced for the perfect browned piece of bread to shoot out of a slot.

"I present speeches. That's what happens at Toastmasters. You learn to give speeches so you don't freak out when it counts."

Taylor feared public speaking more than dying. In college, she nearly passed out during oral communications class. Nate came to her rescue and got her through that class. "I totally suck."

Stephanie's brown eyes warmed. She sat forward. "No, don't say that. You did what you had to do. You don't suck."

189

It took a moment for Taylor's heart and mind to catch up. When they did, air swooshed out of Taylor's lungs, creating a guttural groan.

"You were talking about sucking at giving a speech," Stephanie said with a sigh.

Taylor waved away Stephanie's discomfort from her interpretation. "No worries. What you said was nice. Thank you for that."

Stephanie wavered on a thought, searching the crowded Inner Harbor for something. Then she bowed her head and fidgeted with her fingers. "A part of me wished you were a loser."

"What?"

"I wanted you to be someone with serious life-choice issues." Stephanie bowed her head more. "Terrible, right?"

"Why did you want that?"

"If you were doped up on pills or sipping vodka straight from the bottle, you wouldn't have had the sanity to come back for me. I could've accepted that."

Taylor would've preferred being torn apart by a giant set of plyers to experiencing the hurt in Stephanie's words.

"I'm so sorry."

Should she place a comforting hand on her back and rub it the way her mother would've done or remain a safe distance from her? She hadn't a clue how to operate under such conditions.

Stephanie lifted her chin, and joy resurfaced on her face. "No. I'm sorry. I didn't mean to say that."

"No, it's okay." Taylor braved a step closer. "It's good that you say what's on your mind."

Stephanie pulled in her upper lip. "What I meant is that I never pictured you to be a success story. Well, once in a while that would pop into my mind and it hurt because if you were successful and didn't care about me, I'd be pissed. I struggled less when I pictured you like a homeless person at a traffic light grasping a sign and begging for coins. So that's who I pictured you to be all these years. It neutralized things in some ways."

"So you did have a difficult time?" A vise tightened around her chest, squeezing out her strength one painful turn at a time.

"Whenever I dwell on unknowns, I tend to overdramatize things." Stephanie's cheek flinched. "I tend to complicate things, too, by creating larger-than-life stories in my head—things that couldn't come true. I let them play out anyway."

"That's a storytelling trait, I'm afraid. I do the same thing," Taylor said.

"Then, as a storyteller I need to remember that I control the pen, don't I?"

Stephanie was wise. A swath of maternal pride washed over Taylor. "You do. You control the pen and can write the story as you want it to be."

"When I stopped picturing you as a homeless drug abuser waving a filthy sign, I sometimes let myself imagine us sitting in a café together playing a game of Monopoly as we sipped hot chocolate." Her eyes sparkled again.

"I love both of those things."

"Then I'd bring myself back by remembering that my parents loved me and treated me like their own flesh and blood. They've done so much for me, and I can't imagine if I didn't have them and if they didn't have me. We all saved each other."

"How so?"

"My parents had lost their first child to SIDS. Then I came along. Back then, they lived in North Carolina. A nice woman they knew from church told them about you, a young pregnant woman who wanted to find loving parents."

A cry lodged itself in Taylor's throat. "Ms. Peabody?"

Stephanie nodded. "She urged them to register with the Catholic Adoption Agency. I'm pretty sure she pulled some strings and got their name to the top of that list."

"She had pull," Taylor said. "Or at least the personality to possess it."

Stephanie stared at her for a long pause. Her eyes grew wet in that span, and a few tears rolled down her rosy cheeks. "Ms. Peabody placed me in a home with a lot of love."

The vise across her chest lightened. "I'm so happy you have parents who love you."

"They really do. I'm lucky." Her eyes sparkled.

"I always stressed about that, praying your parents loved you all along just as they had that first day I handed you over to them. I waited to request unsealing the records because I didn't want to interfere when you were too young. I didn't want to mess you up."

"My parents weren't ready for me to meet you," Stephanie said. "Which is why they never contacted the agency to have the records unsealed. Honestly, I'm glad they didn't. I wouldn't have been ready before now."

Her chest squeezed shut again. "I understand."

Stephanie twirled her hair nervously, gazing around the scene at the people bowing their heads into their cellphones. "I don't hate you. It's important you understand that."

Taylor went numb. "I was afraid you might. You'd have the right. You spent your whole life wondering. I'm sorry for that. I hope one day you might be able to forgive me for everything."

"Forgive you?"

The numbness evaporated replaced by painful jabs to her extremities, like the thawing after frostbite. "Forget I said that. That was incredibly insensitive and premature. How could I ask you to forgive me?"

Stephanie's eyes warmed. "I can't forgive you because there's nothing to forgive. I don't blame you for what you did. It was the best thing. For both of us."

Was it the best thing for Taylor? Sure, she may have turned out the dozen bestsellers she'd written over the years with all that time and space on her side. But what she might've gained with Stephanie would've glossed right over that literary opportunity, opening up others with greater value. You can't replace love with a career or things.

It might've been the best for Stephanie, though. She was a success story. Young, intelligent, eager, and curious. Her parents loved and admired her. Taylor couldn't have assured the same level of quality in her childhood by being a single mother, without the guidance of Maya, Nate, and ultimately Oscar.

"I suppose if anything had changed in our history, we'd be different people today," Taylor said.

A sad recognition played across her cheeks. "Yeah, I suppose you're right. Everything happened as it was supposed to." She straightened her lips into a thin line. "I should go now. My fiancé's probably bored by now."

Taylor's heart pinched. "It's been really nice meeting you, Stephanie."

"For me, too." She turned over her shoulder. "That's my fiancé. The guy with the blue hat and funny long beard."

Taylor glanced at him. The guy waved. Taylor waved back.

"I can't drive myself around yet, so he's been my escort."

"Well, I don't want to keep you and him too long." Taylor extended her hand. "It was a pleasure to meet you, Stephanie."

Stephanie opened her arms instead, and Taylor fell into them.

They squeezed each other. She smelled like fresh strawberries, fragrant and lively. The scent lingered on her as she rose. "So until next time."

"Yeah." Stephanie bobbed her head. "Until next time."

Taylor left her with one last smile before turning away and retracing her steps back to where she started out.

"I'll bring my Monopoly board next time," Stephanie shouted.

Taylor glanced back at her, and her heart lifted. "I'll bring the hot chocolate."

"Deal."

"Deal."

~ ~

Later on, as Taylor parked her car on the side street adjacent to The Pet Boutique, she thought more about Ms. Peabody. Then she thought back to that nice man on the bus, Roger Lyles. Had he ever published a science-fiction book?

She pulled out her phone and did a quick Google search for his name. Sure enough, the first three pages of Google included various links to articles, videos, and Amazon. A proud smile spread across her face. Maybe she had played a little part in nudging him toward writing a book.

She landed on his author page, and there sat a picture of him wearing a stylish fedora hat and the same kind smile he showed her on one of the worst days of her life.

He had written four science-fiction books. And all four had won awards, displaying the award's badge on the covers. She clicked on the sample of his first book, *The Angel of Surprise,* and scrolled through the opening title page to the copyright and then to the dedication.

To Taylor, thanks for the conversation that day on the bus and for inspiring me to follow my dream.

Taylor remained planted in her front seat for a long time, riding the emotional journey that Mr. Roger Lyles' words placed in her heart. Once she settled back down to Earth, she purchased the kindle version. Then she visited his website, where she clicked the link to purchase a hardcopy directly from him. She sent along a message with the purchase, asking for that autograph he promised her, a promise that man had made way back before she had learned to love herself again. She added to her message, *I'm glad you're still wearing the fedora hat. And just an FYI, I still have your quarter.*

Chapter Seventeen

Lexie followed her aunt through the front door of The Pet Boutique, carrying the decorative items they'd picked up at Target that morning. Her heart bounced around in her chest as she braced for the excitement when she'd stand before Taylor again, that time with her clothes on.

The night before had been an amazing, thrill-seeking journey of tumbling, flying, and coasting all in one. Taylor had let loose and introduced Lexie to paradise, that place where vulnerability met with passion. Taylor navigated Lexie's body like someone who had studied all the right moves and sensitive areas of a woman many times over. She caused Lexie to moan and arch under her lead.

Taylor rose from a bent position near a set of shelves and smiled at Lexie.

Lexie's legs turned wiggly and limp.

Taylor's face pinked like she'd jogged around the neighborhood. "What do you think?" she asked Maya.

With the rehab almost behind them, the place took shape. It had been a week since Auntie Maya had been in the boutique, and Lexie couldn't wait to see her aunt's excitement over the way she and Ally had pulled some of the décor together.

Auntie Maya walked past Taylor's flushed face and straight toward the bins at the reception counter. "You chose biscuits." She picked up the plastic package of one set of doggy bone-shaped biscuits and gawked at it, turning it over, backwards, sideways.

"Isn't that what you wanted?" Lexie asked her, tossing Taylor a concerned glance.

"It makes sense to have them at the counter," Taylor added. "They always say to entice customers with impulse products at checkout. Nothing says impulse like dog biscuits."

"I do like this leash holder," her aunt said, glancing at the new piece Lexie had found in a vendor catalogue featuring handcrafted items. The artist constructed a hound dog in a hunting pose. He had constructed it using metal with a rusted, old-world vibe. It could accommodate up to six leashes, probably the maximum number of dogs Anne Arundel County allowed in an oversized property lot.

Auntie Maya rubbed her chin, turning over her shoulder and scanning the mural wall, now the backdrop to three bohemian style tables and chairs and an area rug filled with paw prints. Artists had stained each table with vivid flair in muted tones of peach, purple, amber, brown, and honey-mustard yellow. The lacquered pine wood tops boasted a functional, clean look.

Then she swept her eyes to the front window and the card rack display, now accompanied by a chew toy rack, featuring fun stuffed animals like dragons, scarecrows, raccoons, and bears.

She continued to rub her chin, as she turned to the wall across from the mural where the food, wellness products, and beds would go on the shelves Taylor assembled.

"Goldie told me something didn't feel right." Auntie Maya turned over her shoulder at Lexie. "Was she referring to the biscuits?"

Argh, Goldie!

Lexie had enjoyed arranging the boutique. She loved accessorizing it with quirky décor, bold colors, and practical products. Even Ally admired her taste and logic when it came to deciding on décor items. Lexie took that as a huge compliment because Ally was the queen decorator of the family. Her house resembled something out of the glossy pages of *Better Homes and Gardens*. Of course it helped that Tom's salary offered her the budget to play with her dreams. Lexie's budget mirrored that of a college student buying cheap bedding and furniture to cozy up a dorm. Yet she worked it out.

She bought the window treatments, rugs, cute doggy decorations, furniture and small trimmings that tied the place together at online auctions. A maternal pride in the place rose in her and she needed to protect it.

"We're not doing this anymore," Lexie said. "You can't live your life guided by a psychic, Auntie. That's ridiculous. The biscuits are fine. Besides, Goldie likes to stick things in people's minds and get them all worked up over nothing. It's irresponsible."

Auntie Maya glared at her. "She's my friend, and I resent that you said that."

Her glare penetrated Lexie right in the heart. "I'm sorry. I guess I got a little irritated. I'm sure she means well. I just don't think you or I or anyone should follow her every inkling. What if she's wrong and we make a terrible choice?"

Auntie Maya softened. "Did she say something to you?"

Lexie flipped her hair over her shoulders, uncomfortable with the stares from her and Taylor. "No, it's just…I worry about you," she stammered.

"Well, I may have heart issues, but my brain is fully functioning. So no more worrying. Deal?"

Lexie folded her arms across her chest. "Deal."

"I want to show you what I did with the back self-service stalls, Maya." Taylor waved her to follow, and then tossed Lexie an understanding blink as her aunt passed by Taylor and led herself to the stalls.

"Well, are you going to show me or what?" Auntie Maya yelled out.

Taylor's cheeks pinked again, and she dashed off, yelling, "Geez Maya. You're grumpier now than before your heart attack."

"Wait until I get my red pen going again. By the way, I'm waiting for the next three chapters."

"You'll get your damn chapters."

Their voices carried throughout the boutique like a confused song going in and out of pitch and volume. Lexie moved closer, resting her back against the adjacent wall while pretending to read over some inventory sheets.

"Why do you have a weird smile on your face? What did you do?" Lexie heard her aunt ask Taylor.

197

"A few things," Taylor said on a chuckle.

"Well? Fill me in."

"It's kind of premature to get too excited."

"Too premature? What kind of stupid shit is that?"

Yeah, exactly, Lexie thought. *What kind of stupid shit is that?*

Just then, Goldie entered. "Oh, good, I'm glad I found you here." She sailed in, overtaking the room so Lexie could no longer hear Taylor's answer. She carried a box under her arm. "I signed for a delivery." She handed her the box.

Whispers filtered in from the back stalls. Whispers Lexie much preferred eavesdropping on over dealing with Goldie. She stuck her nose where it didn't belong, and it aggravated her now. Goldie no longer charmed Lexie. She was a confusing hazard for her aunt.

"Is that your aunt back there?"

"Yes. And Taylor." Lexie stuck her finger under the packing tape and slid it open.

"How is she feeling?"

"Shouldn't you know that kind of stuff?" Lexie snapped, and regretted it the second it hit Goldie.

Goldie flinched and placed her hand over her heart.

"I'm sorry," Lexie said. "Lack of sleep." She shook her head. "I've been snapping at everyone. I'm always worried about my aunt now and the boutique."

"It's more." Goldie searched her face.

Oh here we go.

Lexie opened the flaps to the box and spotted an order of bone keychains. "I've got to get these priced and into the computer system."

"Just remember that everything is temporary, okay? Whatever you're going through, or will go through, will pass."

Lexie narrowed her eyes. "Stop. No more. Okay? You may be able to get away with feeding my aunt bullshit, but I'm not like that." She bit her tongue and walked behind the desk. She dropped onto the chair, hiding her face from Goldie and her strange revelations.

~ ~

Taylor couldn't wait to tell Lexie about her visit with Stephanie. But when she came out of the backroom stalls and spotted Lexie sporting a weary frown, her excitement faded. "What's wrong?"

Lexie flipped some paperwork over at the desk and stood. "Yeah, I'm kind of preoccupied with inventory, even though the work is *premature*." Her words pelted the space like hail, denting and misshaping it.

Taylor stared at her long and hard. "What's happening?"

"Your voice carries because you talk loudly."

"I do?"

"Yes." Lexie nodded, not taking her eyes from her paperwork. "Last night you didn't act like anything was too *premature*."

Then it dawned on Taylor. She took her conversation with Maya extremely out of context.

Lexie reminded Taylor of an adorable child tossing a temper over not having her turn at hopscotch. "Lexie Tanner, how is it possible you're even more adorable when pitching a fit?"

Lexie met her eyes. "I'm not pitching a fit."

"No?" Taylor moved in closer and traced a finger down her cheek. "I wasn't talking about you with your aunt."

Lexie met her eye. "Fine."

"Fine." Taylor mocked her childish tone.

Lexie playfully slapped Taylor's finger away from her face. "I thought you were."

"Well, I wasn't." She pulled up a step stool and sat. "Though I do find your snooping side sort of charming."

Lexie tucked some loose strands of hair behind her ear. Those hairs tickled Taylor's face the night before as the rest of her hair splayed out across her couch's pillow.

Taylor's heart pulsed the same as it had while she brought Lexie to intoxicating pleasure. She wanted to be in that place again, kissing and teasing her until her body arched below hers.

Lexie peeked up at her with innocent, doe-like eyes. "Well, when you talk loudly, it piques my curiosity."

"What about when I whisper?" Taylor leaned in and placed her lips on Lexie's ear. "Come back to my place with me after this."

Lexie giggled. "Okay, look, if you don't mind. I have some work to do, and so do you. We are shooting for an early November grand opening, and those shelves aren't going to hang themselves."

Taylor kissed the hollow of her neck, inhaling her fresh, clean scent. She nibbled gently on her earlobe, then whispered. "I always deliver on time."

Lexie released a moan.

"By the way," Taylor rose. "I met my birth daughter today, which, of course, was the thing I referred to when I said the whole premature statement you overheard."

Lexie rose to meet her. "You did?"

"I did." Taylor held her gaze. "Just a little while ago. We met at Inner Harbor."

"Oh my God. Really?"

"We met for about an hour. Enough for me to see she's turned into a beautiful young woman with a stable good life. And she doesn't hate me." Taylor beamed, bursting with joy.

"You gave her life. Why would she hate you?"

"Okay, well, not hate, but she had every right to be cautious. I could've turned out to be a wacko or an uncaring soul who lived a reckless life. I relieved her by not showing up with track marks on my arms and missing teeth."

Lexie laughed.

"Come by tonight, okay? And bring Cashmere this time. We'll take her on that walk."

~ ~

Lexie's stomach fluttered as she approached Taylor's front door, gripping

Cashmere's leash. The smell of fall flowers swirled in the air. The setting sun cast sharp shadows along the slate-blue shutters. Everything brought peace and comfort.

She'd always dreamed of a pretty home packaged like a gift box. She pictured it on a street where kids rode bikes and trees grew tall and stocky and dropped piles of crunchy leaves to dive into and splash about.

Another strange bout of jealously wound itself inside of her. Could all of the beauty around her ever become part of her future? Would she ever get to live in a pretty house with a healthy lawn and gorgeous fruit trees in the front and side yard? She needed to stop listening to her aunt and Goldie. They were smothering her in doubt.

She swallowed the bad taste and placed her fist beside the wreath. Then, summoning up a better vibe, she knocked.

When Taylor opened the door, Cashmere jumped to greet her.

"She is super eager about her walk."

Cashmere circled her ankles and barked at them. Taylor danced around her fiery spirit until Cashmere settled. Then Taylor bent to her level, and Cashmere licked her face with slobbery gusto.

"Cashmere stop!" Lexie straddled her, inching up on her leash. Meanwhile, Taylor giggled like a two-year-old, stretching her face closer for Cashmere's ease.

Cashmere snorted and surrendered her curiosity on a huff.

"I'm so sorry." Lexie said, laughing. "She gets a little excited."

"A little?" Taylor touched her face and smeared sticky goo.

"Oh, here." Lexie let go of the leash, dug into her front pocket, and handed her a wad of tissues.

Cashmere pushed forward straight into Taylor's living room. She wandered off, sniffing and trotting.

Taylor leaned against her doorframe.

Lexie fixated on the curve of her cheek as it rose.

"Are you going to let me in or will you be staring at me with those intense eyes from your doorway all night long?"

Taylor tugged on the strings of Lexie's zippered pink sweatshirt. She twirled her finger around one of the strings, not taking her eyes off her. "Well, there's always the couch. I hear it's pretty comfortable. For sitting and stuff."

Lexie chuckled, mesmerized by the lightness in the air between them. "Listen here, Ms. Famous Novelist, I didn't come here to just—"

Taylor pulled her closer and kissed her.

Lexie's knees buckled, and Taylor helped keep her standing with her strong grip and even stronger kiss.

Then, Cashmere barked and bolted out the door, knocking them off balance. She chased after a motorcycle speeding down the street.

~ ~

Lexie launched herself down the front stoop and chased Cashmere. "Cashmere. Come back." She tripped over the divots in the grass, launching herself toward the side yard and over to the street where the motorcycle traveled.

Taylor followed, sinking into the spongy grass and cringing as her brand new Converse sneakers turned from light blue to brown. Lexie continued to call Cashmere's name as they ran through other yards to get back on the street.

The motorcycle's *vroom* disappeared along with any trace of Cashmere.

Taylor wheezed. She hadn't run since high school. And even then, she'd only jogged when on the cross-country team. Now, she sprinted across multiple yards and streets. At one point, Taylor almost blacked out. But she kept her pace because that's what a woman did on a date. She did everything in her power to impress the date. If that meant sprinting down the street wearing stupid little skimpy blue sneakers with no support and Capri pants too tight to be good for blood circulation, then that's what she did. She had an inhaler back at her house. Surely, she'd last long enough to get there. And if not, at least she'd go out on a heroic beat.

Finally, in the distance, Lexie stopped on a patch of grass in someone's front yard. Bent over with her hands on her knees, she gulped air. "We lost her," she said hoarsely. "She's gone."

Taylor coughed and bent over with her hands on her knees too. The two of them panted, and Taylor feared they'd both keel over right there under a beautiful cherry blossom tree in front of someone's dining room window.

"She'll come back," Taylor blurted out, adding, "My friend's dog used to run away all the time as a kid. He always came back stinky and wet from his jaunts to the pond." She took another gulp of air. "She'll come back or the pound will call when someone finds her."

Terror sat on Lexie's delicate face. "She's never quite run like this before. She's lost. We have to find her."

"Of course. Let's catch our breath and keep searching."

Taylor rose. She shaded the sun from her eyes. Well-manicured lawns sprawled in front of them with countless houses. She could be anywhere.

Lexie blinked. "Which way should we go?"

Taylor took the lead. "We'll head down the street to the right. When in doubt, go right."

"Right," Lexie nodded. "Right it is, then."

They walked for what seemed like forever.

Eventually, they rounded a corner and set their eyes on a welcoming sight.

Perched on the front stoop of the third rancher house down on the left, Cashmere stared at them as though she'd never seen them before. A boy of about five years, sporting a crew cut, sat next to her. Breaking the stare, the boy offered Cashmere a dainty water bowl. She sucked that water like she'd spent the past ten years of life crawling through hot sand.

Lexie sprinted down the street, swinging her arms and hips.

She ran up the sidewalk to the house. The little boy stood. "This is my dog. I found her fair and square." His little beady eyes squinted. He puckered his lips and stood his ground.

Cashmere sat there, drooling, staring at the back of the boy's head. Perfect angel. Had the kid drugged her?

Lexie stood still, gripping her hips. Her chest lifted and fell in quick successions.

Sweat dripped down Taylor's face and through her polo shirt. Her mouth dried like the inside of a preheated oven ready for some of that Italian bread she had planned for their dinner. She'd rummaged through every contingency for the night, except how to win a custody battle over a dog who enjoyed the showdown.

So long, Italian bread with olive oil and herb dressing. Bye bye, bowl of ziti smothered in a rich layer of mozzarella cheese. Nice to know you, delicious deep red wine that would've paired so nicely with spices.

Lexie's expression showed more shock than anger.

When she took a step closer, the boy put up his hand.

Taylor played out the scenario in her mind. She could sneak behind the kid and grab Cashmere. She'd end up the hero. Lexie would deter the kid long enough for them to get away. They'd sprint back to her house. The little boy would eat their dust.

Lexie scooted down beside the little boy, ignoring his outstretched hand. "She's adorable, isn't she?"

He eyed Taylor, warning her with a flinch of his cheek that he led the charge in the current situation.

Taylor sat back on her heels. Being the hero on a date was kind of cliché anyway.

"Do you know her name?" Lexie asked.

He shook his head. "I don't know yet."

Lexie stared at him for a moment as a bead of sweat rolled down the side of her face. She opened her mouth and said, "I'm her mommy. So I know her name. Do you want to know it?"

The little boy's eyes filled with tears.

"Her name is Cashmere. She loves to be scratched right behind her ears. Like this." Lexie leaned over and scratched. Cashmere leaned into the indulgence. "Want to try?"

The little boy moved in and scratched the other ear. Cashmere leaned into him, and the little boy chuckled.

"Cashmere has a lot of toys in her room that she loves. So she might be sad if she doesn't get to come back home with me."

The little boy's tears turned his face blotchy. "I like her, though."

"I'll tell you what. My friend, here, lives down the street. We can always walk Cashmere by your house so you can still see her and give her water."

Always walk her by your house. Taylor's heart flipped.

"And pet her behind her ears?"

Lexie's face lit up. "Yes, you can even pet her behind her ears."

Lexie was so perfect. So compassionate. Such a good person. She had a nurturing quality to her that eased the soul.

He hugged Cashmere. "You promise to come visit me Cashmere?"

Cashmere licked his nose, and the little boy laughed. A full-out belly laugh.

Just then, a slender woman wearing an apron came to the front door. "Hello, can I help you?"

Lexie rose to her feet. "My dog ran away. He kept her safe until we found her."

"He loves dogs, and has been begging us for one for some time." She walked over to her son and patted his head. "Sweetheart you can't take one who already has a home."

"Can we please get one, Mom?" He stood. "I'll be a good brother. I took care of Cashmere. She even drank water."

She glanced at the flowery bowl. "I see that." She leaned her son against her hip and spoke to both Lexie and Taylor. "I'm glad your dog is safe."

A weird giddiness rose in Taylor. *Your dog.* As if they were an established couple.

Lexie didn't even correct her.

Lexie grabbed Cashmere's leash. "She's safe because of your son." She walked away. "We'll bring her by soon."

She said we'll. Taylor's stomach did another little flip.

She turned into a full-fledged acrobat hanging out with that woman.

Cashmere entertained. Through her silliness and sneakiness, she offered everyone around her the chance to laugh, feel, and engage with life rather than escape it, as Taylor had spent too much time doing over the past few years. Cashmere reminded Taylor of why she wrote—to engage with life. She built worlds that excited her and teased her to discover what waited for her around the next sentence.

Cashmere the entertainer and teacher.

Her ears flopped as she trotted.

Lexie then broke off into a quicker pace, and Cashmere eagerly matched it.

"Why the death march," Taylor called out, lagging behind and too tired to quicken her pace.

"I'm starved." She giggled and skipped ahead.

Taylor had never seen a woman as beautiful and full of life as the one before her. If her lips could continue to brush against hers, she'd never need another thing in her life.

Well, except water.

Okay and maybe food.

She caught up with her under a tree in her secluded side yard. "I'm starved, too." Their arms brushed as they headed forward. Cashmere continued to lead them with great focus.

"What are we going to eat?" Lexie asked, in a sultry tone. The early evening sky cast a beautiful glow on her face.

In a brave and uncharacteristic move, Taylor gripped her wrist and stopped her. Cashmere propped herself in between their feet.

"Something delicious," Taylor whispered, loosening the grip on her wrist. She stroked Lexie's hand, summoning the courage to once again close the space between them.

Cashmere regarded Taylor with a sidelong glance.

Lexie studied Taylor for a moment. "I'm really glad you invited us tonight."

Taylor buzzed with a desire to indulge in her softness again and be tickled with her teasing touch. Lexie's eyes twinkled. A moment later, her lips swooned against Taylor's tender cheek. Slowly and reverently. Taylor's eyes fluttered as time suspended and her heart swelled. She closed her eyes to drink in the moment. Then, with a gentle touch, their lips met.

Lexie's touch was light, fluid, and poetic. In that brief moment, they connected and the rest of the world faded. The two of them swayed as one in the afterglow of the setting sun. Before Taylor could grasp the delicacy of her beauty, Lexie pulled away on a gentle smile.

Taylor nearly toppled over again.

Chapter Eighteen

"Isn't she amazing?" Rex asked, holding the sonogram picture up to Lexie's face. Lexie stared at an inkblot. "Totally."

"Wait until you experience parenthood. There's nothing like it."

Lexie had wanted a family since middle school when she babysat the neighbor's kids, Claudine and Eddie, twin five-year-olds who could play the piano and sing. She envisioned twins of her own, two boys, best friends and pure souls. They'd be mischievous and full of giggles. Then, as they grew, they'd be protective of their mom, always thoughtful and kind, baking her homemade cakes and crafting hand-written birthday cards.

Even back then, Lexie dreamed of marrying a woman one day. She dreamed of marrying her friend, Clara, a dark-haired, dark-skinned girl on her soccer team. The first girl she ever kissed. She even dreamed up their wedding, both wearing elegant Cinderella-type wedding dresses, the kind with a long, lacy trail. Clara would wear her hair pinned up with delicate flowers. Lexie would wear hers pinned up at the sides with the rest hanging down in cascading large spiral curls.

As life had careened ahead and she began dating Christine, prospects of angling her life in such a way smeared into an oversaturated, blurry mess. Odds never curved in her favor when it came to marriage or kids. But she hoped her luck was changing.

"You and Taylor would not only make a cute couple, but excellent parents." Rex continued to plug for that success story. Wini bounced her head up and down in agreement.

Lexie glanced from Rex to Wini, her heart pinging around like a ball in a pinball machine. "Easy does it. She's got a lot on her plate, and so do I. We're taking it one step at a time."

Rex placed the sonogram picture back in his wallet, right on top of a condom that had gotten comfortable in it. "Don't wait too long and risk her slipping away." He hugged his pregnant girlfriend.

Lexie folded her arms over her chest and glanced at Taylor talking with Maya and Goldie. They laughed about something, and Taylor dipped her head toward Goldie before catching Lexie's eye. A desire pooled in their warmth.

Everything in her wanted to swim with her in that desire. But Lexie didn't want to get too hopeful yet. What if Taylor decided she didn't like the way her breath smelled? What if Stephanie didn't like her? Then what? Ask her to choose between the daughter she's always wanted to connect with and her, a woman she had met in an old, stinky building with a cobweb in her hair?

"It'd be nice to raise kids together," Rex said.

"Seriously, slow down, cuz."

"I'm just saying, it'd be nice for our kids to grow up in the same generation. We can do sleepovers. Camping trips. Swimming dates."

"None of us have a pool." Lexie snapped her finger against his arm.

Rex kissed Wini's forehead. "We will in about sixty days." He turned to Lexie. "We bought the house down the street from Mom's. It has a pool."

Her chest pinched as Rex and Wini's pride grew. Her life sped up and she feared missing out on all those things she wanted—a solid relationship, a family, swim dates at Rex and Wini's pool.

"A house? That quickly?"

"When you know, you know. The best things happen without planning for it. Just like with love. I fell in love the second our hands brushed when Wini handed me a packet of seeds at the hydroponic center. Bam, now here we are. Time doesn't matter."

She understood. Taylor had planted something new in Lexie, something alive, thrilling, and delicious. She hadn't planned it. The seed found its way in and embedded itself without constructing major details on where it should go and how deep. Guided by instinct, it dug in and rooted itself.

"You're more impulsive than me," Lexie said.

"I love being impulsive. It helps me stay flexible with all those bumps along the way. Life is full of them, so the less rigid, the better."

Lexie studied the happy couple.

"Besides," Rex added. "Anything worthwhile is always a bumpy ride. That's the beauty of seatbelts. Buckle up. Simple as that."

Seatbelts had saved Lexie's life in the past. Like that time she spun out five times in an ice storm coming back from a photo shoot after dark. Or the time she and Ally went out for ice-cream and her tire blew out. She couldn't forget the time she slammed on her brakes to avoid hitting a family of geese. They were crossing at the pond in front of Auntie Maya's neighborhood the day she first met Taylor in the back of The Pet Boutique.

"Simple as that, eh?"

"Simple as that," the happy couple said in unison.

Anxiety leaked in around Lexie's chest. It suffocated her hope for a life with Taylor and exposed a troubling layer of fear that something would get in their way.

She would do what she could to prevent the unease from becoming their truth. She had an idea, and would surprise Taylor with it later on that night.

~ ~

Taylor was mid-sentence in her next chapter when her phone vibrated. She glanced down and read a text from Lexie. *Hungry?*

She smiled at Lexie's one-word ability to turn her into a gooey mess. *Always.*

I'll be there in half an hour.

I don't know if I can wait that long.

Lexie responded with a red heart.

Taylor responded with two.

She returned to her sentence, forgetting her place in the story. Typically, when Nate interrupted her in the past, she'd want to pull her hair out of her head. She'd wake extra early to get in a few chapters before he rose. But some days, when in the heat of a scene, he'd walk by her and start a conversation. Poor guy wanted to spend time with her, and she'd glare at him like he had robbed her at gunpoint, forcing her to sacrifice her child. Her words *were* her children.

But Lexie's text refreshed her like a cool shower on a blazing hot scorcher of a day. She would let her words nap while she lived and experienced life. Later on, she'd wake those words back from their slumber. High on freshness, they'd dance before her fingers and tap life into the story.

Life had finally taken shape.

Her writing had returned.

A quiet, accepting comfort replaced her sadness. Her birth daughter was healthy and happy, and left the door open for future visits. And Lexie was coming over to feed her hunger.

Then, just when Taylor couldn't imagine more greatness to her day, the mailman knocked.

Taylor had to sign for a package. A package from a Mr. Roger Lyles.

She didn't even bother to close the front door before digging into it. Inside sat the glossy hardcover copy of his science-fiction book she had ordered. Taylor's heart leaped. She opened to the dedication page and right below it, he signed it with a note: *To Taylor, a gifted writer of prose that stirs the mind and heart. I'm a huge fan of your work, and have read everything you've written. I'm honored you're going to read something of mine. If you ever find yourself on a bus with an old man wearing a fedora hat, be sure to tap him and say hello... Happy travels and happy writing.*

Taylor had autographed countless books in her career and always wondered about the fascination some readers had with them. She now reverently and intimately understood. She hugged the book to her chest and bowed her head in silent praise for the blessing of meeting Mr. Roger Lyles.

~ ~

To Taylor's delight, Lexie arrived with a freshly-baked carrot cake and

212

Cashmere.

"How did you know that's my favorite?"

"I asked my aunt. I wanted to surprise you with something special."

"Well, that you did. So you spoke about me with your aunt?"

"I did. She also told me you have a knack for playing Gin Rummy." Lexie revealed a deck of cards, still wrapped in plastic.

Taylor ushered them in, placing her hand at the small of Lexie's back. "She's sharing my secrets now. Sounds like serious investigative research on your part."

Lexie nodded, playfully. "I like to know my subject on an intimate level."

"How many subjects do you know on an intimate level?" Taylor asked, reveling in the light scent on her neck.

Lexie giggled, balancing the cake in one hand and her pocketbook with the other. "If you keep that up, we may be eating cake off your living room floor."

Taylor grabbed the cake holder and headed toward the kitchen. Cashmere skipped alongside of her, ears perked, eyes wide, and anticipation dripping from each of her strides. "What is going on with the little sidekick here?"

Cashmere twirled.

Lexie crossed her arms across her chest. "Someone wants to go visit her new friend down the street. I'm afraid carrot cake may need to wait."

Taylor placed the cake on the counter and bent down to meet Cashmere. "That sounds like a mighty good plan to me. What do you say?"

Cashmere bolted toward the front door.

"Walk it is then," Lexie said, dropping her hands to her side.

A few minutes later, Cashmere led them down the street of the little boy she had befriended. She began to run when she spotted him riding a tricycle in his driveway. They followed her excited pursuit. Lexie braced to stop her before she launched herself on the boy.

As they approached, the mother rose from a chair on the front porch and waved.

The little boy turned toward them and leaped off his bike when he saw Cashmere. The next few seconds turned into a Hallmark moment, with the little boy running toward her with open arms and pure joy springing from him. Cashmere bent her ears backward, hung her chest low, and wiggled her butt.

The little boy lost himself in a fit of giggles.

They met on a hug. The little boy threw his arms around Cashmere, and she twirled at his little feet, whining and digging into the moment.

"You came back." He squeezed his eyes shut and hugged her tighter.

"This is the cutest thing, ever." Lexie hugged herself, and Taylor swung an arm around her shoulders, joining them together in their own Hallmark moment.

"She led us right here," Lexie said, smiling down at them before meeting the mother's grateful eyes.

"He's been talking about Cashmere every day. When we say grace at dinner, he always asks God to watch over her."

Taylor's heart warmed even more.

"Do you want to walk her around the driveway?" Lexie handed him the leash.

He rose from the hug with a dropped jaw, like Lexie told him Santa Claus planned to eat Christmas Eve dinner with him.

He took the leash with his skinny fingers and began to walk. "Come on Cashmere. Do you need to poopy?"

The mother shared a silent giggle with them, and then she mouthed a thank you.

They spent the better part of an hour chatting with the mother and watching the two new friends bond over a water bowl, walk up and down the driveway, and have a serious chat on the grass by themselves.

By the time they left, they had learned that the little boy had high-functioning autism and excelled at playing the piano. They promised to swing by another night in the near future to hear him play.

When they arrived back at Taylor's, Cashmere walked over to the couch, climbed on top of it, and cozied up to a pillow. Taylor went into the kitchen to round up a couple slices of cake for them.

"Seems someone is giving us some privacy now that she had her playtime," Lexie said in a sultry tone from the living room.

Taylor peeked her head around the corner of her kitchen wall to catch the tease playing out on Lexie's face. "Oh, to hell with carrot cake, then." Taylor advanced toward Lexie's full waiting lips.

Lexie's smile pulled her in every single time. It warmed her and sent her floating.

"I didn't need to bring a cake, did I?" Lexie whispered into her mouth.

Taylor answered that by leading Lexie with a gentle nudge past the recliner, through the archway, down the narrow hall, and into her dimly lit bedroom.

"Vanilla candles, hmm?"

"You're not the only one who can dig up info. Your aunt enjoys playing the role of intermediary."

"We should start asking each other instead." Lexie's pulse quickened as she pulled on the belt to Taylor's cargo shorts.

Cake. Candles. Romance. And Communication. Taylor moaned against Lexie's lips. "We might be onto something here."

Lexie pushed her down on the bed and pulled her shorts down over her feet. Then she straddled Taylor, sweeping her over with playful eyes. "You might want to buckle up for the ride."

A ride she brought.

The candlelit room disappeared around them until she and Lexie existed in a state of heightened sensory bliss in a sea of blankets. Lexie catered to her every whim, tracing her tongue up and down the full length of her, dipping her in and out of pleasure until she lifted her so high, the bed disappeared beneath her. The love in Lexie's embrace kept her afloat.

Lexie was a gift she never thought she'd get again in her life. Lexie moaned into her ear, as Taylor now offered her the same gift of love.

In the beautiful highlights of her bedroom, Taylor grasped that life offered more than one chance to live freely and happily. She'd never be able to go back to who she was prior to meeting Lexie.

Chapter Nineteen

Taylor and Stephanie continued to exchange letters. Getting together was a little tough with Stephanie's college schedule. But she could always squeeze letter writing in between visits, she said.

Taylor asked her a lot of questions about her past, present and future. She learned that Stephanie loved strawberry ice cream, and had an even greater obsession with it than Taylor.

I have it at least four times a week. Jeff, my fiancé, brings over a pint of it every time he eats dinner with us. He loves my mom's apple pie, but something is always missing from it. One day I baked one instead, and wouldn't you know, everyone, including my dad gushed over it. This upset my mom. You see, cooking is her favorite pastime. She says she's nothing without it. I disagree. She's a lot of things, more than a great cook. Now, her baking skills are another story. None of us have the heart to tell her so, except for my gramma. She says it like it is. Always. One time, when I was like ten, she told me she hated my new haircut. My mom took me to her hairdresser and asked her to cut it into one of those bobbed cuts, you know, when it comes down longer near the jaw and stacks up in the back? I felt so pretty until Gramma gasped when she saw me and tried to pull my hair back to length. So if you ever meet my gramma, be prepared. Fair warning! Okay, got to go prep for an assignment. Write back! Steph

Her letters brought a new level of excitement to Taylor's days. All the pieces of her life started to fit together without effort.

That little voice in the back of her mind cut loose, though. It taunted her with questions like, *when will the next whammy in life smack me upside the head?* Because

217

a whammy always followed high times.

At least in Taylor's experience, that's how life played out. So it became even more important for her to enjoy those letters and write back. To keep the flow going.

In Taylor's latest letter, she decided to share a little bit about her personal life in hopes that it might bring more of a bonding and less of a superficial texture to their relationship evolution.

So I had a bad case of writer's block with my latest book. My editor, Maya, who happens to be my best friend, asked me to rehab an old building to get it ready for a new store—a pet boutique. That's where I met Cashmere and my friend, Lexie. You'd like Lexie. She's pretty like you. She has a knack for running into cobwebs. You should've seen her the first day I met her. I thought she would suffer a heart attack because she ran right into a spider in a cobweb and she landed on the ground smacking her head. Ever since, she's been trying to prove her bravery to me. That's the kind of person she is—a woman who has a lot of pride. Too much sometimes! I suppose we all do, though.

I get that way about my writing. I hate to admit when I'm struggling. I spent two months staring at a blank screen before confessing to my editor, Maya, that I might never write another book again. That's when she handed me a hammer. Who would've thought hammering nails, drilling screws into wood, painting, refinishing floors, and assembling shelves would get the words flowing. Wouldn't you know, shortly after doing all that, the words came back to me!

Of course, it could have something to do with my new friend, Lexie. She's sort of a muse. She fills my head with stories. She's a bumbling mess in a construction zone, always bumping into everything and getting paint everywhere. I've recently learned that imperfections are a great story catalyst. When I stopped worrying about being perfect, the words flowed again. So that gives me great hope!

By the way, The Pet Boutique is having a grand opening a week from tomorrow. We're a few weeks late with our goal for it, but still on time for the holiday season.

Maya, Lexie, and Cashmere will be there, as well as a bunch of other fun-loving people who I've turned into characters. But shh...you can't tell them. That's our secret! Oh, and things might get really crazy if the psychic who owns the building shows up to do some readings. She's Maya's friend and trusted confidant. Maya won't make a move without her guidance. It's a bit much at times, but kind of entertaining too.

So anyway, do you want to come? You and your fiancé? Bring your family too. Even Gramma. Let's see what she has to say. Honesty is always a good thing when you're trying to get things right. Maya and Lexie could always use an unbiased opinion. I tell them I love everything. They roll their eyes at me. So what do you say? A week from Saturday? Ten a.m.? I'll confirm that they have strawberry ice cream!

Two days later, Taylor got a text from Stephanie in response to her letter.

I'll be there around noon. My family and I go to daily mass, and Saturdays we always go with the priest and nuns to the nursing home to say prayers with them and sing songs. Oh by the way, can you come to my Toastmaster competition tomorrow? I'm competing in Table Topics. I have to give a two-minute improvisation speech on whatever word or phrase they give me.

Taylor smiled. *Tell me where and when and I'll be there.*

She sent her the details before Taylor could take a sip of water.

Oh and by the way, will that psychic really be at your grand opening?

Why? Do you want a reading? She'd love it!

No! Please no. Everyone will flip. Especially Gramma. She's not open-minded at all. Anything that goes against her ways is off limits in my house.

Taylor's heart clenched. What would her grandmother think of her and Lexie if she couldn't deal with a psychic? She couldn't engineer a decent response. How could she pretend she didn't adore Lexie? And she couldn't hide Goldie. The woman tended to offer advice without being asked to. Anything could come out of her mouth.

She might be there.

Oh.

She's nice. She won't ever tell you something bad. She only reveals the good stuff. Silly stuff. You know like, bring your baseball hat on that walk later because it's going to rain. Things anyone would know, really. She's harmless.

Ok.

Ok?

Yeah. See you tomorrow.

~ ~

The next day, Taylor kissed Lexie goodbye and walked out of The Pet Boutique. She carried a bouquet of delicate, aromatic flowers Lexie had bought for her to give Stephanie after her competition.

As Taylor drove south, away from the boutique, her stomach knotted. She wished Lexie could've gone with her, but she had already committed to a freelance gig photographing a family dog for Christmas cards.

Instead, she invited Maya to join her.

~ ~

Maya followed Taylor into the auditorium of Veteran's Memorial Hospital. The whispers of strangers echoed against the vaulted varnished ceilings, waving in and out like a cicada song.

An excitement filled the space. Contestants of that regional public speaking competition paced the aisles next to their support systems. Their pale faces and quick darts back and forth tightened Maya's chest. Why would anyone torture themselves like that?

Taylor was a ball of nerves. "Oh my God, there she is." Taylor stopped and moved back a few steps, landing on Maya's toe.

"Ouch!" Maya screamed, grabbing her foot. People stopped talking and gawked. "What? She stepped on my toe with those…" She scanned Taylor's hideous boots. "With those things." She glared at them. "We're going on a shopping spree soon, and you're buying me lunch."

Taylor's face went from sick pale to tomato red.

Maya grabbed her elbow and pulled her forward. "You're a hot mess. How would you have gotten through this on your own?"

"She's waving us over." Beads of sweat popped up on Taylor's forehead.

Maya dug for a handkerchief and pulled her up the steps. "First we have to clean you up. We'll say our hello's afterwards. For now, turn and wave at her."

Taylor turned her beet-red neck toward the stage and offered a weak little wave.

Soon after taking their seats, a woman with a screechy annoying voice welcomed the crowd. "You're in for a real treat," her voice bounced around the auditorium. Hands flew up to people's ears as she ineptly worked the mic. "We have a talented lineup of speakers today who are competing for a spot at the national convention in Albuquerque in three months."

"God save us all." Maya muttered, pulling out her cellphone to escape.

Taylor leaned over and snooped. "You should put that away."

"While she's yacking and killing our ears, not a chance."

Taylor's face blotched. "Well, at least put it on silent mode."

"Fine. I can do that." Maya turned the switch to vibrate. Then, feeling the burn from Taylor's annoyed glare, she dropped the phone in her pocketbook. She grabbed the program booklet from Taylor's white-knuckled grip and opened it. "This goes on for four hours! Do they at least give us a snack?"

"Shh." Taylor shot her a dirty look. "Stop fidgeting. You're shaking the entire row of seats."

A man tapped on Maya's shoulder. "Could you keep it down, please?"

Maya turned and met up with a set of wrinkles that resembled a topography map. The poor man needed some serious facial moisturizer. "Sorry, I get a little excited about these things."

He winked. "I get that. You see that girl with the long hair?"

Maya glanced. "Yes, we're here for her."

His wiry eyebrows furrowed. "How do you know her?"

Maya propped on her knee and placed her hand on Taylor's wrist. "Oh, this here is her…"

"Someone here to support her speech today," Taylor finished for her. She

221

elbowed her and hissed, "Jesus, Maya."

The man leaned in between them. "You shouldn't take Jesus's name in vain."

Taylor flung him a wave. "Sorry."

The man needed a toothbrush. He stunk like day-old coffee grinds.

"Do you know her?" Maya asked.

"That's our granddaughter." He clutched the hand of a tired, cranky, white-haired woman.

"Oh, how nice." Maya forced a smile and turned back to face front.

The man tapped her shoulder. "Enjoy the show."

Maya waved, and escaped back into the program booklet. Then a moment later, she glanced around the curved auditorium at the sea of strangers. She loved to people watch. Taylor should've been taking advantage of the cast in front of them, too. People watching lent itself to priceless researching opportunities.

As she settled back against the hard creaky seat, a scary thought poked around Maya's mind. What would Stephanie do to Taylor's creativity? She couldn't afford another blockage.

The woman with the irritating tone and lip-smacking microphone pops interrupted Maya's thoughts. "We're going to start with our famous Table Topics part of the competition. Table topic speeches are unrehearsed, unplanned talks where contestants are given a phrase to use. They'll be judged on how well they incorporate the phrase into the overall delivery."

She continued to kill Maya's ears with instructions for each contestant. She ordered them to wait backstage and come out one at a time. "Ah, the element of surprise," the woman screamed into the mic, causing everyone to jolt in their squeaky seats.

"Jesus," Maya said aloud. She turned to the old man before he doused her in another smelly serving of his poor hygiene. "Oh, sorry. Knee-jerk reaction."

Finally, the first contestant stood on stage awaiting her word or phrase to begin a two-minute impromptu speech.

"Your phrase is, 'Once in a Blue Moon.' Good luck."

The irritating, stage-stealing woman walked away and allowed Maya two minutes of freedom.

Maya suffered through two dull speeches before Stephanie stepped on stage and awaited the table topic phrase she'd use to deliver her two-minute speech.

Stephanie was a beautiful girl and resembled Taylor, even down to her dimples. Her beauty captivated Maya. She had confidence, unlike Taylor at times. She stood tall and ready, a capable competitor who had likely seen a stage or two in her lifetime already.

They *were* in for a treat.

She stood next to the moderator with her hands folded in front of her, a gentle smile resting on her face, the catalyst to the bright speckle of excitement dancing in her sunny eyes.

"The Table Topics phrase for today is, 'Once in a Blue Moon,'" the moderator screeched.

Stephanie didn't even blink. She walked, carrying confidence like a designer handbag, to the front of the stage. She opened her arms wide to the audience and graced them with the same warm tones as Taylor often used during their chats.

"Once in a blue moon, there comes along a person who, by a certain glance, is capable of lifting you to a higher place where it no longer matters what you wear, how much you weigh, or why you fear parts of life. My once-in-a-blue-moon story began the day I got stuck in an elevator with a total stranger and, two hours later, came out of it madly in love. This guy teased me into playing a game of make-believe where we were a couple married five years, stuck in an elevator. We pretended to talk out our marital issues and see how we might improve our relationship."

Stephanie giggled at the memory and walked from the center of the stage to the right, welcoming that side of the audience into her intimate world.

"That same guy proposed to me in that exact elevator a year later. And sometime in the future, he's going to marry me on top of that building in a sunset ceremony surrounded by our closest friends and family. Once in a blue moon, people are lucky enough to meet up with a person who changes their life and sets them on a course where doubts and self-consciousness have no power."

Stephanie continued to tell her tale of love. Her voice tendered at the right places, creating an emotional journey for everyone in that audience. She fed them hope and encouragement, reminding them that if they opened their eyes and hearts, they'd surely experience that special once-in-a-blue-moon moment, too. A moment when destiny met up with the present moment and everything aligned as it should've.

Maya glanced over at Taylor as Stephanie wrapped up her speech. Her eyes brimmed with moisture. Parental love swept across her happy face.

She hadn't remembered seeing Taylor as beautiful before. She glowed, lighting up the space.

Taylor would do anything for that young woman.

Maya squeezed her friend's hand. That's when the tears leaked from her friend's pretty brown eyes and left tracks down her cheeks.

~ ~

Taylor enjoyed when Lexie visited with her. That night, they decided they'd indulge in another cake that they'd make together.

"So I spoke with my parents, and they invited you to join us for Christmas in North Carolina." Lexie stirred cake batter into a creamy swirl, then scooped some with her finger and placed it on Taylor's lips.

"You told them about me?" Taylor licked the batter from Lexie's finger.

She pulled it away before she could lap it all. "Well, yeah." She tapped Taylor's nose with the leftovers. "They'll love you. Much better than my ex. They didn't like her at all. Of course, in the three years we were together, they only met her once by a fluke. They surprised us at Auntie Maya's birthday party. Anyway, my ex had loaded up on whiskey sours, no thanks to Jack. He drinks them like they're lemonade. He loved Christine." She wrinkled her nose. "That should've told me something right there." She wiped her hands on her apron.

Lexie kissed her. She tasted like cake batter.

"You've been licking it too, I see." Taylor nudged her against the counter and tickled her.

She giggled and tossed her head back, revealing her long, sexy neck.

Taylor nuzzled against it. "God, I adore every piece of you."

Lexie stared lovingly into her eyes. "Really?"

Taylor met her gaze. "I do."

"Everything, huh?" she teased on a sultry whisper.

Taylor twisted her mouth, feigning contemplation.

Lexie slapped her arm with a playful wisp.

Taylor massaged Lexie's hair and gazed into her eyes. Lexie's scent swirled in Taylor's head, filling her with desire. She caressed her skin with soft kisses and feathered her long fingers down into Lexie's skirt and undies.

Right there in the kitchen, the two began a wild journey through a sea of loving undulations. Waves thundered in Taylor's mind, matching the intensity of their moans as they rode the rush toward that reeling climax.

Lexie's hunger intensified Taylor's ripples of pleasure as she sent her vibrating with her finely-tuned fingers. Taylor went on a journey all her own, soaking up the smooth delicacy where her undies once covered. They reveled in each other's strokes right there in the space between the kitchen island and the dishwashing machine.

Once satisfied, Taylor scooped her up and swung her away from the counter. "I adore everything about you." She placed her down after two spins, slipping her fingers through her freshly-washed hair. "Everything. Even the way you forget to close the toothpaste cap. Every time I glance at the oozing toothpaste likely covered in germs, I whisper to myself, 'That's my girl.'"

Lexie dipped her head back again, airing her defiance. She landed back on her eyes, staring at her with a seriousness. "So how about Christmas in North Carolina?"

Taylor bit her lip. "I want to say yes, but I want to stay around here just in case…"

"In case Stephanie wants to get together. I get it." She traced a finger over her lips again.

The relief from Lexie's response bathed her in the kind of comfort a roaring fire on a blistery day could bring. "You do?"

225

"Yeah, I mean, this is all new to us both. Last year at this time, Rex and I booked a Christmas cruise. This year, I'm opening a pet boutique with my aunt, single-mothering Cashmere, living in my aunt's attic, and trying to figure out my next responsible step in life. So yeah, change adds different layers to sift through. Everywhere I turn, I smack into a caution sign. So I'm okay with keeping everything in healthy check."

Taylor hugged Lexie. "There's a lot of change going on for us both. So far, I've been pretty happy with how things have been going."

"Me too." She squeezed her back.

Hope rose.

Taylor dangled her arm around Lexie's shoulders. "Stephanie's coming to the grand opening."

Lexie picked up Taylor's hand and kissed her fingers. "Oh exciting. Introducing her to the Merkel gang, huh?"

"Yep. Her parents and grandparents, too. But I'm kind of nervous about her grandmother. She was very grouchy at the competition, and Stephanie mentioned she isn't exactly open-minded."

"About?"

"Well, about psychics, and I'm sure about homosexuality."

"Is that going to be a problem?"

Taylor shifted her feet nervously. "I won't let it be."

Lexie smiled at that, and that smile swam around Taylor's stomach uneasily. What if she couldn't prevent it from being a problem?

"I'm happy being with you, Taylor."

"And I'm happy being with you, Lexie. I never thought it would be possible to be this happy again. I assumed I'd spend the rest of my life alone trying to fill the emptiness with words. Words that, up until meeting you and Stephanie, have been hard to come by. Thank you for opening my eyes again."

"Thank you for opening mine, too."

Taylor would immerse herself in the deeper parts of Lexie, and open her eyes

226

even wider. She could hope for such a thing. But right then, she needed to get some writing in before the grand opening.

"You have a cake to bake, and I have a character about to lose her way with a client."

Lexie swung her hair around, flipping it over her shoulders. A suggestive smirk played across her face. "Oh, you make that sound so much sexier than it is."

Taylor kissed her. With Lexie, everything was always sexier.

~ ~

Time flew by for Lexie. The grand opening fell upon them, and that baked up a bittersweet tug on her heart. She'd miss rehabbing the place with Taylor. Even though they already set plans for indefinite dates, she'd miss hammering nails and sneaking peeks of her climbing up and down ladders.

On the other hand, they did it. Now they'd celebrate the day by opening the doors to the public, and just in time for the holidays. Thankfully, she and Goldie were getting along again after Lexie snapped at her about her psychic advice for her aunt. Goldie agreed to tone it down a bit, and Lexie agreed it was none of her business because her aunt was a grown woman, after all. So they left it at that.

She snuck up behind Taylor who was pouring ice into a pitcher of water. She wrapped her arms around her waist and nuzzled her neck. "I'm so happy you're here today."

Taylor gazed at her, long and hard. "Me, too. I truly adore you."

A smile started at the corners of Lexie's mouth. Her eyes sparkled.

"I hope those eyes will always sparkle as they are right now," Taylor said.

"The day I got caught in a cobweb and you laughed at me, I never would've dreamed in a million years I'd say this back to you. I adore you, too. It's been a crazy, adventurous journey, hasn't it?" She leaned in and kissed her cheek.

Taylor Henshaw was a complicated person with a past littered in heartbreaks and shiny with the treasures of learned lessons and stronger insights. She wiped away Lexie's insecurities and helped her change into someone kind of cool who could swing a hammer and flirt in ways that surprised even her.

All those silly doubts from before had no place in the life they were building together. Things would turn out just fine for them, despite Goldie's threats of clouds.

Lexie led Taylor by the hand, toward the backyard to check on Goldie, Cashmere, and Bella, the cat.

Cashmere and Bella ran loose in the backyard. Bella hadn't a clue what to do with the big white dog who ran wide circles around the yard's perimeter, kicking up dirt and leaping over an occasional patch of tall grass. Eventually, Bella romped and rolled next to Cashmere, then stood her ground with a hiss whenever Cashmere attempted to straddle over top of her back.

"We should get inside," Goldie said. "Your aunt's likely ready for opening prayers. Come on Bella." She whistled, and both Bella and Cashmere sprang toward her.

Taylor laughed. "She's just like a dog."

Goldie nodded. "Without the need for all the walks."

They wandered into the front room where her family gathered. Never on that first day of exploring the grimy place had Lexie ever considered it would turn into the thing that would complete her.

But there she stood alongside people who highlighted her latest trek through life with purpose and value.

She stood by her aunt's side, surrounded by Taylor and the Merkel gang, to pray together before opening the doors for the first time to the public.

Auntie Maya clasped Lexie's and Taylor's hands. "These two designed this moment. Without their efforts, you'd be off grocery shopping or filling your car up with gas. Because they spent so much time hammering, painting, and organizing, you're about to step into an exciting moment. Your father would be happy that they did so in his honor, for me, and for you." She spoke to her children and their better halves. "They started off on the wrong foot. First Lexie with a cobweb stuck in her hair and Taylor with a serious case of blockage the size of this building. Yet they've built something special together."

Jack caved into a genuine smile filled, undoubtedly, with the idea that love, in all its abundance, always won. He nodded at Lexie, his secret way of offering approval for what he once believed to be as idiotic an idea as she did, turning a dilapidated space into something special.

Ally elbowed Lexie's side and leaned her head on her shoulder. The same move she repeated hundreds of times as a kid whenever Lexie cried because her parents dropped her off for the summer.

And Rex, linking his arms around Wini and Goldie, smiling, neck extended, and eyes sealed closed as if connected to God.

They did it. They pulled it off.

"I propose we move our monthly check-ins with your father to the backyard here. He'd like this place. He would've been in his glory working here, passing out treats to dogs, sneaking free bags of kibble to customers, and helping people shampoo their dogs in the wash basins." Her aunt glanced around her bunch of family and fresh tears sprang. "Yeah, he would've loved this."

Cashmere barked at a couple walking by with a golden retriever. "Ah, the song of her soul," Jack said. "Well, if that doesn't scare off the customers, I'm not sure what else will."

"That's her play bark," Rex said.

"How will a customer know that?" Jack asked. "Listen to her. She sounds frantic."

"She's spinning and bowing." Rex did his own version of an eye roll, and right to Jack's face as opposed to behind his back like they always did to him.

The couple pulled on the door handle, but it was still locked. Cashmere's pirouettes increased in height and width.

"Well, the queen has spoken." Auntie Maya drifted toward the front door, and Cashmere circled her with bright eyes and a wagging butt. "Let's do this."

They stood as sentinels, hands cupped around their faces in anticipation of what would come next.

Before her aunt opened the door, she ordered Cashmere to sit. Lexie's heart swelled when her darling girl obeyed. She parked her wiggly butt on the polished laminated floors next to her new cat friend, Bella, and waited patiently for the couple with the retriever to enter their new pet boutique.

When they did, the two dogs bowed to each other in friendly greetings, yipping and carrying on like kids having fun in a playground. The only difference was that dog treasures, spongy mat tiles, and colorful toys filled that playground.

"Well, you know what I see," Goldie said, remaining with the Merkel gang under the bright display of lights hanging from the rafters.

"The sun is shining all over it," everyone said in unison.

Then, they broke out into a relieved laughter as Auntie Maya welcomed their first guests into their charming new pet boutique.

~ ~

Once the couple and their dog finished shopping, Goldie passed the couple a business card. "Next month, an award-winning portrait artist will be on call to oil-paint your cutie-pie dog. She and her family are moving here all the way from Denver to be part of the fun. Be sure to call and schedule an appointment with her."

They nodded, and wished them all well before heading out the door with their bag of organic dog treats and a bottle of essential oils for calming.

Before Maya closed the door behind then, she turned the sign to open. She smiled at Rex's iPhone. "Is that thing recording?"

"By 'that thing,' do you mean this dazzling piece of technology fresh off the shelf?"

"It's a phone," Maya said.

"It's an iPhone XS Max, Mom. It's not just a phone. It's everything in one convenient package. You'll be happy I'm using this to chronicle today. It'll record everything in detail like you can't imagine."

"Are you going to make love to that thing, too," Jack chimed in, coming up behind Rex. He snuck a peek at his mother standing before them with purpose and pride.

"Say the word 'nice,' Mom," Rex said.

"Nice?" Her eyebrow arched in an unusually high fashion. "What happened to the word cheese? Does that thing not work with cheese?"

"Follow my lead, Mother." His voice rose.

"Fine. Nice," she said, and the most natural smile spread across her face.

Rex showed the click to Jack. "See that? Is that not the most gorgeous photo of Mom?"

Jack leaned in. He tapped Rex's shoulder. "You did great, kid." He walked away and left a trace of shock on Rex's face.

After the first hour, Lexie and Maya had welcomed a few dozen friendly guests. One set of guests included Cashmere's best buddy, the little boy from Taylor's neighborhood and his mom. As they browsed, Cashmere gleefully fell in alongside of them, excited to be part of their first romp through the colorful boutique.

"My face hurts from smiling," Lexie said a little while later as she curled up to Taylor's side. "We already sold out of the bowtie cookies with the strawberry sprinkles."

Taylor brushed her hand against Lexie's. "Cashmere enjoys her hostess role."

Cashmere now greeted an older, hippie-style couple carrying a toy poodle. She sniffed the air, pushing her way into their personal space, and the couple responded with lots of *awes* and *cutie pies*. Cashmere's favorites. She rubbed herself against their ankles and demanded petting.

"She's acting like a cat now!" Lexie's face lit up. They stood and admired her for a few long moments.

Lexie glanced at the decorative brass clock hanging on the mural wall next to the big cherry blossom tree. "Are you getting nervous?"

"You could say that." Taylor's face hurt, too, from tensing it every time the second hand moved closer to the twelve o'clock hour.

Lexie squeezed her hand and kissed her cheek. "Everything will work out as it should." Then she walked away, back to greet more new guests as they continued to pour in and glance around the quaint space.

Taylor stood against the mural wall, absorbing the unfolding scene. Maya danced around the space with her typical wide-arm, theatrical moves. She dazzled her customer with a southern charm born not out of the south, but of watching too many movies and editing too many manuscripts with southern belles as the lead.

Ally came up beside her. "I like you."

Taylor stretched her eyes to her. "Why do you say that?"

"Because I mean it. You're good for Lexie. She's happy."

Taylor eased. "She is, isn't she?" They glanced in her direction. She wore her smile like a charm, dazzling everyone who caught sight of it.

"She loves hand-painted pet rocks if you ever want to surprise her. She'll melt if *you* paint one for her."

"Okay," Taylor said cautiously. "Thanks for the tip."

"You're welcome." Ally squared off with her. "Please don't ever forget her birthday. She'd never admit this, but when her ex forgot her last one, it hurt her. And someone like Lexie doesn't deserve that kind of careless hurt."

"I'd never forget it."

"Don't give her a pet rock for her birthday, though. Only I do that. You're free to give her one whenever else she needs one."

She sailed away and joined her mother near the cafe.

Lexie lucked out with her loving, accepting extended family. Everyone with a heart like Lexie's deserved that gift.

She glanced around the happy place. The Pet Boutique served as a similar gift for the lovable pets whose humans could buy them a treat, accessories, and toys to show them that same kind of love they all deserved too. Sometimes great love didn't come from flesh and blood, but from those who extended their love for no other reason than to give it to someone special.

Lexie helped an elderly couple choose the perfect harness for their little Yorkie. Rex and Wini entertained a bulldog while its parents selected a magnet. Jack and Nico charmed an elegant couple dripping in designer flair and gorgeous hair. And Goldie sat at a small round table talking with a man with orange hair and freckles and his cute snowy white fluffy lapdog. Taylor smiled, until her eyes met up with the sign on her table, *free pet readings. Find out what's stressing your pet.*

What the fuck? Where did that table come from?

Stephanie and her family would arrive soon, and the first thing they'd come into contact with would be Goldie and her psychic mumbo jumbo.

"We are so busy," Lexie said. "Amazing, right?"

"Goldie's doing readings today?"

Lexie scanned the storefront and found Goldie's table. "Oh, that's great. She must've found the folding table in her place, after all."

"It's not a good idea."

Lexie glanced at her impatiently. "Why not?"

Taylor didn't want to cause stress on opening day. She'd deal with it when and if it became an issue. "Forget I said anything. What can I help with?"

"Can you help the lady with the two kids and poodle by the kibble?"

"Done." Taylor bowed away and walked up to the woman. She carried the small poodle mix in her arms. It wore a pink bow and harness. The dog stared wide-eyed at Taylor. When Taylor tilted her head, the dog did, too. When Taylor opened her mouth, the dog did too. When the woman walked down the aisle, the dog stretched its neck to keep its eye on her. When the woman crossed to the next aisle out of viewpoint, the dog barked.

Taylor followed them. When the dog spotted her, it stopped barking. "Can I help you find something?" Taylor asked.

The woman pet the top of her dog's head. "I'm just browsing. Tootles loves cute little dresses." She fingered through a row of them. "She turns majestic in them."

"Try one on her."

The woman asked Taylor to hold Tootles. "Do you mind?"

Taylor opened her arms to her. "Tootles is free to roam if you like."

"Her roller harness is in the car. Otherwise I'd say yes."

"Is she paralyzed?"

"Ever since she was two. She doesn't let that stop her, though."

233

"She's faster than her friend," the little boy yelled out.

"Everyone loves Tootles," the little girl said, petting her in Taylor's arms. "She's the popular dog in the neighborhood." The girl smirked, proud of her furry sibling.

"Does the psychic really have the ability to talk to dead pets?" the woman asked.

Just then, the bell above the front door chimed once again, and when Taylor's eyes met Stephanie's, her heart swelled.

"Excuse me." Taylor handed Tootles back over to the woman. Then she inched away from her, failing to answer her question.

She walked toward Stephanie. She wore a sugary smile and no longer needed a wheelchair. She held her fiancé's hand and headed over her way. The nice grandfather and the grouchy grandmother, with her bluish-white hair, followed. So, too, did Stephanie's parents, an elegant middle-aged couple. They stopped in front of Goldie's table and shared a panicked glance at each other.

Taylor froze a few feet in front of them.

So much for shaping a good first impression. That chance choked and died.

~ ~

Lexie glanced around the room.

The boutique filled with lots of people and sang a soulful song. It buzzed and sprouted life in every smile, purchase, and delight.

The space carried products to please the pets and their humans. From home décor items like funky lampshades constructed with copper and fused glass to elegant clocks adorned with colorful gemstones to decorative water and food bowls, The Pet Boutique transformed from its original dilapidated state to something of a destination for the distinctive homeowner and ultimate toy store for pets.

Dogs could have their pick of plush balls, canvas happy faces on a rope, talking stuffed pink pigs, ice cream cooling toy cones, Frisbees, donut rings, you name it.

Cashmere bounced around from person to dog and back to person, sporting her happy face full of excitement. Lexie took it all in, including Taylor as she approached a young woman who struck an incredible resemblance to her.

234

Stephanie.

They hugged, and Stephanie turned over her shoulder at an elderly couple talking with Goldie. Everything else happened in slow motion, the kind like in the movies right before a train collides with a school bus full of happy children. Taylor nudged Stephanie out of her way and leaped toward Goldie's table. Stephanie then stretched her pretty little arms out and mirrored Taylor's leap. Goldie climbed to her feet and placed her fists down on the table. Her eyes widened and her jaw dropped. Taylor took a stand in front of Goldie, now blocking her from the elderly couple. The grouchy woman pointed her finger at Goldie, wearing fear like a mask.

"What is happening over there," Jack whispered, coming up beside Lexie.

"I'm pretty sure they aren't fans of psychics."

Jack folded his arms over his chest. "Well, they can leave, then."

Nico corked his arm around Jack's, united in their stance against the judging rapture of strangers with too much authoritative power over poor Goldie. Her chin quivered and her eyes bled tears that poured down her cheeks.

"I'm sorry, she's doing what?" The old lady's voice cranked out with biting hysteria.

"Gramma, please. Calm down." Stephanie pulled at her grandmother's sleeve.

"We're going to go to hell just being in this place." The lady glanced at the ceiling, wincing at it as though the devil himself lived in the rafters.

Taylor flung Lexie a lopsided frown.

"Why is she doing that with her face?" Jack asked.

"Because she's afraid." Lexie wrapped herself in a hug.

"Of?"

"Of losing her daughter before even having her back."

Jack knitted his eyebrows together. "Please speak English here."

"She gave her daughter up for adoption when she was eighteen, and this is the third time they're meeting."

"Hell of a family she ended up in." Jack rolled his eyes in classic fashion.

"We don't all end up with people like your mom."

They all moved in to help Taylor. The panic rising on her face told Lexie she might've been too late.

"I'm sorry," Stephanie said to Taylor. "My family's religious. I told you she'd freak out about the psychic."

"The psychic has a name. She's Goldie," Jack stammered.

Lexie tapped his stomach.

The old cranky lady pointed her eyes at Jack and Nico and then at the conservatively dressed couple with her. "I've seen enough. Let's go."

"Wait," Taylor said. "Please don't go. You drove all this way."

Cashmere darted up to the old lady and nudged her ankles with the top of her head. The lady raised her chin at Cashmere like she was a rat.

Lexie stiffened. "Cashmere, come."

Cashmere shot Lexie a look like, *what the fuck, Mom?*

"Come," she said more sternly.

Cashmere bowed her head and came to her. Lexie bent and massaged her baby girl's neck, touching her forehead to hers in a move of solidarity, apologizing for the cruelty of humankind.

"Okay," Taylor said swiping her hands together. "This is not going to work. Why don't we head out? Get a cup of coffee across the street. They have a delicious dark roast with hazelnut flavoring."

She motioned for them to move toward the front door.

A middle-aged couple stood their ground. "No," the woman said. "We're here. Let's see the place."

Stephanie and Taylor wore frowns, buckling at the chin. They shared apologetic glances.

The old woman grumbled something and moved away from Goldie, glaring at her as if Goldie had the black plague.

"So, Taylor," the middle-aged man, likely Stephanie's father, stepped forward. "We didn't get a chance to speak much with you the other day. Are you married? Do we get to meet the other half today?"

Taylor inhaled an alarmingly large mouthful of air. Her face took on a green cast. "My husband died a few years back."

The man's face dropped. He exchanged glances with his wife. "Oh, geez. I'm so sorry."

Stephanie's eyes grew large. "I didn't know that."

Taylor bit her cheek. "I tend not to talk too much about it."

"Oh, you poor thing." Stephanie's mother wrapped her hand around Taylor's upper arm. "It takes time to heal and move on. Don't worry. One day, another Mr. Right will come sailing in and help you heal even more."

Taylor met Lexie's eye with a plea as if begging her to stay back.

Lexie's blood pressure rose along with those clouds that Goldie had predicted.

Taylor walked away and toward the café area where Cashmere gnawed on a bone. She bent and pet her. Stephanie and her family followed her lead. The mother placed her hand on Taylor's shoulder. "It takes time."

Jack wrestled for his arm back from Nico.

"What are you doing?" Nico whispered.

"We should tone it down." Jack muttered.

Nico grabbed for Jack's arm. "No. I'm not toning anything down."

"If they fear a psychic, can you imagine how they'd fear us?"

Nico reasserted his place beside his husband. "We can't be gay in front of them?" His voice rose, startling Stephanie and her family.

Taylor rose and walked over to them, after signaling for Stephanie and her family to stay put for a moment.

"Not now, Nico," Jack said firmly.

Lexie turned to Jack. "Yes, now."

Jack blinked, and rubbed Nico's wrist. "Do this for me," he whispered. "It's important to my cousin. We'll straighten it all out later."

"No," Lexie jumped forward. "This is not what I want."

"Please," Taylor pleaded. "Help me get through this right now and I promise like Jack, we'll straighten it all out later." Her voice carried a desperate plea, one Lexie didn't like at all.

"You can't ask them to not be gay in front of other people." She turned to Jack and Nico. "You two, be as gay as you are. The Pet Boutique is a safe zone welcome to anyone. I don't care if you're an alien with five heads. You're welcome here. Drama and judgments stay outside."

Nico grabbed his husband's arm back and latched onto it. Jack stretched his lips into a thin line. "We don't have to do this, cuz."

Tears prickled her eyes. "Yes we do. It's who we are."

By that point, Rex stood on the other side of Jack and rested his hand on his shoulder. Jack responded to the united move by swinging his arm around his brother's shoulder and pulling him in tightly.

Lexie pointed at Jack and Nico. "None of us are going back into hiding." She turned to Taylor. "I did that for Christine with her family in the beginning and I won't do it again. If you want to be with me, you need to leave the apprehension at the door and go all in or don't bother coming in at all. I'm never tiptoeing again." Then she turned to Jack. "And you're not either."

Lexie stormed off, but Taylor didn't follow her. Instead, she followed Stephanie and her family out the front door.

Chapter Twenty

Taylor rummaged through her pantry. She didn't have enough junk food to help her through the crisis. She needed a serious load of comfort that only potato chips and Little Debbie snack cakes could provide.

That's how she got through the first weeks after Oscar passed.

She plowed through a snack-sized bag of Doritos, half a pint of strawberry ice cream, and half a dozen stale chocolate cookies she found behind her Dustbuster.

A few hours later, once her heart settled down and her mind defogged somewhat, she called Lexie.

"Hey," Lexie said, flatly.

"Hey." Taylor hesitated on a shaky breath. "A lot happened today."

"You can say that again."

"I don't know what else to say, except that I want you to know I care about you."

Lexie sniffled.

"Lexie, I care about you a great deal. I told you before, I'm a fucked up person with a lot of history. I need a moment to sift through everything in my mind and make sense of it all. It's messy, and I don't want to screw up any of it. Do you understand? I need some time to sort through it all."

"I do, too. So let's take that time and not say anything we'll regret."

"Okay," Taylor managed. "I really do care about you, Lexie. I hope you know that, and I hope that you care about me, too."

Lexie sniffled and hung up.

The darkness curled up around the edges of Taylor's bedroom shortly after they hung up and she took three Tylenol PM's. Somewhere in between that and morning, she managed to catch a few hours of sleep while holding her treasured quarter from Mr. Roger Lyles.

Despite the usual power in that quarter, she woke with a stomachache and ball of despair lodged against her heart.

She had woken with the same pain before. In the next hour, she expected the pain to turn into more of dull throb that stole any chance of turning the day into something manageable or desirable.

Taylor showered, blow-dried her hair, and got dressed in her lazy clothes: baggy sweatpants and her long-sleeved Orioles t-shirt. She burnt a piece of potato bread, and suffered through eating it plain, her punishment for getting herself into such a mess in life.

Unable to stand the sunshine filtering in the kitchen window or the tight squeeze her sweatpants created on her bloated waistline, Taylor undressed and climbed back into bed.

She lay still, rubbing the silky blanket between her fingertips, reliving the loving, tender moments spent with Lexie a day before. In the few short months they'd spent together, she grew fond of her being a part of her day.

Then, the echo of Stephanie's gramma's words stabbed at her.

"I won't let my granddaughter be around anyone who endangers her chance of getting into heaven."

Was she talking about Goldie or Jack and Nico? Taylor couldn't tell. She could read the fear those words incited in Stephanie.

"Gramma, they're all nice people."

Gramma turned to Taylor. "If my granddaughter has a relationship with you, I can't have you bringing her around friends like you have."

"Like I have?"

"You know what I mean. I will not speak the words. God hears those."

"So what are you asking?" Taylor's heart thumped.

"Choose. A relationship with Stephanie or not."

"She's eighteen."

"And who do you think pays for her college and apartment?"

"Surely you wouldn't take that away from her."

"Surely you wouldn't either."

"I will pay for her college and apartment," Taylor said. By living a modest lifestyle in a simple rancher home, she had plenty of savings to do this for Stephanie.

"I will never let her in my home again if she accepts that offer."

Stephanie's watery eyes still stabbed at Taylor. She rolled over in the sheets, tangling herself in them.

Talk about an impossible decision.

Taylor had fallen in love with Lexie. Not choosing her would be a huge mistake. She did nothing but love people. Her family did nothing, aside from a ridiculous amount of eye rolling, but love people. Same thing with Goldie. They all brought their own slice of heaven to Earth.

She'd never be able to change the opinion of a cranky old lady clinging to the subjective verses in a bible. Whether she feared psychics, gay people, or both, Taylor still wasn't sure.

In a few years, after Stephanie graduated from college, they could try again. If Stephanie didn't harbor those same fears, of course.

If she did, she'd still love her as a person. But she couldn't accept life on anyone else's terms but her own.

Life on Taylor's terms had no room for prejudices formed out of unwarranted fears. Taylor wouldn't add fuel to those fears by refusing to stand up for what she believed in with her own heart. She wanted to teach Stephanie to stand up for what she believed in, too. And only Stephanie could decide what that was.

Taylor could lead by example by living a life true to her calling.

For Taylor to overcome the blockages in her life, she needed to nurture her soul and take steps to move forward and get out of the valleys that had kept the sun from shining its light on her.

She took out her laptop and typed a letter to Stephanie to air out her thoughts.

Dear Stephanie,

This letter is long overdue by decades. Not from anything you've done. From what I've done, which is to abandon my own principles for the sake of keeping peace with those I love most. When I placed you up for adoption, I did so because I wanted to keep the peace with my mother. I wanted her to love and respect me and not see me as an irresponsible person who refused to follow her rules or instructions. I wanted her always to see me in her best light. In hers.

Why not mine?

That's a question that keeps popping into my mind this morning. If I had been courageous enough to stand up to her and speak my truth, life would've played out differently.

Not a day goes by that I don't regret that decision. I'm sad for all we missed out on because I allowed fear of the unknown to direct me. Now we find ourselves at a crossroads again. A place where other people have injected their opinions and fears on us and we must act in accordance with peacekeeping, even if that means sacrificing our ideals for the ideals of others.

I don't want that decision to weigh on you. But I can't stand by and let it weigh on everyone else who I've grown to love, too. It's an impossible decision.

Then, I'm reminded that everything in life is temporary. What is true today will not be true tomorrow, likely. So not everything we decide today is cemented into place for eternity. I can't turn my back on my life to suit your gramma's ideals. I don't expect you to turn your back on your life, and the love you have for your family, to suit my ideals, either.

Perhaps there will be a tomorrow in the future where we can rejoin and set our own ideals.

While you still can, love your gramma. She means well because she's acting in the only way she knows how. You don't want any regrets later on.

Everything in life is temporary. Including all of this.

Let's rekindle things with those we love, and know that when push comes to shove, we have each other's backs.

Always here for you.

Love,

T

Taylor texted Stephanie and alerted her to the email she sent her.

Ten minutes later, Stephanie texted her back.

Just so you know, I'm not afraid of psychics. I think they're pretty cool.

Your gramma isn't reading these texts, right?

No. That's silly. She can barely see the large-print books anymore.

Good. Then let's be more frank, here.

About what?

Gramma is more concerned with homosexuality than psychics. Taylor wrote.

What?

Why are you acting surprised?

I'm genuinely surprised. Who's gay?

Taylor face-palmed herself. *So Gramma only worried about the psychic part? You're confusing.*

Well, I'm also bisexual. I'm in a relationship with Lexie. Well, was. Hopefully still am. That's to be continued in a future text.

OMG! I love Lexie. And Cashmere! Yay!

Really?

I never saw that coming. Lol. You must've been hiding it well.

Taylor stiffened. *Yes, and that cost me dearly.*

I'm sorry. I hope it works out.

A giddy pride coursed through her. *Me too.*

You should marry her and adopt a baby together. You're good mom material.

Taylor froze, staring at the three dots.

More came. *You have a lot of love, and there's plenty to go around for us all.*

Relief washed over Taylor. All those years, she worried her daughter would consider her a monster. Yet talking with Stephanie was so natural. So easy. *I don't even know if she'll talk to me now. So that might be a bit premature.* Taylor smiled at the memory of that reference.

Well, T, everything starts with a thought, as my fiancé always says. So you're welcome! Lol So anyway, back to Gramma. She'll never know if I visit you. We can go back to the café across from The Pet Boutique. After all, they have gluten-free options! And maybe next time, you'll be able to eat something because you won't be so upset.

Taylor laughed. *Yeah, well, I should go work on that now.*

Eat?

That too. And talk to Lexie and see if she'll ever let me back in The Pet Boutique again.

Why did you leave her in there and come with us?

Taylor hesitated. Then she spoke her truth. *Because I was afraid to lose you again.*

Don't worry about that, T. We're straight. Oh wait, I didn't mean straight like that. Argh forget it. You know what I mean. Lol

Taylor loved that kid. *Lol Have a good one. Thanks for being so open and beautiful.*

Aw. Hugs.

~ ~

Lexie swept the floor of the boutique, prepping for the second day opening. The day before had been chaotic and a total rollercoaster. They ended the day with profits and a whole lot of empty shelves, all great signs that at least something would work out in life.

Cashmere barked her tirade out back. The pizza place owner two doors over was probably emptying trash into the bins. That charged her, like a sparkplug kicking an engine to life.

Her barks kept Lexie engaged, at least.

Everything else hollowed and emptied. Pointless really. She tired of losing and of always starting from square one again in the love department. How many more people would she have to date to find that someone willing to take a chance on her?

Willing to take her on and risk everything for the sake of love? She was worth it. Wasn't she?

She was smart and resourceful. Fun and flirty. And decent in the sex department.

Yes, she was worth it. Finally, she could say that. She did everything right that time around.

She swept some more.

She replayed the disastrous scene from the day before in her head for the umpteenth time that morning. Taylor's shameful gawk flashing at her from across the room. Her plea for Lexie to stay quiet. Asking everyone else to change so her new family would accept her.

That group of strangers had no right to judge them.

She had done the right thing, storming off. Normally, she liked to solve things. So if she could solve things, she would, because she hated the echo her pounding heart created in her hollow chest.

She kept trying to figure out a way to ease the blow. Nothing came to mind. She couldn't force Taylor to live a life where she'd have to sacrifice her most important desire. Stephanie had always been her top priority. Lexie understood that going into it. She would never expect to come before a kid. Even if that kid was a grown adult making her own decisions. In Taylor's mind, Stephanie was still that infant she abandoned. Taylor would end up spending the rest of her life in misery if it meant she would have the opportunity to build a relationship with Stephanie.

Lexie would've done the same thing.

Cashmere bolted through the doggy door and up to the front window. Her nub wagged like it was tapped into the electric circuit that powered the city of Annapolis. She moaned, groaned, whined, and yipped at the faint knock on the front door.

Lexie glimpsed out the window and spotted Taylor standing on the stoop. A fresh bouquet of exotic flowers, oddly similar to the ones Lexie bought her for Stephanie the day of her competition, covered most of her face.

She opened the door, and Taylor handed her the bouquet. "Hello."

"Hello." Lexie took the flowers and sniffed their freshness. "So original of you."

The joke fell flat between them.

Taylor shrugged sheepishly. "You always have the eye for these kinds of things."

"I do." Lexie took that compliment and carried the flowers to the reception counter.

Taylor handed her a white square gift box with a pink bow, her favorite color. "This one you might find a little more original."

Lexie stared at it, not ready to ease up on her hurt.

Taylor placed it on the table.

It took an outrageous span of seconds for Taylor to speak. "I shouldn't have left with them."

Her words sat empty at Lexie's feet, like the fur she swept from the day before. It created a dusty film that didn't ease the hurt that had sunk in her heart overnight. "Then why did you?"

"Because I let a complication trip me yet again. I'm not using that as an excuse this time. I fully admit to my missteps. I'm sorry I walked away and crossed that line of choice before I considered my actions. Only a fool would walk away from the woman she loves."

Taylor loved her.

Taylor used her sincere voice, not the *I'm tired and cranky and need to eat* voice. The nice one with the creamy texture that always turned Lexie into a puddle. She had a ways to go before she'd cave, though. "That hurt like hell."

Lexie wanted to go toss her arms around her neck, kiss her and tell her she forgave her. But she wouldn't. She needed to be sure.

Taylor stepped closer to her. "I should've come back yesterday."

"I wish you would've." She did, but that pain vanished with each inch closer Taylor stepped. Still. She needed to be sure. Maybe she didn't come to make up. Maybe she wanted to ease her mind of more guilt for abandoning her. Maybe she would walk out the door after issuing her apology and wish her a nice life as she headed south to be closer to her daughter and her daughter's Christian extremist ideological family.

Where was Cashmere when she wanted her to start barking?

Taylor landed right before her. Lexie caught her sensual scent.

"I want to fix this," she said with her delicious tone—another one in her receptacle of smooth-talking, puddle-inducing equalizers.

Lexie's heart pounded.

Taylor traveled her gaze around Lexie's face, as if taking in all the freckles and contours. She circled her fingers down the length of her arms until she caught up with Lexie's trembling fingers.

"I've gone and added more complications to my life. Something you've taught me over the past several months is that nothing is ever permanently tangled. I mean, you escaped your massive spider web."

"True," Lexie whispered.

Taylor arched her eyebrows, playfully, and that little move granted her a finger squeeze.

"I never want to get so tangled that I lose sight of what captured me in the first place," Taylor said. "That's you. You captured my heart, and I don't want to lose you."

Spoken more like a romance than suspense writer. Lexie could wrap herself in that any day. "I don't want to lose you, either."

"I've still got things to work out."

"So you're saying you're a fixer-upper, hmm?" Lexie smiled and released a sigh. The tension oozed out of her and rolled out of sight.

"You can think of me as a rehab project."

"I do have a thing for…"

"Imperfections," Taylor finished for her.

"They evolve into the best kinds of stories. A writer and a mural artist told me that once." Lexie brought their entwined hands to her lips and rested against them.

Taylor lowered them and kissed her, replacing all the drabness of the morning with beautiful highlights. Those highlights accentuated all those hidden parts that, up until that moment, never saw the light of day.

"I'm so sorry I hurt you, Lexie," Taylor whispered in between kisses. "I felt torn apart and without all the pieces to put myself back together."

Lexie wrapped her arms around her neck. "I shouldn't have pressured you with my dramatic ways. I saw us being ripped apart and it freaked me out."

They stared at each other for a long pause.

"Life is one big learning process, isn't it?" Lexie asked.

"It is. You know what the best part of learning is?"

"What's that?"

"It never ends," Taylor said.

Lexie cupped Taylor's face. "I'm willing to give this learning process, or whatever we're calling it, a try." She paused, and stared deeply into her eyes. "I love you, Taylor. I have from the moment you first opened up to me."

Taylor's eyes sparkled. "Well, I fell in love with you the moment you tore off your shirt and did your little spider freak-out dance."

Lexie giggled, then grew serious in the next beat. "I don't ever want you to regret this conversation."

"How would I regret it?"

"I don't ever want to be the person who gets in between you and Stephanie."

"You'll never be. Even if she didn't dig you and Cashmere, I'd still be right here with you."

Her body lightened. "She digs us?"

"I texted with her this morning. Oh, and she thinks that psychics are pretty cool, too." Taylor chuckled.

Lexie pulled away a few inches to take in Taylor's laughter. "What will Gramma do with that?"

"We concluded that there are some things Gramma will never understand. It's not up to Stephanie to force any of her beliefs on her. Just as Gramma shouldn't force hers on Stephanie. None of us are perfect."

Just then, Cashmere bolted through the doggy door again on a full sprint toward them.

"Except Cashmere." Lexie laughed. "Her timing is not only perfect. It's impeccable."

Taylor kissed Lexie's forehead. Then she walked over to grab Cashmere's leash. "You want to go for a walk so your momma can get the boutique ready for another opening?"

Cashmere couldn't contain her excitement. She tried her hardest to sit as trained, but with Taylor, that old, tired training went out the door. Instead, she choose to leap, bow, and repeat until that leash went on and Taylor opened the front door.

"Open your gift. A little birdie told me you love the kind of thing that's inside."

Before Taylor could walk out the door, Lexie perked her ear toward the speaker above the reception counter. "Ah, I love this song. "You're My Best Friend" by Queen. That's my and Cashmere's song."

Taylor's jaw dropped, and she stood her ground on the front stoop despite Cashmere's insistent pull and whine on the leash. She looked ready to cry. Her chin buckled as she looked up to the bright blue sky.

"What is it?" Lexie asked, coming to her side.

"A sign."

"A sign?"

Taylor looked at her with watery, bright eyes. "I've been waiting for a sign, and Goldie told me I'd get one eventually."

"I don't understand." Lexie cradled her hand on Taylor's wrist.

"Nate and I used to sing this song to Oscar every night when we tucked him into bed." The tears broke free and a grateful smile spread across her face. "They're giving me a sign."

Lexie hugged Taylor, and Cashmere sat calmly, peering up at them as if understanding the gravity of the moment.

Taylor began to chuckle and lighten in Lexie's arms after a few long moments. Then she pulled out of the embrace and bent to hug Cashmere. "You and Oscar have the same song. How about that?"

Cashmere leaned her forehead against Taylor's, her beautiful signature move.

They stared straight into each other's eyes. Taylor released another chuckle before rising. "Ready, Baby Cakes?"

"Baby Cakes?"

"My nickname for her."

Cashmere responded to her new special nickname from Taylor with a jolt to all fours.

"Let's go, then. We'll leave your momma to her gift." Taylor winked and walked out the door, following behind a very excited doggy who was ready to explore the streets of Annapolis with one of her best friends.

Lexie watched them trot away, both happy for their own reasons. When they passed the corner, Lexie walked back to the reception counter and grabbed the box. She stared at it, the thrill of surprise lapping at her heart. With a giddy rush, she opened it. She looked down at a pet rock painted pink with "The Pet Boutique" written across it in white. "Aw Ally, you told her my little secret," she whispered.

She hugged it against her chest and savored the moment, the moment when everything finally felt right.

Then, Lexie glanced around The Pet Boutique with fresh eyes full of hope. She had the rest of her life to look forward to keeping life's gifts in their best shape. If she could take that dilapidated old building and turn it into the cheery and welcoming pet boutique, she could polish anything life tossed her way by sprinkling it with love.

As her Auntie Maya once told her, *where there is love, there is life.*

EMMA AND HALEY

Curious about how Emma and Haley, the couple featured in *The Pet Boutique*, first met? Check out The Fiche Room, which is the story of their love. (http://bit.ly/FRsuziecarr)

SPECIAL CONTRIBUTION

As with all of my books, I enjoy giving a portion of proceeds back to the community by donating to Hearts United for Animals www.hua.org. Thank you for being a part of this special contribution.

A SPECIAL REQUEST

Word-of-mouth is crucial for any author to succeed. If you enjoyed *The Pet Boutique*, I'd be so grateful for your honest review of it. Even if it's just a sentence or two. It would make all the difference and I'd be so appreciative. Also, if you could share your thoughts of this story on social media (especially in reader groups on Facebook!) that would be amazingly helpful. – Thanks! Suzie

(www.amazon.com/author/suziecarr)

www.ingramcontent.com/pod-product-compliance
Lightning Source LLC
Chambersburg PA
CBHW021425200626
46814CB00015B/656